Sandy is a serving police officer.  teacher but soon traded her hock has recently received her twenty ! Good Conduct Award.

When her local paper printed an unflattering picture of her in a charity marathon, Sandy felt compelled to respond with an amusing account of her training programme. This led to regular contributions and a taste of national publications. Her writing has never stopped. *Girl Cop* is a drama based on real events in the British Police Force.

Sandy lives in the West Country with her husband and two sons. She enjoys tennis, rugby and still keeps up her first love of gymnastics – proudly demonstrating back flips and the splits to amazed friends.

Girl Cop

SANDY OSBORNE

To, Eloise,

With best wishes,

Sandy

SilverWood

Published in 2012 by the author using
SilverWood Books Empowered Publishing®
30 Queen Charlotte Street, Bristol, BS1 4HJ
www.silverwoodbooks.co.uk

ISBN 978-1-78132-066-2
epub ISBN 978-1-78132-067-9

British Library Cataloguing in Publication Data
A CIP catalogue record for this book is available from the British Library

Set in Sabon by SilverWood Books
Printed on responsibly sourced paper

Acknowledgements

Without the help of the following people I would never have got this far. A big thank you to:

Annie Penn for her advice, inspiration and giving it to me straight. Dr Louise Shaw for her medical expertise. Antonella Collyer for her authentic Italian input. Dympna Brooks for her inside knowledge of the NHS. Valerie Cuff for allowing me to use the collar number 2679 in memory of her son, Sergeant Andy Cuff. All my friends who 'agreed' to read and comment on my draft copies.

Thanks also to The Bath Priory Hotel, Mallory and Baskervilles Gymnastics and Fitness Centre for their support and allowing me to name check them.

And finally to the three men in my life for tolerating all the tears and tantrums (mine and theirs) – I hope this makes them worth it.

A percentage from the sale of this book will be donated to the Police Dependants' Trust and St Peter's Hospice.

Chapter One

"They're either lesbians or slags!"

PC Dunbar was voicing his opinion of his female colleagues.

Sally stared at the title on the front of her pocket notebook. The gold embossed letters stamped into the tight black leather cover read POLICE CONSTABLE 1759 GENTLE – that title was going to take some getting used to. She sat feeling somewhat conspicuous, having arrived a little too early for her first shift as a newly trained police officer at Bath Police Station. She felt like the new girl at school. Her pristine uniform made it glaringly obvious to any bystander including PC Dunbar that she was fresh out of training school, commonly referred to as a 'sprog'.

Sally took a deep breath and wondered how she should respond to the 'lesbians and slags' declaration. Safe in the knowledge that they were alone in the room, she decided to start how she meant to go on. Brushing a stray blonde hair out of her eyes, she looked straight at her fellow officer who was leering over a wooden lectern at the end of the table and replied, "That's OK. I'm both!" before returning her attention to her notebook.

She heard PC Dunbar 'humph' and wander off, obviously unsure whether he had managed to impress or not. Sally glanced at his back as he retreated and noted his unkempt appearance. The mud caked on his boots and splashed up his trousers together with his shirt hanging out over his backside like a nappy showed that he no longer wore his uniform with the fresh pride that Sally wore hers.

Not a great start, Sally thought to herself. She had been in the station barely an hour and it looked like she had made an enemy already. She pretended to be engrossed in her notebook reading through all the scenarios she had dealt with at training school. They all seemed so far removed from the reality she was about to face as she drew a line underneath the last entry and wrote today's date: *Thursday 9th September 1993*.

The briefing room was a pretty grubby affair with a collection of odd chairs around a large ancient-looking, Formica-topped table. Sally looked round at the tired paintwork on the walls which was camouflaged with an assortment of mug shots and posters displaying information that she guessed would gradually become familiar and relevant to her.

As 2pm drew near, her new teammates began to arrive. They were all polite enough to say hello. Some even introduced themselves, but after that they just talked amongst themselves as if she wasn't there. Disappointed by the cool reception, Sally suddenly felt an overwhelming desire to stand up and run from the room. She would never fit in here.

She sighed as she looked around the table and wondered if she had made the wrong career choice. The team was made up of an odd mix of men of varying ages, along with one female, who looked around Sally's age but wasn't interacting with anyone. Sally scanned the faces of these strangers with whom she was about to go and fight crime and face potentially life-threatening situations. From their first reactions, it would seem that they couldn't give two hoots whether she lived or died by the end of the shift.

The two shift sergeants, one male Sergeant Morley and one female Sergeant Baron, entered the room and headed for the wooden lectern at the end of the briefing table from where PC Dunbar had earlier tried his crass chat-up line. Sally looked at the two supervisors who would influence and mould the start of her career. Sergeant Morley was in his mid-forties and wore his long service ribbon proudly on his tie showing that he had completed at least twenty-two years' police service. He had a kind face, albeit hidden in part by a full beard and moustache. Sergeant Baron, by contrast, was a hard-faced woman who wore her auburn hair pulled tightly off her face into a neat bun at the nape of her neck. Sally estimated she was in her mid to late thirties and watched her as she placed the clipboard she was carrying onto the lectern and took a pen from her shirt pocket. Sally clocked the lace bra that was clearly visible through her shirt, which she thought at least showed a potentially softer side to the woman.

The sergeants were closely followed by Inspector Creed. He was a tall, thin, grey-haired figure aged around fifty, which meant that he was nearing retirement. The lines etched on his face were evidence of a life of shiftwork. Added to that, the fact that he wore his inspector's flat cap in the briefing room showed that he was 'old school' with old-fashioned police values. Spotting the pips on his shoulders, Sally made a movement to stand and salute him as had been a requirement at training school but, noticing the lack of response from everyone else, she quickly took her seat again feeling her cheeks flush to a ripple of suppressed giggles.

The briefing started. It comprised a synopsis of what had

happened on the district since the team had last been on duty, followed by what was expected to happen during the next eight hours, together with the crews for the shift. It was then that she was welcomed by Inspector Creed and introduced to the team.

He had barely finished her name before saying, "Sally, it's customary for the junior officer to make the tea at the start of the shift."

"Oh, I...I..." Sally looked around apologetically. She had heard that this was a tradition and one that she wasn't going to enjoy – but if needs must..."If someone could show me where the kitchen is..."

"Yeah, get yer pinny on," said PC Graham Butterworth, a pudgy man in his mid-thirties who looked like he'd worn his uniform to bed.

A couple of younger members of the team snorted and nudged each other, obviously glad to be passing this task on to the new girl. Sally flushed again but she immediately stood up to show willing. It also offered her the chance she was looking for to leave the room and its uncomfortable atmosphere.

"Come on, I'll show you."

Sally looked in the direction of the owner of the voice that had offered her the first hint of friendliness since she had entered the room. However, he had already turned away from her and was heading for the briefing room door. She followed him gratefully. It was only when she was safely out of the room that she was able to look at the face of her guide who turned towards her and extended the hand of friendship.

"Hi, I'm Alex, Alex Moon. I'm your buddy." He smiled a warm smile at her. A 'buddy' was a more experienced officer who was paired up with a new recruit for their first ten weeks to 'show them the ropes'. Sally beamed appreciatively back at him as she shook his hand – an ally at last in this battle zone she had found herself in.

"We don't actually have a kitchen. We use the kettle and sink in the Custody Unit," Alex explained as Sally followed him along numerous corridors and through even more doors. As she followed, she took the opportunity to check out the finer details of her buddy. Hmm, not bad as policemen go, she smiled to herself, considering the standard of the rest of the team. He obviously kept himself fit and being six feet tall and sturdy would be useful when the need arose to grapple with a drunk. His short dark hair was kept tidy with a touch of gel and, without wanting to sound like PC Dunbar, had a rear view she wouldn't be complaining about.

Eventually, they reached a reinforced door where officers had to press a button then wait until someone from inside released the lock to allow them entry. As they waited, Sally glanced at Alex and found him looking at her. They both smiled awkwardly.

"A bit nerve-racking, your first day, isn't it." Alex offered to fill the uncomfortable silence. "Don't worry, you'll soon settle in."

Sally tried to smile back at him but she was sure it was more of a grimace, and they were both relieved to hear the sound of the buzzer indicating that the door was open. Once inside, Alex pointed out a small room and said he would meet her back in the briefing room. With that, he was gone, the reinforced door slamming behind him.

Sally looked with dismay at the array of filthy mugs and tea-making paraphernalia that covered the worktop. She filled the kettle and, whilst waiting for it to boil, began to wash the encrusted mugs, making a mental note to bring her own mug in the next day. Finally, she had ten mugs of tea on a flimsy tray ready for her trek back to the briefing room.

The route back seemed to have even more doors than she remembered with most opening towards her – meaning that she had to keep putting the tray down to wedge the door open with her foot whilst coordinating picking up the tray and manoeuvring through each one. At the final door, she was just at the point where she was picking up the tray – bent over, legs apart and unable to quickly right herself – when the weight of the door was taken by someone behind her. Standing up, she looked at her mystery helper to see PC Dunbar grinning from ear to ear.

"Thanks," she said tersely, not wanting to sound ungrateful but, at the same time, aware that he had obviously enjoyed a full and unexpurgated view of her uniformed backside.

"The pleasure was all mine," he oozed lasciviously – the sneering grin still stuck to his face.

Feeling decidedly hot and bothered, Sally continued to make her way into the briefing room. She couldn't hide her disappointment when she saw that the room was deserted, with the exception of Sergeant Morley who was standing writing at the lectern. He looked up at her as she stood scanning the empty room, holding a tray of steaming mugs of tea. He noted her puzzled face before returning his attention to his paperwork.

"Pub fight in The Grapes," he explained without looking up.

Not only had her efforts with the tea-making been wasted, but she had also missed her first shout, a pub fight – how exciting was that?! – and whilst she was making the goddamn tea! Impatiently, she put the tray down on the table causing her careful journey back to be in vain as the contents of the mugs slopped over the sides.

Sergeant Morley helped himself to a mug. "Better not let your efforts go to waste, had we."

Sally also picked up a mug and walked over to one of the noticeboards to study the faces displayed there more closely. She winced as the hot liquid burned her mouth.

Sally decided that her first day was not going well.

Alex Moon returned to the station surprisingly quickly. Apparently the fight was all over before they got there – a situation which she came to realise was fairly common for such calls and always welcomed.

"Run to a fire and walk to a fight," Alex told her as they gathered up their hats, coats and folders containing their paperwork, and made their way to the forecourt of the station. He led her to one of the Ford Escorts lined up in the bays along the front of the building and opened the back door on the driver's side slinging his kit on the back seat. Sally followed his lead and did the same on the passenger side.

"OK?" Alex asked once they were sitting beside each other in the car. He reached for the logbook to check the mileage was correct before they set off.

Sally nodded and felt her spirits lift as Alex started the engine and manoeuvred the car off the forecourt. Within seconds of him pulling out onto the road, they got their first call from the Control Room.

"Foxtrot Bravo 2679," a female voice crackled from the speakers in the dashboard.

"That's me," said Alex and nodded towards the handset of the radio. "You gonna answer it?"

"No way!" Sally exclaimed, her heart racing. "You do it – please?"

She was very nervous about using the radio because everyone on the district could hear the transmissions and she was terrified of getting tongue-tied.

Alex didn't protest but leaned forward and took the handset. "Go ahead, 2679."

Oh, my God! Sally thought to herself. *This is really it! I'm a real policewoman in a real police car en route to my first job!* She smiled as she looked out on to the streets of Bath to see how many members of the public were looking at them and wondering where they were going, just as she used to do when she saw a police car.

"We've got a domestic for you, Alex," continued the control room operator, "though not your usual husband and wife argument. This one's between parents and their teenage daughter. Good luck!"

"Thanks for that!" replied Alex good-naturedly.

Sally, remembering her training, jotted down the address the operator had given together with the time of the call.

"We don't often get called to domestics in that area – it's quite upper class – let alone a teenage girl being the cause of it!" Alex enlightened her as he accelerated up Lansdown Road. "I'm sure they have domestics just as often as the ones living on the estates we usually go to, but they're normally far more reluctant to call us. This should be an interesting one."

Soon, they were pulling into Lansdown Park. There were no house numbers in this impressive leafy cul-de-sac. *Trewellyn Haven* was nestled amongst the detached residences where prestige cars not housed in double garages were displayed on spacious drives beside neatly ordered gardens.

After Alex had pulled up at the bottom of the drive, Sally got out of the car and put her hat on. She checked her reflection in the car window before following Alex up the driveway where a spotless Mercedes was parked. They had been told on the radio by the Control Room that the fifteen year-old daughter had argued with her parents before slapping her father in the face, smashing a vase and then barricading herself in her bedroom.

They were greeted at the front door by the tearful mother, Mrs Stringer, who immediately apologised to them for wasting their time. She invited them into the hallway where she explained the situation and said that this wasn't the first of these incidents, not by a long chalk. She had only called them this time because she was at the end of her tether.

Alex turned to Sally. "Shall we go on up and see what's what then?" he said, standing aside to allow Sally to lead the way up the stairs. She paused for split second, having expected Alex to go first, but checked herself when she realised that he was indicating that she should lead the way. Unsure whether he was being gentlemanly or whether he thought she would be better at dealing with a teenage girl, Sally placed her hand on the banister and began the ascent. An array of school photos lined the wall, starting with one girl smiling dutifully at the camera who was joined halfway up the stairs by a younger sister displaying the same dutiful smile.

They stopped outside the room Mrs Stringer had indicated. On the door there was a large sign stating *Laura's Room, Keep Out!*

"You call out to her," Alex whispered. "She might respond better to a female voice."

Sally could see the logic and knocked lightly on the door. "Laura, can I come in?"

15

They waited for a reply.

Nothing.

Sally knocked again. "Laura? It's a police lady here. I just want to have a chat with you. Can I come in?" she said in a calm and, hopefully, friendly voice.

Again, nothing.

Hmmm, what should she do now? Was Laura going to let a police officer in if she wouldn't even let her parents in? Sally was thinking back to her own teenage days.

She knocked for a third time and, when there was still no reply, Alex pushed the door handle down and tried to open the door. It opened a couple of centimetres but was blocked by something on the inside. He put his shoulder to the edge of the door and, with considerable ease, pushed it open wide enough to get through despite the barricade behind it.

He stepped inside first, closely followed by Sally. They were faced with a diminutive, blonde-ponytailed teenager who was standing at the far side of the room by the window. She was assuming the stance of a bulldog, snarling at them with her face down but her eyes looking up at them.

Alex stifled a laugh and looked from Laura to Sally. "I think I'll leave this one to you. I'll be outside if you need me." With a muffled giggle, he slipped out of the door.

Sally looked back at Laura who hadn't moved from her defensive stance. Sally knew the confusion she was feeling must be showing on her face and so she shrugged her shoulders at the girl. She wasn't sure what to say or do next. The decision was made for her as Laura relaxed her body. She let out a frustrated 'oowl' as she took a few steps forward and dived onto the bed, burying her head in the pillow and howling in frustration at her futile attempt to be intimidating.

Alex popped his head back round the door. "OK?" he enquired, looking at the crumpled mass on the bed.

Sally nodded and moved towards Laura. Alex retreated, leaving Sally to tackle this angry young woman.

Laura looked like your average teenager – jeans, pink sweatshirt and her ponytail held with a matching pink scrunchie – not the scary image her mother had portrayed. As Sally approached the bed, she could see that Laura's arms were wrapped round a pink teddy bear.

"Can I sit down?" Sally asked calmly.

There was no response.

What now? Sally thought to herself.

"You want to tell me what's happened?" she asked in a tone she hoped sounded non-threatening. The only sound was the ticking of the clock beside Laura's bed. Sally looked around the room. It could have been hers not so many years ago. Laura's school bag was thrown in a corner and recently played CDs were scattered over the surface of the dressing table amongst an assortment of make-up and hair paraphernalia. More cuddly toys scattered around the room showed that this young woman hadn't yet let go of her childhood and was still trapped in the confusing maze that led to adulthood. Sally blew a deep breath out as she sat down on the edge of the bed. The only chair in the room was also full of cuddly toys.

"Parents, eh?" Sally said giving the pretence of exasperation as she placed her hat on the bed beside her. "So, what won't they let you do then?" she continued, remembering what the majority of her own arguments had been about.

Laura turned her head from where she lay to look at the next adult she had to contend with. To Sally's surprise, Laura sat up at right angles to her, her knees tucked up underneath her

17

chin squashing the teddy between her legs and torso. Her face was red and blotchy. It evoked memories of so many similar arguments that Sally had had with her mum. She remembered how she had fought with the temptation to vent her anger on something tangible whilst teetering on the edge of blind rage.

Laura looked at Sally and shrugged her shoulders before blurting, "I want to go on a sleepover tonight and *they* won't let me. All my friends are going – I'm going to look really stupid." She sobbed into the teddy bear.

"Phew, that's a tough one," Sally empathised. "What are their reasons?"

"I haven't finished my homework and it's my mum's birthday tomorrow. Mum said I could go if I finished my homework but Dad said 'No' because of Mum's birthday."

"Ah," Sally said, agreeing by her tone that it was a tricky situation. She thought for a couple of seconds before deciding that she hadn't got any suggestions on how to resolve this dilemma other than to try to turn it around. "How would you deal with it if you were them?"

Laura stifled a laugh and lifted her chin up from her knees for the first time. "I'd have let me go…" The futile answer hung in the air.

"Yeah, but what about now – after the events that led them to call us – slapping your dad and smashing your mum's vase? Was it a valuable one?"

"No, it was really cheap. I gave it to her." Laura sniggered at the irony of her statement and swung her legs round so that she was sitting alongside Sally.

"You know what Mums are like though – they cherish the crappiest of things. My mum's still got the pie funnel that my sister and I bought her the first Christmas we were old enough

18

to buy our own presents. It must be a health hazard by now, it's so chipped and cracked, but she still insists on using it and regularly tells us she's still got it."

Laura turned her head to look at Sally grabbing the edge of the bed as she did so causing her teddy bear to fall to the floor. She leant forward and picked it up, hugging it back to her chest. With wide eyes she turned to Sally and asked, "Are you going to arrest me?"

"That wasn't my intention." Sally reassured her whilst also letting her know that this could have been an option.

Laura visibly relaxed. "I guess I would ground me too then," she conceded, picking up Sally's hat which had been lying between them and fiddling with its shiny new badge.

"Parents are such a pain at times!" Sally offered, trying to lighten the atmosphere. "They're only good for free taxi rides and cash at this age, aren't they!"

"Yeah, too right," Laura agreed in a tone that was a little too impertinent for Sally's liking. The cash and free taxis had obviously been doled out a little too liberally thus far in this privileged teenager's life. Then Sally spotted a collection of sports trophies which, from the badges in the centre, she could see were for gymnastics. That was it: a common theme.

"I see you do gymnastics – and it looks like you're pretty good at it too." Sally nodded towards the display of trophies. "Which club do you belong to?"

"Baskerville's. I'm in the elite squad," Laura added with fervour.

"Baskerville's? I used to train there, a few years ago now though, before they moved to their new premises."

"Wow, did you?" exclaimed Laura forgetting her troubles for a moment, seemingly astounded that Sally could have a normal life outside the police.

"Yeah, and I can still do the splits, though not in these." Sally indicated her uniform trousers. "I'd probably split them!"

With that, Laura stood up and elegantly slid down into perfect splits in front of Sally. "Like this?" She held her head high with her arms aloft showing impressive poise.

"Well, maybe not as good as that now. I'm a bit out of practice." Sally giggled at the thought of trying it in her police uniform.

From there, they launched into a discussion of favourite moves and champions. Sally could see that Laura was basically a good kid but just struggling with growing up like so many other teenagers. Her family's wealth had probably hindered the journey rather than assisted with it.

Once Laura had given her a guided tour of her trophies and medals, Sally brought her back round to the matter she was there for.

"So, what are you going to do now?" Sally waited for Laura to reply with a suggestion of how to make amends, but it wasn't forthcoming.

"What would you expect?" Sally probed further.

"An apology," came the sullen reply.

"What about suggesting that, if you finish your homework, maybe you could go over to your friend's for a couple of hours but not stay over?"

Laura tutted before Sally continued, "I'm sure, if you explain to your friends that it's your mum's birthday, they will appreciate and understand, won't they? That way, you can leave without looking like a kid whose parents won't let her sleep over..."

Laura pursed her lips in thought. "I don't think they would

even allow that now that you've been called," she said miserably.

"Possibly, but it's worth a try, isn't it? At least it would show that you're sorry and you realise the repercussions of your behaviour." Sally paused. "I'll go downstairs and prepare the way for your apology, shall I? I'll suggest that a bit of give and take on both sides will probably reap better results than a completely inflexible resolution – but I can't work miracles, you know." She stood up and waited for a response from Laura that wasn't forthcoming. Instead she reached for a tissue from her bedside table.

"You really frightened them, you know," Sally added in a more serious tone.

Laura's head went down again. "I know, I deserve to be grounded," she replied despondently.

"Come on," Sally said brightly, not wanting to ruin the rapport she had built up. "It's time to build some bridges."

They both knew that this wasn't the first of this kind of incident, but hopefully it had provided enough of a short sharp shock to make sure it was possibly the last on this scale.

"I'll do my best, but you know I can't make any promises, don't you?" Sally reiterated as she made her way towards the bedroom door. "Come on, help me move this out of the way."

They both dragged Laura's chest of drawers back to its normal place.

"Hey, you're pretty cool, you know. What's it like being a cop?"

"I dunno," Sally replied. "It's my first day. And it's seems like only last week I was rowing with my mum and, yes, I was grounded on more than one occasion!"

Laura beamed back at her admission. "I...I don't know your name."

Oops, novice mistake, Sally thought to herself. She should have introduced herself at the start as per training school manual – all part of the ice-breaking protocol!

"God, sorry! It's Sally, Sally Gentle."

Sally felt she had made a friend and pulled out one of her contact cards – the first she had handed out to a member of the public although she had already given them to all her family and friends. "Say 'hello' at Baskerville's from me – though you might want to make up a different story about how we met."

Both of them laughed as Laura placed the card amongst her trophies before following Sally onto the landing.

"Good luck. With your new job, I mean."

Sally looked back. "Thanks and good luck to you too, Laura," Sally replied as she started her descent back down the stairs.

Sally entered the lounge where Laura's parents were waiting. Mrs Stringer, having apparently recovered from her earlier state, was proffering a plate of chocolate biscuits to Alex and offering him another cup of tea. Alex politely shook his head and they all turned to Sally with a look of expectation on their faces.

"Can I get you a cup of tea?" Mrs Stringer offered.

"Thanks, but I think Laura will be coming down to apologise shortly," replied Sally, remaining in the doorway, indicating that it was best if they left the family alone to deal with the reconciliation. Laura's parents looked at each other. Their astonishment was clear to see.

Sally related her conversation with Laura making it clear that she had made no promises to their daughter. "I guess it's up to the three of you to sit down and discuss the way forward," she said to the still worried-looking parents. "I think our visit has probably brought things to a head, and it can hopefully only get better from here."

Mr and Mrs Stringer were full of thanks and apologised again for calling them. As they all shook hands, Alex reassured them. "It really wasn't a problem. I hope PC Gentle has been able to help turn things round."

As soon as they reached the car and saw that the front door was closed, Alex turned to Sally. "Very impressive, PC Gentle. What's your secret?"

"Oh, you know, a bit of girl talk. I plaited her hair and she painted my nails..." Sally trailed off as they both got into the car.

"Really?" he replied, glancing down at her nails. This man had only just met Sally a couple of hours ago and wasn't up to speed yet with her sense of humour.

"You're gullible for a cop, aren't you?!" Sally said and pulled the car door shut, waving her unpolished nails towards him.

"Yeah, good one, Sally!" He gave her arm a friendly punch.

She returned the punch and they both laughed out loud as they drove away. Sally beamed at his smiling profile. She knew that they were going to get on just fine.

The 'get-to-know-you' conversation was one that Sally came to realise was repeated every time she worked with someone new. It comprises a synopsis of your marital status and family background, together with length of service, current aspirations and a resumé of your career pre-police. As they drove around the city, Alex went first.

"I'm twenty-eight and joined up when I was twenty.

I'm a local boy, born and bred in Bath. I've been married to Ann-Marie for five years and have a little boy, Max, who's nearly four." Alex fished a photo of them both out of his wallet as they were stopped at some traffic lights and showed Sally.

"She's French," Alex continued, "and Max speaks it better than me already." He smiled affectionately as he studied the familiar faces. "I don't 'live for the job' as so many colleagues do but I 'work to live'."

That sounded like a pretty good philosophy to Sally. "I'm hoping to get on to the drug squad sometime in the next year before I start studying for my sergeant's exam. That's the plan anyway!"

Then it was Sally's turn. "Well, I'm twenty-three, and I live with my boyfriend of four years, Julian, who works for Sulis Marketing. I trained as a teacher but, when I got to the end of the course, I decided to plump for a job with less of a routine and with the added bonus of having a bit more power to my elbow!"

"Aha! So you have previous experience of dealing with moody teens then!" Alex scoffed.

"Hmm, maybe," Sally replied, not wanting to confess that she had been a 'moody teen' herself not so long ago. "My dad and uncle were both in the police. My dad was a sergeant but he died when I was fourteen after battling with cancer."

"Jeez, that must've been tough," Alex sympathised. "Have you got any brothers or sisters?"

"Yep, a sister – five years older, married with two girls, who works as a researcher for the BBC. We were quite close – well, we still are really, but since the kids came along they seem to have taken over," she said fondly, thinking she must make more effort to get together. "My mum lives near me and works part-time in the office of a primary school."

The conversation flowed easily as Alex gave Sally a tour of their patch; the trouble spots where she would be spending a lot of her working hours and the best place to sit and enjoy an ice cream without the public gawping at her. He showed her the tourist sites including the impressive Royal Crescent and the Circus, and pointed out a busker whom he had arrested a couple of months back for beating his wife.

"I've got a secret network of tea stops which I'll show you over the next few weeks if you promise not to tell anyone else! Damn useful when you're on foot patrol in the rain."

Sally would later find that these tea stops were in a variety of settings from the homes of members of the community who always had the time to make them a cuppa to official workplaces like the Pump Rooms where the caretaker Paddy would lead them around the bowels of the ancient setting.

Before Sally knew it, Alex declared, "Come on, time for grub."

Sally made a face at the unsophisticated term. "Grub?" she echoed. This was not an expression that she was comfortable with using but she would soon learn that it was a widely used and accepted term for a meal break – whether you were grammar school-educated or not.

Alex chuckled at her reaction and, as he headed back towards the station, continued, "We have to make the most of a break when we have time. It's often considered a luxury as, more often than not, we won't get one due to the demands of too many jobs and not enough police officers. We take our grub fairly early on a late shift so that we're available for when it gets busy later on."

*

After their grub break, they were sent to an abandoned stolen vehicle. Sally was excited to have a look at the souped-up Escort XR3, a favourite of the local joyriders. She was eager to look inside and wondered what the thieves looked like; how they had broken into the car; how they had got it started; where they'd been; what they'd done in it…and why they had chosen to abandon it there.

As soon as they drew up, she leapt out of the police car to examine her first stolen vehicle. She looked back to check that Alex was following but, instead, saw him smiling broadly from in the driver's seat where he was talking into the radio handset. She paused realising that he was smiling at her novice's enthusiasm but then he nodded towards the Escort indicating that she should continue. She didn't mind if he was amused by her keenness. She wanted to have a look at her 'find' but had to remind herself not to touch it before it was examined by scenes of crime officers.

It wasn't long before Sally would understand Alex's smile that day. Stolen vehicles would become a run-of-the-mill job – a chore in fact – unless the vehicle was moving, of course. Then the chase was on!

They remained with the car until it was recovered by a local garage ready for it to be examined by scenes of crime officers. They then spent some time carrying out PNC – Police National Computer – checks on a few parked cars. This allowed Sally to get used to the radio procedure and test her knowledge of the phonetic alphabet. All letters given over the radio had to be spelt phonetically, which Sally found a challenge in itself.

Alex continued to show Sally around their patch until

their next call came in. This time it was the activation of an alarm at a restaurant in the town centre.

"Probably just staff closing up," said Alex calmly, reaching for the panel of buttons on the dashboard and turning on the blue lights and horns.

My first blue light run! Sally inwardly screamed to herself, her heart dancing. She looked for the heads turning to look at them as they sped through the streets feeling *so* important with everyone hurrying to get out of their way.

They pulled up outside Franco's Trattorio in Milsom Street which was, coincidentally, one of her favourite restaurants. However, it was going to be different going in as a police officer rather than as a customer!

They were greeted at the door by Franco himself.

"Oh, officer, I'm so sorry, so sorry to waste your time," he said in his heavily accented English, raising his hands apologetically to his head.

"It was my new waiter. He does not know how to use the alarm. I'm so sorry, officers, to waste your precious time!"

"It's no problem," said Alex, "as long as everything's OK?"

"Yes, yes, everything is fine, officer." Franco looked from Alex to Sally. "You want a cappuccino? You got time for one of Franco's cappuccinos?"

Sally looked at Alex who, she would soon learn, was a caffeine junky and never turned down the offer of a cup of tea or coffee.

"That would be great thanks," Alex accepted graciously, "as long as you won't think it rude if we have to rush off if we get called to another job?"

"Of course, of course. Come, come."

Franco ushered them inside and they perched on the bar

stools at his counter. It was clear that he was enjoying having 'celebrity' customers in these uniformed police officers as he set about making them their drinks. The guilty new waiter smiled apologetically at them as he lifted the chairs onto the tables ready to sweep the floor.

Franco was the head of his family who had come over from Italy with his wife, when they were newly-wed, to seek their fortune, and they had never gone back. He was a distinguished-looking man in his late fifties with a full though greying head of swept-back hair. Sally had often seen his wife who worked in the kitchen – a large archetypal Italian woman who wore predominantly black, with her hair twisted into an elegant glossy chignon and who still caused Franco's eyes to light up whenever he saw her.

Alex revealed it was Sally's first day which drew admiring comments from Franco.

"Oh, you are looking very smart in your uniform. You must make me a regular stop on your patrols."

"There you go, Sally." Alex toasted her with his coffee cup. "You've just found your first tea stop!"

Fortunately, they weren't disturbed and Sally enjoyed the first of many of Franco's cappuccinos whilst on duty. He got to know just how she liked it: one shot of coffee with plenty of froth.

"Come again anytime," said Franco as they walked back to the car, "and thank you again for coming so quickly. You are good people."

"I think you were a hit there too," said Alex as they headed back to the station to finish their shift. "Keep it up and you'll be my sergeant before you know it."

They sat up outside the station and wrote up their pocket

notebooks, detailing the jobs they had been to during the shift, before gathering their kit together and heading into the building.

They walked into the sergeants' office to return their radios. The sergeants were both sitting at their desks doing paperwork. Neither lifted their heads as Alex and Sally bustled in. Alex was teasing her about how she had talked the stroppy teenager round.

"Hey, we've got some talent here. Sally's managed to sweet-talk her way round everyone we've met today!"

Sergeant Morley looked up and smiled in approval but Sergeant Baron kept her head down as she retorted dryly, "Well, let's hope her policing skills show the same talent. See me before you go off-duty, please."

Sally looked at Alex who gestured with his head to follow him out of the office.

"What was that all about?" she said, somewhat bewildered by the unfriendly comment.

"Don't worry about it," Alex reassured her. "She's a bit of a tough cookie at times. You would be well advised not to get on the wrong side of her. She's a great one to have on your side though and she's very influential at this nick, hence her nickname 'the Baroness', and they call Sergeant Morley 'Maureen' cos he acts like an old woman at times!"

Sally chuckled at the nicknames but her stomach was in knots at being summoned to see the Baroness and she wondered what it could be about. She'd had a great first day, but somehow knew that her bubble was about to burst.

After the shift had been dismissed at ten o'clock by Sergeant Morley, Alex and Sally returned to the sergeants' office to find the Baroness alone. As Sally walked in, closely followed by Alex, the Baroness snapped, "No need for you to stay, Alex."

"Oh OK." Alex stopped in his tracks and flashed Sally an anxious look. "I'll…I'll see you tomorrow then, Sally. 7pm start don't forget." He gave Sally a smile that he hoped was reassuring before he left the two women alone.

"Sit down," instructed the Baroness as she walked towards the door and, before closing it, slid the signage to show 'engaged'. Sally sat at the desk directly opposite the Baroness, a pang of nausea gripping her stomach. The Baroness, obviously enjoying the moment, smoothed back her hair and relished a pregnant pause whilst staring at Sally's worried face.

Alex had described the Baroness and her husband as 'bohemian types' who enjoyed an uncharacteristically contrasting hippy lifestyle outside this job, and who regularly attended Glastonbury Festival where it was alleged that they smoked dope just like the rest of the festival goers. He joked that her dogs were her child substitutes as she made it clear that she did not intend to bear any children herself.

"Sally, I'll come straight to the point," the Baroness began. "I have been contacted by the training school who have reported to me that, on the night of your passing-out dinner, you displayed what can only be described as 'unpolicewomanly-like behaviour'." She paused, waiting for a response.

Sally's jaw dropped open at this unexpected allegation – unable to respond having had her breath drawn from her. The Baroness didn't like this response, or lack of it, one bit and had obviously already made her mind up about Sally's guilt. Moreover, due to the colour rising in Sally's cheeks, she clearly assumed she was onto a winner.

Sally slowly began to regain her composure and asked, "What exactly is unpolicewomanly-like behaviour?" She had to know this before she could address this allegation, surely.

"Oh, come on, Sally, you don't want me to spell it out for you, do you? You were there. You know what happened," said the Baroness, impatiently.

"No, no, I have no idea what you're talking about." Sally shook her head through her shocked daze.

"Right, OK then, if you want to play it that way," bristled the Baroness. "I have it on good authority that you were caught engaged in an indecent act within the grounds of the training school after guests had left. I've called you in here now to warn you that, if behaviour like that continues, you may be flavour of the month for a while, but you will make yourself a very unpopular young lady in the long run. I've seen it before and you're making a very big mistake."

Sally was in a total state of shock – this woman was acting like she was doing her a favour when, in reality, she was accusing her of something which Sally knew nothing about. In short, Sally stood accused of performing an alfresco sex act on an unknown male which had apparently been witnessed.

She desperately tried to recall the events of the drink-fuelled evening which had marked the end of her police training. She and her fellow students had all returned to their accommodation blocks after the coach transporting their guests had left and, although the revelry had continued, she had no memory of anything like the calibre she stood accused of.

Sally's silence and reluctance to confess all was clearly infuriating the Baroness.

"You surprise me, Sally. I would have thought that, with your graduate skills," she emphasised the word 'graduate' with disdain, "you would have at least tried to talk your way out of this."

Sally, dumbfounded, sat staring at her accuser.

"Look, you were seen by some senior officers' wives who were appalled and shocked and want you spoken to. Life as a policewoman isn't always easy and it's tough enough in this man's world without some of you letting the side down. The wives all hate us anyway, without this kind of bad press. We have to be whiter than white to maintain a healthy reputation, and you'd do well to take my advice on board if you want to survive in this job." The Baroness spat the words out at Sally's drained and bewildered face.

In response, Sally changed from shaking her head in disbelief to nodding in acknowledgment at the advice she was being given.

"These things stick, Sally," the Baroness continued, "and only time will tell whether you can rise above it – but I can tell you, from the outset, you've done yourself no favours."

Sally opened her mouth to protest but didn't know what to say. Her mind was buzzing with trying to recall the evening – she couldn't have been so drunk that she would have forgotten such an event. The only way to get to the bottom of it was to get in contact with some of the other students whom she had spent the evening with and check her facts before trying to refute the allegation.

The Baroness picked up her bag and walked out without another word, making it clear that she was extremely unimpressed with this new recruit who didn't even have the good grace to defend herself, let alone admit to anything. Sally, shaking and sweating, followed her.

Chapter Two

Sally had to put on a brave face as she took off her tie and epaulettes and put a civvy jacket on over her remaining uniform, having arranged to meet Uncle Jack for last orders. She considered calling the pub to pass a message to him to cancel, but she knew how disappointed he would be. Uncle Jack was her mother's brother. Due to an argument that happened when Sally was a child, the cause of which was never discussed, her mother and Uncle Jack had not spoken for as long as Sally could remember. Sally strongly suspected it was to do with Uncle Jack choosing a wife her mother disapproved of. She knew that they had been very close growing up, and that only served to make the divide between them even more raw all these years later. Sally's vague memory of Aunt Bridie, a fiercesome Irish woman, made her not altogether surprised at the resulting situation. Unbeknown to her mother, Sally had contacted Uncle Jack after her father had been taken ill, and she had remained in secret contact with him. She had almost succeeded in persuading him to make contact with her mother when Sally's father had died but, despite Sally's best efforts, Uncle Jack had decided that it wasn't an appropriate time to intrude on her mother's grief.

Uncle Jack had also been a police officer, and it was through him that Sally's mum and dad had met. Since his retirement, he had worked as a security officer at the university. He had encouraged Sally in her decision to join the police, following her progress with interest. She often met him in his local pub where he sought solace from his miserable home life with cigarettes and alcohol.

"How's it going, poppet?" Uncle Jack asked as Sally walked in the Old Crown.

No matter how old Sally was, she was always going to be his poppet particularly as he and Aunt Bridie had not had any children themselves. Sally adored him and prayed for a reconciliation with her mother so that he could adopt more of the father figure role she yearned for.

Sally tried to put the recent conversation with the Baroness to the back of her mind and focus on the remainder of the shift that had gone so well. She didn't want to relate the Baroness's accusation, primarily because she was very embarrassed about the whole situation. She decided she would tell him about it after it had hopefully been resolved.

"It's been a great first shift," she forced herself to say as she bent to kiss him on the cheek and sat down opposite him, his half empty pint of bitter on the table between them.

"What are you having, poppet?" he asked, standing up and taking his wallet from his pocket. He opened it as he spoke and Sally glimpsed the well-worn photo he always carried of himself and Sally's mother as children sitting on Slapton Sands laughing, their faces covered in ice cream. A memory of happier times.

"Better have an orange juice," Sally replied. "Got to practise what I preach these days."

As he returned to the table with Sally's drink and another for himself, Uncle Jack asked excitedly, "Come on then, tell me about the jobs you went to."

Sally started to relax as she related the events of her first shift, including the troublesome Laura. "She was actually quite like me when I was that age." Sally giggled.

"Still, you didn't turn out so bad, did you!" Uncle Jack smiled affectionately at his niece. "What about your shift-mates? What are they like?"

Sally went through the main members of her group. Despite her best attempts, apart from Alex whom she described with enthusiasm, she didn't seem to have too much positive to say about her new colleagues.

"You'll settle in in time, poppet – it's early days – they'll become some of your best friends, working in such a job together."

He should know, Sally thought to herself.

When she left Uncle Jack outside the Old Crown, Sally felt a bit more upbeat and went home to make contact with her fellow students from police training school. She suspected that Julian wouldn't have waited up for her. He was in the middle of some major takeover bid at work and was constantly exhausted – too wrapped up even to have wished her 'good luck' for her first day. She didn't mind. She knew that, if he pulled off this deal, the big promotion he was after would be well within his reach.

Thankful for small mercies, Sally found him snoring on the sofa with paperwork strewn all around him. She crept in to the bedroom glad of the opportunity to be able to make some phone calls in private. The last thing she wanted was to have to explain the situation to Julian, which she couldn't actually explain, before she got to the bottom of it.

Fortunately for Sally, the fact that all her training school buddies were working shifts too meant that to her relief the first one she called picked up the phone after a couple of rings having also just finished a late shift.

"Hi, Ian, it's Sally here..." She paused not knowing quite how to broach the subject she wanted to discuss.

"Sally!" he replied, clearly pleased to hear from her. "How's it going?"

Ian, who was from a neighbouring constabulary, had been one of her closest friends due to him being in her syndicate – a smaller group within the class that made up a shift of officers for role-playing purposes when dealing with mock incidents. He had endeared himself to her by showing his feminine side when he struggled with home sickness throughout the course. She had spent many an hour persuading him to stick it out, and that it would be worth it in the end. Having spent four years away at university herself, the six months at training school had been a breeze, but Ian couldn't see the end of it. He had thanked her profusely while both drunk and sober when the end of the course drew near. She knew they would remain friends when they returned to their respective forces.

Sally decided to come straight to the point but, at the same time, tried to make light of such an embarrassing situation.

"Ian," she asked, "I'm in a spot of bother...did I take part in any alfresco sexual activity with you or anyone else at the passing-out dinner?"

Ian's initial stunned silence was followed up with an outburst of laughter. "What are you on about, girl?"

Sally repeated her question.

"No, but I can make arrangements if you want to rectify it!" he replied.

The silence from Sally told him that this wasn't the time for crass jokes.

"What's up, Sal?" he asked with genuine concern.

Sally related the facts she stood accused of.

"Fuck me!" was his inappropriate reply. "Sorry, Sal, that's serious shit."

He paused for a second before recalling what he could remember of the events after the coach left taking their guests to the local Holiday Inn. He recounted seeing her hanging out of a window on the top floor of the female accommodation block along with several of the other girls shouting for him and Moose, the nickname of another student, to sneak into their kitchen for a nightcap and, in doing so, to flout the strict 'no opposite sex' rule in the accommodation blocks.

"But, by the time we had managed to sneak over to your block without being caught by the security staff, you were nowhere to be seen. That's when we checked your room and found you comatose on the bed still in your ball gown. We decided it was best just to leave you there and carried on without you."

"Speak to Jackie," he continued. "I was stood beside her when she took a photo of you – you looked really unattractive, snoring and dribbling. She put you in the recovery position and left a bucket by the bed…"

All that made sense to Sally. The bucket had come in very useful in the early hours of the following morning but not before she had vomited down the front of her expensive Laura Ashley silk ball gown first. She still hadn't managed to get the red wine stains out.

It took Sally over twelve frustrating hours to make contact with Jackie who called in response to the answerphone message Sally had left. "I know what you want to speak about – what a scream! Not a great start, is it? – but I've offered to apologise to the wives and I think they'll all see the funny side!"

"Err, no Jax, I don't think we can be talking along the same lines here," Sally replied before going on to relate everything to her, including Ian's recollection of the events. Sally's account was interspersed with guffaws and delighted shrieks from Jackie which Sally couldn't understand. She was becoming quite narked by Jackie's lack of sympathy.

Jackie waited for her to finish then explained. "Sally, I know it sounds really awful but I can confirm that all Ian said is correct – the photo is hilarious! I know exactly what you're talking about though." Jackie explained that she had already been taken to task over the incident although, fortunately for her, the facts hadn't got quite so twisted by the time they had reached her supervisors.

"What actually happened is that some senior officers' wives who were staying in the block next to the boys' block heard us shouting and thought we were shouting 'moose' at them to insult them! Apparently they couldn't see the blokes we were shouting at and got their arses in their hands about 'unpolicewomanly-like conduct'!"

Bloody hell, thought Sally. She couldn't decide if that made her feel any better or not. It was all very embarrassing. She took the contact details for Jackie's sergeant, who, it seemed, had accepted Jackie's explanation with good humour, with the intention of getting the Baroness to speak with him to clarify the situation and clear her name. She still felt as if someone had kicked her in the stomach though – nothing was lifting that feeling.

The following day, Sally arrived early for the evening shift and left a brief message on the Baroness's desk asking her to ring Jackie's sergeant for an explanation regarding their previous conversation. She felt some reassurance by the fact that, when she walked into the briefing room, the team seemed to make an effort to greet her with smiles and to acknowledge her presence in a friendly enough manner. She was further reassured when Alex chose to sit next to her and asked how she had slept and how she had spent her day before coming to work. Her feeling of security, however, was completely deflated as, immediately briefing ended, the Baroness had the audacity to address everyone about the passing-out dinner fiasco.

Her face deadpan she announced, "I'd just like to say that Sally has been totally exonerated from her alleged misdemeanour at the passing-out dinner. It had all been blown out of proportion." With that, she turned her attention back to the pile of papers in front of her on the lectern.

The explosion of laughter amid various references to oral sex from around the room let Sally know that the allegation had been made public to everyone. This was the Baroness's way of letting her and everyone else know it had been a mistake – and in the process making it quite clear that she was in charge, holding their careers and reputations in her grasp.

Sally was mortified and realised that this was the cause of the false attention she had received on entering the briefing room. The wave of nausea she had experienced after the conversation with the Baroness the previous evening swept over her once again.

As the laughter died down and people began to wander off, the Baroness explained to Sally that she had been contacted by Jackie's sergeant. It was clear though that she wasn't going to let Sally off the hook completely. As she tidied the briefing papers, she added, "I'm afraid the damage is already done though, Sally, and you're going to have to work extra hard to shake off the reputation you've earned yourself so soon after arriving here."

"Or charge extra for an audience!" came the response from Graham who was still lurking nearby.

The Baroness didn't react to the comment. It was obvious that she didn't give a damn about Sally's reputation – a reputation that she had succeeded in tearing to shreds within two days of starting at the station. It was also clear to Sally that Sergeant Baron had no intention of helping her recover from this nor was she going to admit to or apologise for having got her facts wrong before she had accused her. Besides, it was old news now.

"Ready?" asked Alex who had appeared beside her, carrying his hat and coat.

Sally reluctantly picked up her belongings and followed him out of the station. Sally felt herself fast slipping into one of PC Dunbar's definitions of a policewoman and she had no idea how to extricate herself from it.

Cringing with embarrassment, Sally slumped into the car next to Alex. She screwed up her face at the lingering smell of body odour from the previous occupants which magnified her nauseous feelings. Sally didn't know what to say for the best so she said nothing and just stared unhappily out of the window.

Alex drove them out of the city and parked up overlooking Warleigh Valley. The landscape dropped away steeply in front of them before slowly climbing far away into the horizon, showcasing the impressive Warleigh Manor. Alex switched off the engine and they both sat taking in the scene in front of them. The brightly-coloured canal boats nestled along the bank of the Kennet and Avon Canal below them against the backdrop of a collage of fields dotted with grazing sheep.

As they sat in pensive silence, Sally became aware of the faint smell of Alex's aftershave. She couldn't help but think to herself that he was probably wondering what kind of probationary officer he was going to have to put up with for the next ten weeks. She was mortified by the revelations during the last twenty-four hours that had served to unjustly stake out her reputation for her. She didn't know what, if anything, she could do to live it down.

The first signs of autumn were showing with the leaves edged with rust and gold. This was Sally's least favourite time of the year with summer behind her and the prospect of an English winter ahead. A solitary magpie flew onto a branch of the nearest tree as if to epitomise Sally's bad fortune.

"One for sorrow." Sally broke the silence.

"Not if you greet it," offered Alex. "Go on – wish it a good evening and ask after its family," he encouraged.

Sally chanted miserably, "Good-evening-Mr-Magpie-how-are-your-family-today?"

When they stopped laughing at the ridiculous notion, Alex spoke quietly and with genuine sympathy. "Sally, I know it hasn't been a great start, but you'll be fine. The police service is notorious for gossip. In time, you'll get over it and even be able to laugh about it. And it won't be the last time you get gossiped about; you're a good-looking girl and good-looking girls attract the most gossip! Take it as a compliment!"

"Thanks, Alex," Sally replied not able to turn the feeling around just yet. "I just feel so excruciatingly embarrassed. It's not as if people even know me well enough to be able to make a proper judgement of me."

"I know. I can see how upset you are. If it makes you feel any better, I had no doubt that the gossip was bollocks even before it was explained. I'm sticking up for you, girl, and I'm the one who will get to know you best. Come on, you've got to move on or the buggers will really start getting to you. Rise above it and keep your chin up. It'll be old news soon."

Sally wanted to believe Alex, and truly hoped that what he was saying was right. She smiled at him. "Thanks for the reassurance. I guess only time will tell whether I can rebuild my reputation or not."

"Come on, let's go and kick some motorist's arse!" Sally managed a smile as Alex started the engine and they headed off in search of a defective light.

Alex managed to lift her spirits a little with several stories of when he had been the butt of jokes early in his service at the mercy of his teammates: the time they taken his car keys and moved his car from the station car park leaving a pile of broken glass beside where it had been, and the fake letter he had been completely duped by from the local sexual health clinic after he had a brief relationship with a local barmaid.

Sally started to feel a little more relaxed about things, albeit she was still very hurt, and she decided to do as Alex advised: put a brave face on it and march on. This was her first of many experiences of the joys of Chinese whispers in the police service.

When the night shift came on duty, the evening shift took on the role of Community Awareness Patrol. This comprised a crew bus with a sergeant and as many of the remaining available officers as possible which patrolled the city centre in the late evening and early hours of the morning when the pubs and clubs were closing. Although apprehensive about trying out her restraint techniques that until now she had only used in practice situations, Sally was excited to be part of this crew and to have the opportunity to put the defence tactics she had excelled in at training school to good use.

Senior man Roger drove the crew bus with the Baroness sat in the front passenger seat manning the radio. She positively purred with delight as Roger sycophantically fawned over her, helping with her seatbelt and asking if she was comfortable before he drove off. The remainder of the team were housed in the back. Sally climbed in and sat in one of the back rows of seats. No sooner had she lowered herself down when Graham pointed at her. "Oi, you, that's your seat," he said, spinning himself round so his horrid, stubby finger was pointing at the single seat just inside the door. It became evident that this was known as the 'sprog's seat' – that is, the most junior officer's seat that was positioned closest to the door so that the 'sprog' had to get out first to deal with the job.

Sally didn't reply but obediently moved, allowing him to lower his bulk into her former seat. She winced as a waft of BO filled her nostrils as he squeezed his repulsive mass past her.

As they cruised the city centre, Sally took in the motley crew around her. Tom 'Basher' Bishop was the next officer in line to Sally with regard to length of service but, despite his junior position, he had undoubtedly been accepted as 'one of the lads'; relating lewd jokes and anecdotes obviously helped his standing amongst his peers. As a single bloke, he had plenty of stories to tell and his top of the range Volkswagen Golf GTI, afforded him by courtesy of still living with his parents, assisted with his status.

Dan had just over five years service and was a little over-confident, particularly when it came to his driving. He aspired to be a traffic officer as soon as he could persuade the bosses to transfer him to the traffic department. He was often reminded of an incident where he had landed himself in trouble after showing off in a police car having spotted his wife in her car in front of him. He had pretended to be on his way to an emergency and put his blue lights and sirens on to overtake her. In doing so, he collided with a car belonging to an innocent and unsuspecting member of the public.

Gavin was in his late twenties, although he looked much younger and was a timid type. His weak spot was the moustache which the others claimed he had grown to make himself look older. Watching him perched on the remaining part of the seat left by Graham's bulk, Sally observed how he laughed exaggeratedly at all of Graham's jokes and pranks – but never seemed to have quite enough oomph to step out of line and take the lead himself. It was an odd partnership as Gavin should have been an ideal target for Graham's bullish behaviour but, instead, appeared to be his sidekick or 'yesman' as Sally privately labelled him.

Dave was the sensible member of the team – and had just celebrated his fortieth birthday. Sally discovered that he had recently returned to general policing duties after spending many years on the traffic department. He was very willing to share his knowledge of which she would often take advantage. Despite this, he wasn't interested in impressing anyone or needing to be 'one of the lads'. He wore an unkempt, full beard and had a passion for hill-walking which he would describe with fervour to Sally on the occasions they worked together. He spent his grub breaks engrossed in Stephen King novels.

Finally, there was Neil whom Sally had taken an immediate liking to because of his infectious sense of humour. He was nearing forty – a gifted policeman and natural communicator which reflected in his role as a community beat officer having responsibility for a specific area of Bath. His vast knowledge of the city and the individuals who came to the notice of the police was something Sally would often draw on as she learned her trade. He had been a respected rugby player in his time, and his stature together with his smooth weathered complexion gave the impression of a gentle giant.

Every time the crew bus's call sign came over the air, a cheer would go up before they tuned in to hear details of the job. Pub fights were followed by a "Yessss" and domestics got an "Uughhh." The jokes and stories that were all part of the fun on board the crew bus started as soon as they set off as Basher related a prank he had played on an annoying colleague on a recent residential course that he had attended. Apparently, the annoying party had wound his course mates up to the extent that they had sought revenge on the last night by taking his toothbrush and doing some unspeakable things with it before returning it to his room. To that day, the officer was still blissfully unaware of where the instrument he used to brush his teeth had been. Sally couldn't help but laugh, but also made a mental note not to irritate anyone on any future courses she might attend.

The first call was, to the team's delight, a pub fight. Sally felt her heart rate quicken, realising that this was actually the real thing and not something an instructor would call a halt to if it looked like it was getting out of hand. However, as usual, it was all over by the time they got there.

As Sally got out of the crew bus, having taken the initiative herself and not waiting for Graham to order her out, she was met by an extremely drunk young man in his early twenties sporting a bloody nose.

"I've been hit and my nose is bleeding," he slurred as he lurched towards her so that she could have a better look.

"I can see that," she said, taking a step back onto Alex's boot. She looked at Alex for inspiration but he remained silent; it was obvious he wanted her to take the lead.

OK, Sally thought, *let's start with the obvious.*

"Do you know who did it?" she asked, reaching for her pocket notebook to record some details.

"No, you're too late, he's legged it," the man replied, angrily swinging his arm in the direction he thought his assailant had gone in and clearly holding Sally personally responsible for not appearing on the scene in time to lynch him.

"Do you need medical attention?" Alex interjected.

Whoops, she'd forgotten that priority. She was too interested in finding the culprit and making her first arrest – and, in fairness, the injured party did seem capable of looking after himself. It was no surprise that he didn't want medical attention. He merely wiped his nose on his shirtsleeve as if to prove this and was clearly non-plussed at the sight of his own congealed blood. It turned out that he didn't want to make a formal complaint; most likely because he was as much to blame as the person who had hit him.

Alex turned to Sally and said, "I don't think we're going to get much out of him at the moment – he's too pissed. Give him a calling card and tell him to come in to the station tomorrow if he wants to follow it up."

Sally was grateful for the advice and, as Alex spoke to the Control Room on his radio to ask for an incident log number, she pulled a calling card out of the pouch that was attached to her belt and filled it in with her details. The bloodied male took the card and put it in his back pocket without looking at it whilst half listening to Sally's instructions.

"Yeah, yeah, alright," he said as he wandered off back into the pub having been handed a full pint of lager by a lookalike mate.

It was only then that Sally noticed the remainder of the crew armed with clipboards appearing from the crowd that had gathered to watch the goings-on. They had been attempting to gather information from witnesses to the fight whilst she was engaged with the 'victim'. This was obviously the task that she would aspire to when she was promoted out of the 'sprog' seat. That seemed a long way off at this moment.

Sally climbed back in the crew bus first – or so she thought. Graham was already in there. He looked nonchalant as it became obvious that he hadn't actually got out. Nor had the Baroness who was busying herself with giving an update of the incident to the Control Room.

As they moved off, Sally became aware of a conversation going on between the men in the crew bus.

"Are you up to the challenge then, Basher?" Roger asked.

"Yes, bring it on!" replied Basher.

Sally sat back and watched with anticipation as Roger drove the crew bus towards Snow Hill just outside the city centre. Roger stopped the crew bus and shuffled over beside the Baroness while Basher got into the driver's seat.

Sally looked across at Alex quizzically.

"Watch and take note, this will be you in due course – if you agree to take on the challenge!"

And then the ascent started. Up the steepest hill Sally had ever seen either before or since. It transpired that it was an in-house ritual that you had to successfully complete the 'Bennett's Lane Challenge' before you were considered a competent crew bus driver. This involved driving the manually operated vehicle up this 1:3 gradient without faltering, stopping or stalling, and included pulling out onto the road at the T-junction at the top with a perfect hill start.

The hill start was a challenge in itself without the extra pressure of the passengers jeering and doing their best to put the driver off. As the crew bus tilted up, Sally found herself gripping her seat and involuntarily tensing her body. The engine screamed as Basher scraped the gearstick into second gear and immediately back down to first which increased the volume of the jeering. The wheels spun for a few seconds before they managed to regrip the road surface and continue up the incline. It was more adrenalin-inducing than a fairground ride.

Sally was as relieved as Basher when he made it to the top and out onto Camden Road to a round of applause, cheers and subsequent backslapping. No faltering, no stopping and no stalling. He was officially 'one of the lads' and he could now take the helm on a Community Awareness Patrol.

Sally leant her forehead against the cool glass of the crew bus window as they made their way back into the city centre. She was beginning to realise it was all about proving yourself in this job. She would have to pass the police driving course first to authorise her to drive any police vehicle, let alone this monster.

Another pub fight was next. Turning into Sawclose, they could see that this one was still in progress – a mass of bodies with arms and legs flying in all directions in the road outside Joe Banana's nightclub. This time, Sally wasn't even given the chance to open the sliding door that she was dutifully sitting beside. Instead, she was unceremoniously pushed out of the way by everyone else as they piled out in front of her to get stuck in. Sally stood for a split second watching it all, not knowing whether to wade in or whether she would just be in the way.

Pretty soon, the two main protagonists were taken to the ground at which point Alex turned to her and shouted, "Pass your handcuffs!"

Sally leapt forward and handcuffed the male being restrained.

"Nick him for Section 4," Alex said quietly to her as she wrapped the metal bracelets around the wrists of the youth being held face down on the floor.

Sally recited the magic words for the very first time, "I am arresting you under Section 4 of the Public Order Act." She continued with the caution. "You do not have to say anything but anything you do say may be given in evidence," before escorting her trussed-up prisoner to the cage in the back of the crew bus. The word 'prisoner' seemed a bit over the top to Sally, but it was a term used to describe anyone who had been arrested. Her prisoner stepped without protest into the back of the crew bus. Obviously, it wasn't the first time for him and he knew it would only be a matter of hours before he was back out again.

As the cage door clashed shut behind him enclosing him in a four feet by two feet enclosure, he looked through the bars at Sally and jeered, "I haven't been arrested by anyone as cute as you before, darlin'."

Sally reached for the crew bus doors and slammed them shut.

*

49

Sally soon became very conscious of her lack of ability to use brute strength to overcome those in breach of the law. As a small-in-stature police officer, she had to adopt a totally different approach than some of her male counterparts: she talked. She found it to be a woman's best defence mechanism and it often had far more successful and less violent results than the fisticuffs approach favoured by many of her colleagues. She got stuck in when she had to, but she soon found that she could put her slight form to nimble use, stepping in with her handcuffs at the crucial point when her colleagues' hands were engaged in restraining the prisoner.

The rest of the shift was quiet. They picked up Ruth, who was the other female on the team, from where she had been taking a statement from a security guard who had witnessed a window being smashed at the Empire Hotel. As they drove her back to the station to deal with the man arrested for the damage, Sally chatted to Ruth about a concert she was playing in at the weekend. Ruth played the French horn and obviously to a high standard – an art form quite alien and incomprehensible to the majority of policemen.

When Basher overheard their conversation, he turned to Ruth and asked in an impressively serious tone, "Can you play 'Fellatio' by Goblé?"

Everyone snorted and looked at Ruth for a reply which came with all innocence as she stepped out of the crew bus. "Err, no, I don't think I've heard of that one."

The crew bus erupted with raucous laughter and Sally found it hard to resist laughing too. However, she tried to make her smile a reassuring one for poor Ruth who remained unaware she was the cause of the hilarity as she headed into the station.

During her well-earned rest days, Sally enjoyed some time to relax. She spent the days catching up on a few chores and the evenings vegging out in front of the telly with Julian. She suggested a shopping trip to Wells to her mum who jumped at the opportunity to spend time with her daughter. They managed to fill the whole day wandering round the shops and enjoying lunch together. It was good to forget the police for a while and become an invisible member of the public, allowing her to relax and recharge her batteries.

Sally returned to work for an early-turn shift feeling refreshed and ready for action at the 6am start. As soon as briefing was over and the Sergeants had left the room, Alex turned to Sally.

"Come on, grab your coat and hat. The Baroness and Maureen don't allow any hanging about after briefing. They like us to get on out there." He picked up Sally's hat and patted it onto her head.

"What? Not even time to finish my cup of tea?" asked Sally. Her probationer tea-making duties were made even more demeaning if she didn't even get the chance to drink it. Reluctantly she put her still half-full mug down and reached for her coat before following Alex outside for their shift on foot patrol in the city centre.

The sharp morning air nipped her cheeks, and she pulled her coat closer around her.

"Don't worry, just follow me!" Alex winked at her and strode off towards Orange Grove.

Sally fell in beside Alex and, within minutes, they were walking into a newsagent's in Gay Street. The owner looked up as they walked into the shop and smiled as he nodded towards the back of the shop and reminded them that his was milk with two sugars.

Sally paused at the magazine display.

"No looking at the dirty mags, Sally!" Alex ribbed her, placing his hands over her eyes and steering her towards the back of the shop.

"I wasn't..." Sally started to protest in horror at the suggestion that she would do such a thing before peeling Alex's blindfold away and seeing his cheeky grin. She made him make the tea as his punishment whilst she helped herself to a newspaper she found on the table.

With perfect timing, when they had just finished their last mouthful of tea, Sally's radio crackled into life. "Foxtrot Bravo 1759."

Sally feigned a look of terror at Alex as she recognised her collar number.

"Answer it then!" He giggled back at her.

"Can you attend an alarm at Next in Union Street please?" asked the radio controller.

"Yes, all noted. En route," replied Sally as calmly as she could.

Alex explained that alarm activations this time in the morning were rarely genuine intruders. This one was no different with cleaners having opened up and failed to deactivate the system within the required time limit. It felt odd walking through the near deserted streets at this early hour with only a handful of people walking with purpose to work, cleaning shop windows or clearing the litter.

Alex then watched as Sally completed her first fixed penalty ticket which she issued to a car that had overstayed the eight o'clock restriction in Stall Street. She thought this was a bit mean.

"I expect the owner is just running a bit late," she sympathised.

Alex laughed at her sensitive approach. "You're gonna have to shelve your personal sympathies if you're going to generate the amount of traffic-related paperwork that's expected of you during your probationary period."

Sally then spotted a car displaying an out-of-date tax disc and she gleefully pulled out her pad of red warning notices without a problem with her conscience.

"Ah," deduced Alex with his hands on his hips, "you can ticket a car with no tax, then? Let me guess – you would never allow your car tax to run out but you can see yourself oversleeping and incurring the wrath of an overzealous probationer. Is that about right?"

"Got it in one, buddy!" Sally retorted as she slapped the self-adhesive notice on the windscreen in direct view of the driver.

"Foxtrot Bravo 1759," the radio announced again. Alex looked on amused as Sally tried to juggle putting her pad of tickets back into the pouch hanging from her belt whilst trying to fumble for her radio mouthpiece and dropping her pen as she did so.

He saved her the trouble. "In company. Go ahead," he replied on her behalf.

"Thanks, Alex," came the reply from the radio controller, obviously recognising his voice.

"Can you attend a burglary at Wynnes and Lee Solicitors in Queen Square please?"

"Yep, en route," he answered, turning on his heel and heading back up the city.

Sally was fascinated to discover that the burglars

had forced a sash window in the basement, out of view of the pavement, before rifling through the offices leaving a considerable mess behind them. Gratefully accepting another cup of tea, Sally completed the necessary forms under Alex's guidance, taking the details from the two shaken-up secretaries who had discovered the break-in.

Before they left, Alex turned to the women and said, "Would you like me to ask our Crime Prevention Officer to visit to advise on a suitable alarm system?"

Sally couldn't help but notice the pair of them swoon at the attention Alex was bestowing on them and she rolled her eyes from where she stood behind them, smirking as she gathered her papers together.

As they stepped outside, Sally felt the warmth of the sun on her face, relieved to see that the sharp morning air was slowly beginning to ease, lightening both her step and her spirits. From there, they headed for the Royal Victoria Park with its tennis courts, mini golf course...and cafeteria. The café owner also welcomed Alex as a regular visitor.

"God, Alex, I can't manage another cup of tea," Sally whimpered, "but I'm going to have to make use of the loos."

Sally left Alex chatting to the kitchen staff who were preparing for their daily onslaught of tourists. Going to the loo in full uniform was no easy task and it proved a juggling act to avoid losing her radio and notebook down the pan. She would have to curtail her tea drinking if this was the resulting effect.

After eventually winning the battle, she made her way back to Alex who was sitting in the window slurping his fourth cup of tea of the morning and perched on the seat opposite him.

"You were a long time. You constipated or something?"

"No, I'm not!" Sally started to protest, blushing as she did so, before realising that he was teasing her again. She sat back smiling in defeat at having been caught out once more by his sense of humour.

"You ought to try it in all this garb. It's alright for you blokes!" she said, indicating the bulky uniform and equipment around her midriff. Alex laughed at her feigned indignity.

Sally liked early turns. To be up and about before everyone else gave her a strange feeling of satisfaction; watching the world gradually come to life as people made their way to work, and shops and offices opened their doors.

"Foxtrot Bravo 1759," came the voice from the Control Room.

"Go ahead," replied Sally into her mouthpiece.

Alex downed his last mouthful of tea and they made their way to Charlotte Street where there had been a minor shunt between two cars as rush hour started. She enjoyed a busy shift learning the basics of her new trade.

After three early turns, they reverted to late shifts. The mornings before a late shift passed in a flash and, before Sally knew it, it was time to go to work. She had to be disciplined not to overdo things beforehand as, by the time 9pm came and the city was hotting up, she was feeling decidedly jaded. She learned this the hard way during this first late shift as, after seven hours of walking the city, she arrested a teenager for smashing a shop window at 9.45pm. This resulted in her working into the early hours of the morning with her concentration levels battling against extreme tiredness.

The following late shift, she and Alex were crewed together in a car. This was definitely Sally's favourite deployment as they were sent to much more interesting jobs than when they were walking the city. It had just started to get dark when the call that Sally had been waiting for came in.

"Any unit for a burglary in progress in Bloomfield?"

Sally forgot her fears of being heard on the radio and grabbed the handset, almost screaming down the mouthpiece, "Yes, we'll take that one!"

"Sally, you forgot to give our call sign," Alex said calmly, "but they probably guessed who it was." He activated the blue lights but not the two tone horns, explaining while they sped towards the location that they didn't want to alert the burglar of their approach.

Alex reached for the radio handset as he drove. "2679," he began with his collar number, "can you see if there's a dog handler available?"

He threw the handset on the dashboard, his hand returning to grip the steering wheel as he concentrated on his driving.

"Take my advice and stay still when there's a dog about," he said as he negotiated Churchill Bridge with skill and confidence. "I learnt the hard way and got a nasty nip on my arse. No joke!" he continued, his eyes fixed on the road and a broad smile on his face.

The comical advice left a tempting opening for a cheeky comment about the aforementioned pert part of Alex's anatomy but, as the engine screamed in protest, it seemed inappropriate and, besides, she hardly knew him. Instead, she whimpered with a mixture of fear and delight as they negotiated the right-hand bend at Bear Flat with an audible wheel spin.

"Yeh hey!" she cried out with sheer enjoyment of the ride as Alex accelerated up the Wellsway. She dug her feet into the footwell and held on to the handle above the passenger window – commonly known, as she would later discover, as the 'FM handle' in reference to a frightened expletive – her eyes wide with excitement and anticipation.

They arrived in no time and leapt out of the car. They were met by a man from the neighbouring bungalow who greeted them wearing his coat and slippers. He explained that he had called them because the occupants were away on holiday and he had heard a loud bang at the back of the house.

"You go that way," Alex instructed Sally, with the most serious face she had seen on him in the short time she had known him, as he disappeared around the far side of the bungalow. Two more police cars screeched to a halt behind theirs. Sally felt smug that they were the first unit on the scene and disappeared down the side of the bungalow to seek out her first burglar. She reached the back of the property before Alex and immediately noticed a small window that was open with an overturned patio chair beneath it. Shivering with excitement, she slowly crept up to the window and peered inside. There was nothing obvious to be seen at first glance so she moved across to see further into the room. Suddenly, she saw a figure moving inside and immediately backed out of sight, her breath coming in short involuntary bursts and her heartbeat thudding in her brow. She leapt and strangled a yelp when Basher grabbed her arm.

"You OK, Sal?"

Now shaking with nerves, it took her a few seconds to respond, but Sally managed to point in the direction of the intruder before finding a few words.

"He's still inside. I've just seen him through that window there!" She gesticulated wildly at him speaking in a stage whisper and hitting him on the nose in her panicked state.

Basher pulled her back to the corner of the bungalow and reported her find on the radio. Sally was in no fit state to speak on the radio, but was annoyed at him taking the credit by reporting her find.

Within minutes, Sally became aware of the baying of an over-eager German Shepherd dog accompanied by the purr of the police helicopter which appeared overhead.

God, thought Sally, *this is so exciting. This is what I joined up for!*

Inspector Creed appeared beside them and clarified with Sally which window she had seen the burglar through. She proudly indicated which one before turning to Basher.

"It's like a scene from The Bill, isn't it!" she squeaked excitedly as she watched in awe as the Inspector complete with his flat cap lifted a loudhailer to his mouth.

"This is the police. This house is surrounded. Make yourself known with your hands above your head."

Sally held her breath with anticipation and pressed herself against the smooth Bath stone wall of the bungalow. Her heartbeat was clearly audible in her head.

What was he going to look like? Was he going to make a run for it when he came out or was he going to give himself up quietly?

Inspector Creed nodded towards her which she interpreted as him being pleased with her for spotting the intruder. She smiled and raised her shoulders with exhilarated delight. The burglar would never make a successful getaway with so many police present.

Inspector Creed repeated his instructions twice before asking Sally to approach the window again to confirm her sighting of the burglar. Sally, adrenalin racing through her veins, did as she was asked and sidled up to the window slowly leaning across to look inside. She looked at the point in the room where she had seen the burglar. He wasn't obvious so she slid across a bit further to get a better look inside.

Suddenly the blood rushed to her head as she stared through the window pane with the realisation that what she had seen was in fact her own reflection in a full-length mirror! She staggered back a couple of paces burying her head in her hands, causing Alex, who had been standing at the opposite corner of the bungalow, to run to her aid. He placed his hand on her shoulder and looked through the window.

"Oh shit!" he said quietly so that only Sally could hear, before shouting, "It's OK, it's OK. Everyone stand down." With that, he bent over double and started laughing.

"Sally, you're a scream!" he said when he was finally able to speak again. "This one is going to go in your probationer report. What a classic!"

With Sally wishing the ground would swallow her up, everyone made the necessary noises and poked fun at her before drifting off, obviously having enjoyed the incident at her expense. Fortunately, Inspector Creed saw the funny side and tried to reassure her that her intentions had been honourable and that it was an easy mistake to make.

Once alone in the car, Alex and Sally remained outside the bungalow and logged the incident in their notebooks.

"We'll keep the details brief, shall we?" Alex said, still not able to stop laughing at his probationer's well-intentioned mistake. Sally just held her head in her hands and apologised to Alex for the umpteenth time. She was relieved that Sergeant Baron hadn't turned up, but she knew she still had to face her when she returned to the station.

Chapter Three

To Sally's surprise, Sergeant Baron didn't make a big issue out of the burglary incident – apart from a comment that she was 'making quite a name for herself'. Sally thought it could have been worse.

The remainder of her buddy weeks with Alex thankfully passed without any further mishaps or hiccups and she was beginning to get to know the rest of her team. They were helpful and supportive when she asked for help – with the exception of Graham who seemed to delight in taking every opportunity to mock her. She knew she wasn't the only one who got this treatment, but she wasn't looking forward to finishing her buddy weeks with Alex who she felt had acted like a human shield protecting her from Graham. It seemed that Graham was just biding his time until he was able to hound her unhindered.

On an early shift during her eleventh week, she was summoned to the superintendent's office to be 'signed off' as suitable for solo patrol.

"Put your tunic on and carry your hat," Alex advised her. "You want to create the right impression."

Sally heeded the advice and took her smart tunic with its silver crested buttons out of her locker. As she brushed her uniform down, she couldn't help dwelling on whether the superintendent knew anything about the blunder she had made at the burglary or, even worse, the Chinese whisper from her passing-out dinner.

Alex seemed to sense this as she appeared from the locker room.

"Don't worry, Sal. Superintendent Keely is so far removed from everyday policing, he won't have heard any station gossip and, besides, I've written you an excellent report." He placed a reassuring hand on her shoulder. The temptation to rest her cheek on it was almost too much. She wasn't so convinced and wouldn't have put it past Sergeant Baron to have put her pennyworth in. She pensively smoothed the rounded dome of her felt hat before making her way nervously to the superintendent's office.

Taking a deep breath, she knocked on the door. The light on the wall beside the door immediately turned to green and she reached for the handle and let herself in. The room had an air of calmness and still about it as she shut out the hustle and bustle of the station. An impressive glass cabinet boasted a host of silverware, certificates and photos of smiling people shaking hands.

Sally needn't have worried. Superintendent Keely man-oeuvred around his large oak desk and strode towards her with his hand outstretched to greet her before guiding her towards two armchairs which were separated by a coffee table next to the window. She guessed he was in his late forties and he wore his uniform well, decorated with impressive coloured crowns on his epaulettes. A neat greying haircut gave him a decidedly distinguished look. He conveyed an aura of authority and Sally could see how and why he had made it to the top.

Sally sat beside the window sill where a proud family

photo was displayed. Superintendent Keely sat opposite her and opened the file bearing PC 1759 SALLY GENTLE on its cover which he had placed on the table in front of him.

"An impressive start, Sally," he began.

Sally visibly relaxed. Alex's prediction had proved to be true. She wondered why she had doubted him.

"The constabulary needs young, intelligent and motivated officers and you obviously have all of those qualities."

Sally blushed at his praise and was even more flattered when he suggested she put her teaching skills to good use for the constabulary, asking if she would be prepared to give some talks at local schools that had particularly requested female officers.

"I'd love to," Sally gushed with enthusiasm – though she thought it would be a strange experience returning to the classroom as a police officer.

He asked her about her background and empathised with losing her father at such a young age having suffered the same loss in his teens. Sally sat and studied him as he spoke. She liked to think that her father would have reached this distinguished rank had he been given the opportunity and not been snatched from this world so prematurely. In fact, it could have been him sat in front of her, she mused, before pushing the thought away, not allowing herself to dwell on the idea.

"Watch out for the probationer pranks." He waved his finger towards her in a friendly manner. "I got caught out going to a report of a hanging down in the depths of Somerton. Turned out to be a mannequin swinging in the wind but, by God, it gave me nightmares for months afterwards."

Sally laughed politely, finding it mildly reassuring that the pranks were considered par for the course for a probationer.

"Yes, I am having to watch my back," She raised her eyebrows in recognition of his warning whilst at the same time dreading what lay ahead for her.

After an easy flowing twenty minutes or so, Superintendent Keely shook her hand and wished her well in her future.

Sally was beaming when she returned to the briefing room and found Alex hovering waiting for her.

"That went well then?" he stated, noting her pleased expression.

"Yep – don't know what I was worried about – he's really nice. He even asked me to do some school talks."

"Ah well, that's what has got him to such a heady rank. Being able to spot talent when he sees it."

Sally gave him a friendly shove as he got up and made towards the briefing room door with Basher. It was strange seeing him crewed up with someone else. But, high from her visit to the superintendent, she picked up her hat and checked her reflection in the window before stepping out of the station and heading into Henry Street for her first solo patrol in the city centre.

It wasn't until she started going to work in the knowledge that she wasn't going to be paired up with Alex that she realised how much she had relied on him and, in fact, how much she missed his company. She had felt so safe with him, as if he was somehow invincible – facing danger together seemed to heighten his attractiveness and, occasionally, she had to give herself a reality check and banish all thoughts of a fairytale she often played out in her mind. From talking with her training school friends, she discovered that they mostly felt the same way about their buddies.

Alex had told her to expect to spend most of her time on foot patrol in the city centre during her probationary two years. With this in mind, she made a point of introducing herself to as many shop owners and other regular faces in the city centre as possible from the refuse collectors to the mayor. Everyone was pleased to talk to a police officer; to bend their ear with their tales of woe and to tell them how nice it was to see an officer on the beat. On a warm day, when you were feeling well rested, it was the best job in the world, but on a cold day, feeling down and with a lack of sleep, Sally found that this could also be one of the loneliest jobs on the earth. She even found herself on a bad day taking pity on the street beggars, an undesirable feature of Bath's streets, who sat looking miserable and dejected on the pavements close to the cashpoint machines. She fought the temptation to sit down with them and pass an hour or so, just to be able to rest her weary feet and aching back.

A week of nights followed and, having walked the city every night for the first six shifts, she was delighted to hear her collar number called out on the final night's briefing to crew one of the cars. The delight was short-lived when she realised that her crewmate was Graham; the audible 'tut' from him confirmed the feeling was mutual. His dislike for her had been obvious from the start and although Sally didn't know what his problem was, the fact that he was the more senior meant he had the upper hand when they were working together. And it was a position he was going to damn well take advantage of.

The minute briefing was over, he stood up and turned to Sally. "You ready, sprog?"

"If you mean me, my name is Sally," she replied flatly,

without looking at her tormenter. This prompted a snort from him.

Sally wasn't actually organised and could have done with a trip to the loo before going out. You never knew when you would have the chance again. Instead, she quickly gathered her things and dutifully followed him out to the car.

Graham drove straight to the Sulis Ranger's football ground. She knew from general conversations in the station that he was 'on the board' of the football club and obviously considered himself very important. He often asked for Saturdays off so that he could run the line at home matches.

"Damn lucky to be in a car you are," he lectured her en route. "When I was a sprog, I never got so much as a sniff of the inside of a patrol car."

Sally didn't bother to reply. Instead, she glanced at his belly hanging over his belt resisting the urge to say that he would benefit from a bit more foot patrol himself.

As they pulled up outside the clubhouse, Graham released his seatbelt and said, "I just need to pop in here for a bit of 'S and D'." Social and Domestic – a phrase given for using work time to get your own errands done. "You don't need to come in."

She really didn't want to go in. However, she saw this as an opportunity to use the loo and undid her seatbelt whilst stating her intention to the sound of another 'tut' from Graham.

Immediately as Sally walked in, the lewd comments started from a small gathering of men stood at the bar.

"Wey hey – got some female company tonight, have we?"

"Not going to get much work done tonight, eh, Butts?!"

Sally pretended she hadn't heard and looked around for the ladies. The function room had seen better days in its

Vauxhall Conference history. The busily patterned carpet was threadbare in places especially alongside the bar and the smell of stale smoke gagged in her throat. The walls were dotted with faded photos of bygone stars, and an elderly woman in a navy tabard was wiping the tables and arranging the chairs that were positioned around the edges of the room.

"Your usual?" asked the barman as he put a shorts glass on the bar in front of Graham who looked awkwardly at Sally and replied, "Oh, very funny, Terry, just my usual orange juice please."

His friends laughed knowingly as Sally spotted the door she was looking for. She excused herself and walked off in the direction of the toilets. Before she reached the door, she heard one of them say, "She going to get her kit off for you tonight, Gray?!" They all guffawed.

"She going to sit on your truncheon for you?" Another guffaw, but this time louder.

Once alone, Sally splashed her flushed face with cold water as she stood in front of the mirror. "Sexist pigs," she muttered to herself, seething at this bigoted attitude which she had no choice but to go back out and face.

"What's yours then, love?" asked Terry when Sally reappeared. She looked at the typically dressed football committee members: a half-hearted attempt to look smart with a collar and tie was let down by an over-washed V-neck club jumper and polyester trousers finished off with training shoes.

"Can you do her a slow comfortable screw, Tel?!" drawled one of them lecherously before sucking on his cigarette and winking at Graham as he blew the smoke out.

Sally had heard enough and, retaining as much dignity as she could, picked up the car keys from where Graham had left them on the bar and turned on her heel. She didn't make eye contact with any of them and hoped that her lack of acknowledgement of their foul behaviour would communicate more than trying to put them down with a few well chosen words that weren't presenting themselves to her at that moment. No such luck. Sally left this chauvinistic melting pot to the sound of "phwoars" and other equally inappropriate and unwelcome comments.

She took in a few gulps of smoke-free air as she made her way back to the car. Once inside she looked at the clock on the dashboard: 23:00 hours. Seven hours still to go. It was going to be a long night.

Sally woke up early from her final night shift. She was looking forward to spending some quality time with Julian. They were going to his parents for a family meal that evening to celebrate his father's sixtieth birthday. His family always made her feel welcome and showed their pride in her as if she was their own daughter. She was grateful to Julian who had been very supportive when she had told him about the passing-out dinner business. In truth, it was a drop in the ocean to what he and his colleagues got up to on their corporate weekends, which made Sally more than a little uncomfortable when he retorted with a comment reflecting this – particularly as he had a corporate weekend coming up. He had no understanding however of the extent of the embarrassment it had caused her within her working environment and was obviously not going to make any attempt to understand. Sally decided this wasn't altogether a bad thing and didn't mention it again.

They spent a relaxing day with an indulgent lunch at The Moon and Sixpence before wandering around Bath choosing a gift for his father. She succumbed to a catnap when they got home before heading to his parents' impressive country home near Corsham.

She returned to work re-energised and ready to face another week of shifts. She was starting to feel confident in her role and soon learned where and from whom she could seek advice when she didn't know how to deal with an incident or was unsure of a certain procedure. Alex was the obvious choice but, if he wasn't available, she had made enough friends in the station that she could turn to. Sally also found who not to ask. Sergeant Baron gave her advice in such a demeaning manner, intimating that Sally should have known the answer already, that she avoided asking her.

Graham also proved himself the weasel she had suspected he was from the start, as the one time she resorted to asking him for help, he intentionally gave her the wrong advice about which paperwork she needed for a particular job and then watched her fall – she didn't bother to ask him again. Sally couldn't make up her mind whether he genuinely didn't like her or whether she was just a convenient target for his bullishness. Practical jokes were really funny when they were played on someone else, but when she found herself the butt of jokes continually, Sally found the humour wore a little thin. So far, Graham had sabotaged her sandwiches, which she had briefly and foolishly left unattended, by putting paper in with the filling which caused her to gag to the amusement of the remainder of those sat in the canteen. He had also thought it funny to put salt in to her coffee – again left unattended – which caused a similar reaction from all parties present. Sally made a mental note not to leave anything unattended and spent many an hour dreaming up ways to pay him back.

It seemed that everyone else thought that these pranks were funny too and that they either supported Graham in what he was doing or were too frightened to challenge him for fear of being victimised themselves. Even Alex was reluctant to get involved and advised her again to just rise above it. To Sally, this was easier said than done especially as it appeared that Graham was beyond reproach. She had tried talking to the sergeants about him, but he was clearly the Baroness's golden boy. In her eyes, he could do no wrong so there was no point in moaning. In addition, it was becoming clear to Sally that, although there were two sergeants assigned to her team, Sergeant Baron undoubtedly had the upper hand when it came to decision-making and discipline matters. Whilst Sergeant Morley was a sweet man, it was obvious from the way Sergeant Baron spoke to him in front of the team that she was the one who wore the trousers in that working relationship. Sally's only ally in all this was Ruth who, being the only other female on the group and also still in her probation, was also on Graham's hit list. She was far less vociferous about the unjustness of it though, choosing to remain quiet though obviously unhappy about the situation.

Sally walked the city centre with Ruth the day after the coffee-contaminating incident, and ranted and raged at her about the detestable Graham and his immunity from being disciplined because of his senior position and his close friendship with the Baroness.

It was drizzling lightly and there was a cold nip in the air which added to Sally's low spirits.

"Don't let him get to you," Ruth advised in her sweet,

hushed voice as they walked along Cheap Street towards Westgate Street where a delivery van had been reported as causing an obstruction. "I'm a great believer in fate and that one day things will come full circle and he will get his comeuppance."

Sally wanted to believe that she was right but was finding it difficult to find such faith.

"He's been like it to me since the day I started," Ruth revealed after they had spoken to the delivery van driver and moved him on, "and I soon discovered, like you, that I'm powerless to do anything about him. I'm studying hard for my sergeant's exam and hoping that will be my passport out of here. If I don't pass then I'll put in for a transfer."

"What a shame that someone should be allowed to make others' lives so unnecessarily unenjoyable," Sally voiced her opinion to Ruth. "We ought to get him back with a well planned prank, but I just can't think of anything that would fool him, wily old bastard."

"Wily, fat old bastard!" echoed Ruth and they both threw their heads back and laughed with a sense of sisterhood solidarity before they were called on their radios to a shoplifter in a nearby department store.

The remainder of the team made it clear that they didn't like working with Ruth and, although the two girls often put the world to rights whilst pounding the pavements together, Sally soon found that Ruth really didn't have a lot of conversation or interests beyond classical music.

As a result, Sally didn't find walking the city for eight hours with Ruth what she would call scintillating, in contrast to when she had walked with Alex and the time had flown as conversation between them rarely ceased. Ruth was a sweet girl whose career choice was a mystery to everyone, not least her parents after graduating with her Fine Arts degree. Unlike Sally who was of a new breed of policewomen who preferred to wear more practical uniform trousers, Ruth insisted on sticking to the 'A' line heavy polyester skirt. She balked at the sight of Sally's size four Dr Marten boots – Alex had told her he thought they looked cute. Sally couldn't help think Ruth's desire to conform to the conventional women's uniform harked back to her boarding schooldays where she had obviously been happy and secure – no doubt as head girl or something equally as foreign to Sally's own schooldays. Ruth was a source of much amusement and a glut of associated jokes from many other members of the team who particularly homed in on the fact that her father was a vicar. This fact, at least, explained her unassuming nature which contrasted greatly with Sally who preferred to stand her ground rather than kowtow to people whom she judged unfair. Both were unhappy with this helpless situation they found themselves in.

The three rest days that followed and that Sally had been so looking forward to were taken up with unrelenting arguments with Julian. It had started with Sally breaking the news to him that she was unable to get the time off to accompany him to his work's Christmas dinner and dance. She knew it was important to him, but was also aware that he didn't require her presence purely for her company but more as a conduit for the promotion he hankered after.

"It doesn't portray a good image to the bosses if I don't show that I am settled and reliable," he protested as he dawdled behind Sally, pushing the trolley in Sainsbury's as they did a late night shop. He hated doing the shopping at the best of times and Sally's shifts sometimes dictated they did it at such an unorthodox hour.

"Julian," she replied as sympathetically as she could in view of the number of times she had repeated herself, "you know I have asked three times now if I can take the shift off, but others have got there ahead of me. It's obviously a prime weekend for Christmas functions."

The date fell on a late shift and the answer was a definite 'no' from the Baroness who, Sally noted, had managed to get the shift off herself.

"Take a sickie," he suggested petulantly as he studied with a critical eye the packaging of a box of designer muesli.

"Yeah, right." Sally laughed sarcastically. "Like you'd do that for me?" Julian never went sick. He would crawl off his deathbed if it meant getting his damned promotion. "Anyway, that would be too obvious after I've made such a fuss of trying to get the shift off."

Julian didn't seem to understand there was nothing she could do about it despite her best efforts to assuage him. As a result, there was a frosty atmosphere between them whilst Julian sulked.

Sally related the argument to Uncle Jack when she met him at their usual haunt. He empathised with her and could remember similar incidents with Aunt Bridie.

"That's the trouble with shift work, Sal. Doesn't do anything for your social life. You'll just have to make sure you book the day off in plenty of time next year."

Sally had already tried to reassure Julian with this promise, but the promotion he was after would have been handed out by then. He needed her on his arm this year.

*

The next week of night shifts came round all too quickly and, before she knew it, Sally was again sitting at the briefing table being told she was walking the city with Ruth. It was a quiet week as the cold had set in and discouraged criminals from venturing out. Sally's spirits were at a pretty low ebb, only lifted by the fact that Julian seemed to have got over the disappointment of the Christmas dinner and dance, and was back to his normal self. In fact he seemed to be making more of an effort than usual having spent the week cleaning and tidying the flat and had even sorted through all his boxes of stuff that had been stacked in the spare room untouched since he had moved into her flat nearly two years ago. He sympathised with her plight of having to walk every night with Ruth, but reassured her that it was only whilst she was the most junior on the group and that there would soon be other probationers to take her place. Sally knew this was true, but the eight hours that stretched ahead of her every night seemed like an eternity.

Time and time again, she fell foul of Graham's practical jokes and, together with her own naivety, the week saw her tormentor raise his arms in sick victory on more occasions than she wished to remember. On the first night, he had pulled up beside her and Ruth in a patrol car and called them over to speak through his open window. As Sally stooped to see what he wanted, she felt a cold jet of water hit her square in the face from the windscreen washer that had been redirected to target an unsuspecting probationary officer.

"A direct hit with the washer water!" Graham announced over the radio for the whole shift to hear as Sally walked away trying to retain as much dignity as possible.

He gave her a break for a couple of nights, but scored again when the Control Room asked the two girls to

RV – rendezvous – with a patrol car in York Street beside the Roman Baths to pass on a message. This wasn't altogether unusual when a message was either very long winded or of such a sensitive nature that they didn't want it to be picked up by radio scanners. On seeing Graham was the passenger, Sally hung back and allowed Ruth to speak to him. He wound down his window leaning his pudgy elbow along the rim. Sally could hear him talking about an observation request given out at briefing. Suddenly he broke off from what he was saying and pointed across the road at the surrounding wall of the Roman Baths. "Christ, there's someone in there. Come on, Dave!"

Sally turned to see what he was looking at. Sure enough, she could just make out a figure through the stone balustrade of the Bath's perimeter wall. Sally immediately broke into a sprint towards the intruder. As she ran, the patrol car sped by her, its blue lights flashing, and screeched round the corner.

"Sally!" Sally could hear Ruth calling after her. "Sally – stop!"

Ruth caught up with Sally as she was looking for a way to scale the wall from the Abbey Churchyard. "It's a statue," Ruth gasped. "He got me with the same trick a while back."

Sally stared at the back of the head of a stone statue of a Roman soldier that was just visible over the wall, her fists clenched with rage against her temple. She heard the radio controller obviously sharing the joke with a comment about being met with stony silence. She fought hard to choke back the tears of frustration. He wasn't worth it, she told herself. Nonetheless, she followed after Ruth, her blood boiling and a feeling of sheer helplessness at the unrelenting hounding she felt she was being subjected to.

As if that wasn't enough, Sally managed to drop herself

in it without anyone else's help after attending a street fight when the clubs closed a few hours later. She and Ruth, being on foot, had arrived on the scene later than the police cars, and the main protagonists had been taken away. Sally and Ruth mingled with the crowd that had gathered and took details of those who had witnessed what had happened. When they returned to the station for their grub break, Dave and Graham who had been the arresting officers at the fight asked for the witness details they had taken. It was past 3am and Sally looked wearily at the notes in her pocket notebook and relayed the information.

"I've got two girls, Claire Packer and Lisa Watson, and the boyfriend of one of them – an M Mouse..."

As she said it, she visibly shrank. *God, what a fool,* she thought to herself as the outburst of laughter hit her. Sally laughed with them pretending that she found it funny too. It was funny if you weren't responsible for being so gullible. The two girls were quietly contemplative as they left the station after their break commenting to each other that they hadn't heard the last of Sally's inexperienced blunder. Graham, of course, took full advantage of it and, as the shift drew to a close, she heard him pass an observation message over the radio for a male by the name of Michael Mouse who was being sought as a witness to an earlier incident – the only description available was that he had big ears and a squeaky voice...

Sally reached for her radio and turned the volume down. She didn't want to hear any responses that may have been elicited from the gag. Neither Ruth nor Sally felt the need to comment on it as they turned at the top of Milsom Street and started to make their way back to the station. Sally knew it wouldn't be the last she heard of it. How right she was.

Every night during this week of night shifts, two officers were assigned to sit up in an old warehouse that was being converted into executive apartments. It was being regularly targeted by burglars stealing the boilers and kitchen fittings and there had been a tip-off that another strike was imminent.

The task was shared out amongst the team. Sally was due to pair up with Basher on the Saturday night, if the job hadn't 'gone down' by then. Sally wasn't sure whether she wanted something to happen before her turn there or not as it sounded so exciting but terrifying at the same time. They were given strict instructions that they shouldn't confront any intruders. They were there as an early-warning system, purely to observe until back-up arrived. This seemed all a bit risky to Sally. What if back up didn't arrive in time? But she wasn't in a position to question the plan. Many times she would find herself in a potentially precarious situation, having to rely on her common sense and not try to be a heroine.

When Sally's turn came on the penultimate night of the week, she chose her outfit carefully – they had been told to be in civvies – and armed herself with a few magazines to keep her awake and occupied when it was her turn to take a break whilst they took turns acting as look out. When she arrived at work however, she was mortified to find that, instead of being paired with Basher who had reported in sick, she was told that Graham would take his place. 'Why him?!' Sally screamed inside her head. A whole night with no getting away from that slimy git! She picked up her sandwiches and jacket and waited in the foyer for the lift that had been organised to take them there.

When they arrived, Graham instructed Sally that, from midnight, they would take it in turns to look out or to rest –

which Sally knew meant sleep. She nodded in agreement. At least it meant they wouldn't have to sit in uncompanionable silence all night. They settled themselves on a first-floor landing that gave them a good view of the approach to the warehouse but where they would not be illuminated by any approaching car lights. Graham immediately took out his sandwich box and proceeded to devour his foul-smelling garlic sausage sandwiches.

Sally wondered whether things could get much worse but, when midnight arrived with nothing but Graham's bad breath to note, he announced he was going to 'get his head down'. He found some hessian sacks in an adjoining room and, using his sandwich box encased in a coat as a pillow, settled himself on the floor. Within minutes, he had turned into a grunting, snoring and farting mass of blubber.

Sally checked her watch. It was going to be a long night. If only she had a camera or camcorder. Revenge would be so sweet to capture the saliva which oozed from the corner of his mouth with beads of white phlegm down its length, until it formed a reservoir on the hessian sack, accompanied by rhythmic and noisy exhalations.

Sally initially made a mental note not to lie on that patch when it was her turn to rest but, as she continued to study her tormenter as he lay in such a defenceless and personal form, she decided that she would forego her chance to sleep and leave him slumbering rather than allow him the opportunity to survey her in such a vulnerable state. Besides, the opportunity to be 'alone' was singularly more attractive than having to interact with him.

Sally looked out across the wasteland that fronted the warehouse. It was dimly lit by the moonlight flickering through a row of leylandii obscuring the site from any other form of civilisation. The morphing shadows being cast over the ground made Sally want to double-check that her radio had a good signal. It was a needless task as she could hear the occasional transmissions, but she wanted the reassurance, suddenly feeling anxious about the responsibility of her task and the fear of what might happen. Only the greater fear of waking the sloth that lay comatose beside her stopped her from carrying out the check.

As the long hours ticked away and as Graham continued to enjoy his slumber, Sally flicked through the magazines struggling to make out the words in the limited light coming through the window. Sergeant Morley did call up a couple of times for welfare checks which fortunately had failed to rouse the snorting mass of blubber but, apart from that, it was a solitary and uneventful night. At just after 5am, when dawn started to make an appearance, Sally was startled by the sound of an engine. Remembering her recent embarrassing experience at the house burglary, this time she waited until she was sure of what she was seeing before alerting the Control Room. She was learning fast.

It was the first of the workmen arriving in their uniforms of faded jeans, fluorescent tabards and scruffy boots. Carrying their lunchboxes and hard hats, they made their way to the entrance. Sally took a long, slow intake of breath and stretched. Beside her, her still comatose colleague, who was usually so full of bravado, lay stripped of his power and dominance. She decided to leave him as he was.

Collecting her things and tightening her ponytail, she made her way down the stairs to the entrance hall before calling up on her radio for a lift.

Alex and Ruth arrived within a couple of minutes. Sally suspected they had spent the shift not far from the warehouse in case they – or rather she, since Graham had been asleep all night – had called for back-up.

"Where's Butts?" enquired Alex through the open window as Sally approached the car.

"Oh, he must have forgotten to put his alarm on," Sally replied as she cast her eye to the first-floor window behind which the oblivious Graham slept on alone.

"Allow me," said Ruth opening the car door and making her way into the building. Sally got into the front seat as, although she did not in any way regret leaving Graham in situ, she didn't relish a journey back to the station sitting beside him and knowing she had just scored a minor but moral victory.

"Nice one, Sal. That was brave of you but he's not going to be happy."

Sally shrugged her shoulders. "He deserves a taste of his own medicine. Anyway, he's picked on the wrong person to humiliate all the time. I'm obviously quite capable of doing that myself."

"Ah, that's better – fighting talk!" Alex replied, grasping her hand as he did so. Sally didn't pull away until Ruth appeared from the warehouse laughing and clapping her hands as she related Graham's stunned look as he awoke disorientated and then looking sheepish when he realised the time. She got into the back of the car understanding Sally's need to be as far away from Graham as possible. He appeared a short time later looking even more dishevelled than usual and remained silent throughout the journey, aware that he had been made a fool of. He wound down the window seemingly conscious of his bad breath that created a foul stench within the confines of the car.

Sally smiled, choosing not to make any conversation, aware that the awkward silence was all part of Graham's punishment. A good night's work. She was looking forward to some well-earned sleep herself.

Sally woke up to find Julian sitting on the bed beside her with a cup of tea and some toast. She found it difficult to put her finger on it, but there was definitely something different about him just of late. After sulking for so long over the dinner and dance business, he seemed to be having a change of heart. This made her feel good about herself, added to the fact that she only had one more night shift to go before four lovely days off.

"How do you fancy popping out for a bite to eat before work tonight, Sal?"

"Yeah, yeah, great idea," Sally replied, still rousing from sleep and surprised by the suggestion. It was Sunday night and she would have preferred to go the following night when she didn't have to go on to work but she knew a week night wouldn't suit Julian as he was often expected to stay late at his office.

He disappeared into the study. Sally pulled on her dressing gown, wandered into the living room to eat her toast and switched the telly on. As she placed the remote control on the arm of the sofa, it slid off landing in Julian's open briefcase on the floor beside it. Sally looked over into the briefcase and scooped the remote out. As she did so, an envelope caught her eye. They had never had any secrets between them and, being the inquisitive kind, she took the letter out and unfolded it. She took an involuntary intake of breath as she scanned the letter of congratulations from Julian's boss with the offer of the promotion he had so wanted. She was carefully replacing the letter in the position she had found it when another piece of paper caught her eye. She recognised the crest at the top of the page as that of Mallory, the jewellers in Bridge Street. She stared at the sheet and saw it was a receipt for a deposit on a diamond-cluster ring. She had spent many quiet moments on her night shifts admiring the ring in the jeweller's window which she had often pointed out to Julian on shopping trips. The sound of Julian's footsteps made her hurriedly replace the receipt and she did her best to look innocent as he joined her in the lounge.

"Shall I book Franco's for eight? I can go straight on to work then," Sally enquired, hardly able to keep her voice even and calm.

"Yeah, fine with me," Julian replied as he picked up the television remote, lowered himself into an armchair and started to flick through the channels.

Sally's stomach flipped with excitement and anticipation. She leapt off the sofa and whilst she was waiting for the bath to fill up, she dialled Franco's number from the bedroom. If she was going to be proposed to in a restaurant, she couldn't think of anywhere better!

"Can we have the table in the corner by the window please?" she asked Franco. "It's a special occasion but I can't say too much!" she said in a hushed tone, hardly able to contain the excitement in her voice.

"Of course, of course, anything for my favourite customer. I'll see you at eight," Franco enthused sensing the occasion.

As they got ready, Sally could feel Julian's unease. She smiled behind his back. It must be awful being the one who has to engineer this part of the relationship. No matter, she was intending to make it easy for him by coming back with a resounding "Yeessss". Her last night shift would fly by, even though she knew she would be walking the city with Ruth again, because she would be able to dream of her impending wedding. She'd make straight for the bridal shop in St James Parade when she left the station after the briefing to window shop at the wedding dresses. Just wait till they told her mum and his parents. She knew they would all be pleased. She was positively tingling all over.

They walked hand in hand into Franco's. Sally's only regret was that she wasn't going to be able to celebrate in style with a few drinks – well, maybe just a small glass of champers. After all, she wasn't going to be driving that night.

Sally watched with amusement as Julian shifted uncomfortably in his seat throughout the meal. With their cappuccinos steaming in front of them, they sat there mirroring each other, elbows planted either side of their coffee cups and hands clasped over them.

With a pang of sympathy for his plight, Sally reached forward cupping his hands in hers. She was taken aback as he flinched and withdrew his hands with such force causing an opposite and involuntary movement of his feet which knocked the table legs and spilled some of their cappuccinos onto the saucers.

"Oops!" Sally said, smiling reassuringly. "Are you OK?"

There! That's your cue! Sally thought, wondering where he was hiding the ring.

"Sally..." He paused.

"Yes?" she replied, perhaps a little too eagerly. *Yessss, yessss, yessssss*, she was repeating inside – her stomach doing somersaults. *Come on, get on with it!* Her mind was buzzing with excitement. Should she wear the ring tonight? Would it be the right size? Maybe she would just put it in her locker in case she got into a fight. She didn't want to damage it…

"This is really difficult for me."

Oh, how sweet, Sally thought. He was really struggling.

"This is really difficult for me," he repeated, "but…" He trailed off.

But? But what? What is there to 'but' about in a proposal?

"I…I haven't been happy for some time now…"

What? What? Is this his humorous way of making a proposal? Sally thought.

The pained expression on his face together with his grey pallor made it register with Sally that this was no joke. His eyes were stony and unfeeling.

She suddenly felt dizzy and the vision she had of Julian in front of her became blurred. She felt as though she was falling, falling, and she forced a swallow to try to moisten her parched throat and bring her surroundings back into focus. She reached for the remains of a glass of water on the table unable to release the tightness that gripped her throat.

As Julian sat and smoothed the pristine white brocade tablecloth, Sally listened to his spiel.

"Our careers are both taking off and, for what it's worth, I think you've made the right decision to leave teaching and join the police…but, for me, having a police officer as a partner isn't compatible with my corporate position." He cleared his throat awkwardly before continuing. "My final decision came after you couldn't get the time off to accompany me to my Christmas dinner. It's a really important evening," he rushed on to explain himself, "to impress the bosses and to display a happy and stable home life which they believe reflects one's ability to meet targets et cetera…" He tailed off, waiting to see how Sally was going to react.

Targets et cetera. What was this bullshit she was hearing? This was the multi-faceted twentieth century, wasn't it? She was too taken aback to point this out to the man she had been expecting to be her fiancé by the end of the evening. Sally was in shock and this time it was his turn to lean forward and cup her hands in his. She, in turn, opened her hands wide and recoiled back in her chair.

Franco suddenly appeared at the table proffering the complimentary glasses of the lemony liquor he always offered at the end of a meal.

"Or can I recommend the house champ—?" he started to ask knowingly before stopping short when he saw the pained expressions on their faces.

"Oh, OK. I leave you to it. You call me over if you want anything. OK?" He placed the glasses down and brushed Sally's shoulder with his hand as he left them alone again.

Julian was talking again but Sally couldn't hear what he was saying. He was pulling notes out of his wallet whilst scraping his chair back as he stood up. Finally, he picked up one of Sally's hands and held it between his. This time she didn't resist; she didn't have the energy. She managed to take in the fact that he was going to move his belongings out whilst she was at work and he would be in touch next week to "sort out the rest". And, with that, he was gone.

Sort out the rest? Is that how he saw their relationship? Four great years that could be sorted out next week? Sally sat staring blindly out of the window as Julian disappeared from sight.

Franco came scuttling over and pulled up a chair from a nearby table so that he was sitting at right angles to her.

"Oh, Sally, Sally. It was not as you expected, no?"

Sally couldn't speak but just shook her head as a large tear rolled down her face. Franco caught it with her napkin.

How could I have been so stupid? she thought to herself. And how ridiculous did she look? All dressed up to the nines to be unceremoniously dumped.

Franco tried his best to console her. He called Rossana out to try and persuade Sally to go back into the kitchen with them, but Sally just wanted to be alone. She wasn't going to let herself sob right there in front of him, though God knows she wanted to.

She reassured him that she would be OK and politely told him that she wanted to be alone to have time to think. Franco pushed the cash that Julian had left on the table into her pocket and Sally, being too weak to protest, thanked him and reassured him again that she would be fine. She promised she would be in touch soon and walked out into the cool night air.

She didn't actually want to have time to think. She just wanted to sob, big deep sobs, and let out her grief, shock and whatever other emotions she couldn't quite identify at that moment. She couldn't go back to the flat as she presumed Julian would be gathering his belongings. It was too early for work, but Sally headed for the police station anyway. She held it together as she entered the building and nodded at people she passed, making her way to the locker room in the basement.

Once she had closed the door behind her, she threw herself on a pile of kitbags in the corner and sobbed. Sobbed for her four years with Julian, for the diamond-cluster ring she had believed would be on her finger by now, and for her stupidity and presumptuousness that had allowed her to get to this state.

It all made sense now: his restless behaviour, his sorting of his wardrobes and the spare room in preparation for an easy exit. What didn't make sense was the deposit for the ring.

Eventually, Sally lifted her head and found she was lying amongst an assortment of camping gear. She focused on the name stamped on the side of what looked like a sleeping bag: PC 1481 GRAHAM BUTTERWORTH. Was there no getting away from him? How typical, Sally thought, that her tears were falling on something of his – someone who had succeeded in making her life as miserable as he possibly could and, she had no doubt, would continue to do so.

Where is my life going from here? Sally thought in her wretched state. She had never felt so low in all her life as she attempted to tidy herself up and managed to nip unseen across the corridor to the ladies' toilets where she threw cold water over her swollen and blotchy face.

Sally knew she had no choice. She had to pull herself together somehow. She had a job to do and she was determined not to let the likes of Graham know that she had been crying – or why, for that matter. Sally changed into her uniform, reapplied her eye make-up and headed for the briefing room as the now single PC Sally Gentle.

After briefing Alex called her into a report writing room.

"You OK, Sal? You look a bit flushed."

They made eye contact. God, what she would have given to be crewed up with him tonight; to have the opportunity to pour her heart out to him. Instead, she took a deep breath and exhaled before replying, "I'm fine – really. I didn't sleep that well today. You know how it is – the end of a long week of nights."

He lifted his hand and gently stroked her cheek, both of

them aware that the door was open and anyone could walk past. His touch was soft and genuine. What she really wanted was for him to put his arms around her and to bury her head in his broad chest. Instead, she took another deep breath, managed a smile and walked away knowing she wouldn't be able to stop herself from crying again if she didn't.

After a brief conversation with Ruth, who was going to be staying inside to catch up on some paperwork, Sally pulled on her heavy coat and hat and headed for the city. She made her way on to the rooftop of the shops in Stall Street – a little known fire escape route that Alex had shown her. From the three-storey high parapet, she could see a good proportion of the city and observe it unnoticed. She wasn't interested in what was going on in the city tonight, though. Instead, she sat on a cold iron step, leant back against the railings and stared at the cloudless sky, her head awash with unanswered questions about her future. She stayed there for an hour or so until she realised she was shivering uncontrollably and her body was tense in response to the falling temperature. She slowly made her way back down to ground level and started a lap of the city.

At 4am, with nothing happening on the city's streets, she returned to the same step and this time leant forwards and hugged her knees in an effort to keep warm. As usual, the Sunday night was dead. The radio had been mostly silent with the exception of a drink driver for Alex and Basher. She was deep in thought staring at the ground in front of her when she suddenly became aware of someone approaching. Startled, she jumped to her feet, but Alex had already seen her.

"Knew I'd find you here," he stated, a kindness in his voice she was desperately in need of.

Sally looked defeated and shrugged her shoulders.

"Come on," he continued. "Jump in the car with me for a while and warm up."

Sally looked unsure about the idea and looked around as if the Baroness could see her – knowing she wouldn't allow this or like it one bit.

"Basher is in the station dealing with a drink driver," Alex explained. "Come on." He put his arm loosely around her shoulder and guided her down the staircase. Sally opened the door of the car and, feeling the warmth from inside on her face, gratefully slumped into the passenger seat, her body weary from a week of nights as well as what the previous evening had thrown at her.

Alex started the engine and drove to the top of Lansdown on the outskirts of the city. He parked up out of sight from public gaze.

"You're not OK, are you." He reached over and squeezed her hand. The floodgates opened. Sally told him the whole saga and, although he couldn't change anything or make it better, she felt a huge sense of relief when she had finished just from having told someone, especially him.

Alex tried to offer words of sympathy and advice, but both of them knew that no words could really ease the pain she was suffering. It was something that she had to get through on her own before she would be able to move on.

"I miss working with you, Alex." She paused briefly before carrying on to qualify the statement she had just made. "I'm fed up with walking the city with Ruth. She's nice enough but you can get too much of one person." She finished with a sigh overcome by intense fatigue. At that moment, she didn't care much about anything.

"Everyone gets attached to their buddies. It's just a question of confidence, and you're doing just fine."

"But Graham…and everyone joins in with him – he's so spiteful and our supervisors do nothing about it."

"Yeah, I have to admit, he does overstep the mark at times. And the sergeants don't always address it. I don't know what the answer is. It'll stop in time…when the next probationer comes along. I…I can't really say too much…you know how it is in this job, they'll only start talking about us if I try to stand up for you. We don't need that, do we."

Sally knew what he was saying and she knew he was right. But she couldn't help asking herself: When was her life going to start looking up?

Chapter Four

Sally spent her rest days sitting mulling over her break-up firstly with her mum and then with her sister. They did their best to make her feel better and to be positive about the future but there was little anyone could say or do to ease her heartache.

When she returned to work, she was relieved to be told that she would be working in the enquiry office for a few days. Whether Alex had had a word with the sergeants or not, Sally didn't know and, for that matter, didn't want to know. It offered her some welcome respite from patrol duties and involved dealing with phone enquiries and with the public who came into the police station. As well as being a breath of fresh air from the pressure of looking for work to impress her sergeants and constantly having to keep her wits about her for fear of practical jokes, Sally was amazed at what services the public expected from the police. From lost and found property, vehicle document production, domestic and neighbourly disputes to civil matters and other trivialities far removed from criminal matters. A particular favourite was asking for directions: "How do you get to the Roman Baths?" was a thrice-daily request. It was extremely busy with phones constantly ringing and a steady flow of people coming to the front desk.

Sally enjoyed working in the enquiry office, not just because it was so diverse and the time flew but the staff were kind, helpful and, most of all, fun! 'Stumpy' was a PC nearing his retirement who was spending his last few years in the enquiry office and had many an amusing anecdote to tell. Despite warnings from HQ about conforming to equal opportunities and political correctness, he was the most un-PC PC Sally would ever come across, but he did so in the most hilarious and inoffensive manner possible. He always had a brochure handy with a picture of 'his yacht' he was going to buy with his retirement cheque. Often, he could be found showing it to some unsuspecting member of the public and charming them so much that they often forgot their reason for coming in and left with a different and positive view of the police.

Stumpy's funniest trick was to make use of his lack of height, which he had obviously been ribbed about for the whole of his service. He always said he was in fact a whole foot taller when he had joined up, as there had been a height restriction in those days – but the weight of crime during his service had caused him to shrink! Whenever he had to fetch something, he would announce to the waiting member of the public that he was just going to pop downstairs to get the item. With that, he would proceed to walk alongside the counter bending his legs with each step as if descending a flight of stairs whilst smiling and waving at the customer as he did so. Invariably, they were looking away when he returned but he was equally capable of doing it in reverse. It was hilarious to watch, however many times he did it, and Sally never tired of his Pythonesque humour.

On a rare occasion, Stumpy managed to upset a customer.

He politely tried to tell one of the local 'street drinkers', which Bath was afflicted with alongside its beggars, that his tale of woe surrounding the alleged theft of his giro money didn't quite add up. The inebriated man insisted that he wanted to make a complaint about Stumpy to an inspector. Stumpy left the office stating that he would go and find the duty inspector. He returned a short time later crawling along the floor out of sight of public view with an orange crate which he left where he had been standing. He then disappeared for a few minutes before returning wearing an inspector's flat cap. He stepped onto the orange crate and proceeded to take details of the complaint from the unsuspecting drunk. He gave his assurance that PC Malpass would be reprimanded and, with that, saluted the drunk who saluted back and left the station as 'happy as Larry', as they say. Stumpy turned away from the desk and threw the flat cap frisbee style onto Sally's desk before screwing up the paper he had written on and drop-kicking it into the bin.

The enquiry office was the hub of the station, and everyone popped in and out during the shift whether it was for a specific reason or just to say "Hello" to Stumpy – and pinch one of his extra strong mints which he always had in endless supply – and chat to whoever else happened to be working with him. The pace of life in there and the constant demands from the public took Sally's mind off her broken heart, and she got to know a few colleagues from other shifts who seemed so much more friendly than her own team. By her last day in there, she was feeling in better spirits. Alex popped in a couple of times every shift which didn't go unnoticed by Stumpy who would look over his half-moon glasses at them before returning to his paperwork, which invariably was disguising his newspaper, whilst listening to their every word.

"OK, Sal?" Alex would ask, draping an arm over her shoulder and bending to see what she was doing. "Do you know what you're doing in here yet?"

"Course she does – she's got me to guide her, hasn't she?" interjected Stumpy.

"Yeah, I bet he's loving having you in here for company," Alex smirked at Sally.

"Well, it beats working with the rest of your hairy-arsed shift, doesn't it, eh?" confessed Stumpy.

Sally frowned in mock disapproval at him.

"Are you courting then?" Stumpy asked her during a brief quiet period.

"No, single, I'm afraid," Sally replied more abruptly than she had meant to.

"Hmm, you sound like a woman scorned," he probed in true police officer style.

"Yes, very recently single – so if an eligible bachelor comes in wanting some assistance, you make sure you send him my way!"

"Oh, I'm sure you'll be snapped up soon – pretty young thing like you."

Sally wasn't so sure. She had finally plucked up the courage and nervously phoned Mallory the day before enquiring casually about the purchase in the name of Mr and Mrs Julian Locke for a diamond-cluster ring. She had been shocked when she heard the well intentioned reply.

"Oh yes, the item is still awaiting collection. Do you wish to make an appointment to collect it?" Sally made her excuses and hung up, confused as to why Julian had paid a deposit in the first place – although it didn't surprise her that he hadn't reclaimed it. It would be one of the last things on his mind with his new life and longed-for promotion to enjoy.

She was miles away when Stumpy broke her train of thought.

"Can't beat a good woman behind you," continued Stumpy. He always referred to his long suffering wife as 'Mrs M'. "Mrs M has ironed seven thousand shirts and prepared as many packed lunches for me in my twenty-eight and three-quarter years of service. I'm going to name my yacht after her."

"I'm sure that will mean a lot to her and so it should. Lucky lady!" enthused Sally, thinking how times had changed since his days as a new recruit. Any husband of hers could iron his own damned shirts – and hers whilst he was at it – though she didn't voice her thoughts.

"How did you know what I was gonna call her Lucky Lady?" he flirted with Sally.

Sally threw her head back and laughed as she approached the counter to deal with a woman with a distressed look on her face.

"Can I help you?" Sally offered sympathetically, noting the woman's scruffy, yet designer clothes which included an expensive-looking navy body warmer with a horse emblem on the breast.

"Yes. I…I was driving along the A39 and noticed this dog tied to a gate." She indicated down towards her feet. Sally leaned over the counter to look at the golden spaniel which looked up with its big sad eyes as the woman continued, "I stopped to check it out and I found this note attached to its collar."

She produced a crumpled note and opened it out on the counter.

To whoever finds me – please look after me – I am friendly and love children. Honey

"Oh, my God!" exclaimed Sally as she walked round the counter and let herself out through the security door into the public area. She knelt by the pathetic creature who leant in to Sally as she smoothed its silky coat.

"How could anyone do such a thing? It must have been terrified," Sally gushed.

"Yes," agreed the woman stepping back to allow Sally to pet the dog which was quivering as she enveloped it in her arms.

The woman was equally upset about the abandonment of this helpless and innocent creature.

"What will happen to it?" she enquired, genuinely concerned for its future.

"I'll put it in our kennels while we wait for the dog warden to come and pick it up," Sally explained as Stumpy pressed the button that released the lock allowing her access back through the security door.

Sally checked the Lost and Found Dog Register but there was no matching record so she took the woman's details and completed a new 'found' entry. She then checked the faxed log of incidents that the police had attended so far that day and those for the day before. There were no reports of lost dogs and no way of telling just how long this wretched animal had been left beside a busy main road.

Sally went back through the security door. "There haven't been any other reports about it so hopefully you spotted it soon after it had been left there. I can't believe someone would do such a thing. They need bringing before the courts and punishing," Sally added angrily. As she reached down to smooth the dog it leaned its body weight up against her again, glad to find someone who was showing it some compassion.

"I know," the woman empathised, "I've always had dogs. I just don't understand some people." She plunged her hands into her body warmer and shrugged her shoulders.

Sally looked at the woman. She was obviously an outdoor type from her attire and rugged complexion.

"There is the option of hanging on to it, until the owner hopefully gets in touch. You can even apply to keep her if she isn't claimed," Sally offered.

"No, no, I've got too many of them already...much as I'd love to..." the woman added.

"OK," Sally replied, taking the lead from the woman and moving back towards the security door. As Sally waited for Stumpy to release the door for her again, the woman stepped forward and stroked the dog.

"Bye then, girl. Hope you find a good home."

Sally was toying with the idea of adopting the dog herself if it wasn't claimed – she could do with the company. She made her way down to the kennels in the rear yard, passing the Baroness on the way.

"Oh, my goodness, who's this?" The Baroness bent to scratch the dog's floppy ears.

Sally related the tale of woe. The Baroness was appalled and accompanied Sally to the kennels showing her where the dog food and keys were kept.

As they walked back to the front office, the Baroness said, "I think we should contact the Chronicle and ask them to put a press release out. It might prick the conscience of its owner to come forward. Disgusting behaviour, the poor animal."

Hmm, Sally thought to herself, *the Baroness, it seems, has a rarely-seen softer side.* Sally knew she was an animal lover and it didn't surprise her that she wanted to follow this up.

"Call the woman back and ask her if she'll agree to be interviewed for the story. I bet it'll make the headlines if they have a quiet news day."

Sally agreed it was a great idea and phoned the woman to discuss it. After a little persuasion, she agreed giving her consent for her name and phone number to be passed to the Chronicle.

Stumpy had been monitoring the situation.

"Hey, get your hat cos they'll want a picture of you posing with the dog."

"No way." Sally guffawed and landed a friendly punch on his arm.

It was a station habit to put newspaper clippings on the noticeboard in the foyer to invite witty comments. Sally didn't feel she could cope with that at the moment, especially as some comments could be a little too personal with colleagues taking the opportunity to anonymously write things they wouldn't normally have the courage or audacity to say to your face. Admittedly, she enjoyed reading the comments but wasn't ready to be the butt of such humour herself just yet.

The phone line to the newsroom was engaged on the few opportunities Sally had to try it during the next hour or so. She was kept busy dealing with a never-ending queue of people producing their driving licences, registering with the immigration department and reporting various minor crimes. Sally pushed a pile of papers to one side to finish when there was a lull and looked up at the next person.

"Can I help? Oh..." Sally paused as she recognised the woman who had brought the dog in earlier. "Is something wrong?" she enquired softly, noticing that the woman had obviously been and in fact still was crying.

"I...I can't speak to the Chronicle," she whispered. "I...I..." She looked self-consciously over her shoulder at the people shuffling impatiently behind her.

"Hang on," said Sally. "Stumpy, I'm just going to one of the interview rooms."

He peered over the top of his glasses from where he was sitting writing up his reports and nodded in acknowledgement when he also recognised the woman from earlier. He pushed his chair back taking his half-moon specs off as he approached the counter to deal with the next waiting customer. He waved Sally towards the direction of the interview room as he did so.

Sally opened the door and ushered the woman in. "Rachel, isn't it?"

The woman nodded and blew her nose, trying to compose herself.

Sally was surprised that she was so upset and reassured her. "You don't have to speak to the Press. We can do it. It's just that they prefer a human interest story, but it really isn't a problem." She placed her hand on Rachel's shoulder as she tried to show she understood but was taken aback when, instead of being consoled, Rachel dissolved into sobs.

Sally's bewilderment grew as, in between sobs, Rachel revealed that the dog was in fact hers. "I just can't cope any more. I made the story up because I know that the cats' and dogs' home are reluctant to take on pets in these circumstances."

Sally was dumbfounded. What an extent to go to, to get

98

rid of a dog. She asked a few more questions. The dog had never been tied up beside the road; Rachel had written the note herself.

"We've got two other dogs and one of them has just had a litter of puppies. My husband is at the end of his tether. It's… it's all just become too much to cope with. I thought I was doing the right thing."

Still sobbing, she apologised and Sally left her to compose herself whilst she spoke to the Baroness.

The Baroness swept in to the interview room with the foreboding air of a headmistress, her head held high in contempt of what this woman was doing to a helpless animal. She gave Rachel a serious telling-off about being an irresponsible dog owner stating she should be reported to the RSPCA who would remove all her animals. In addition, she had wasted police time. Rachel nodded in agreement accepting all that the Baroness threw at her. She knew she was lucky to leave with no more punishment than a flea in her ear.

And Sally had a new dog…

The team 'Christmas Do' which was talked about with eager anticipation at briefing times loomed over Sally like a big black cloud. She had already had the embarrassment of reducing her booking from 2 to 1 after her split from Julian and, quite frankly, she didn't want to face it on her own. Ruth was going to be away on annual leave and everyone else had a partner to take, resulting in Sally viewing the event with much trepidation.

As the taxi came to a stop outside the hotel, she paused and looked back the way they had driven in.

"Not keen to party then, love?" asked the driver.

"Is it that obvious?" Sally replied, trying to raise a smile.

99

"Go on. You'll be fine once you've got a few drinks inside you," he encouraged.

"I've already tried that," confessed Sally, having gulped two glasses of wine before leaving home with the intention of giving herself some Dutch courage. Unfortunately, it didn't seem to be working.

She paid the driver and stood outside the hotel taking a couple of deep breaths. She had arrived intentionally late with the plan that, with her gooseberry status, she would look less obvious in a crowd. She had chosen a close-fitting, purple, velvet dress with a ruched neckline and wore her hair down. She looked very much a different woman to the one her colleagues saw in the station. She fixed a smile on her face and made her way in determined to try her best to bestow the joys of the festive season.

As she entered the function room, she could see all the lads standing at the bar and she could just make out the Baroness holding court in the middle of them in a little black dress with her hair in a heap of curls cascading from the top of her head. As Sally approached them, a hush descended on the room and, as she drew near, they all simultaneously turned round to greet her. As she surveyed the sea of faces in front of her, she saw that every single one of them was wearing a set of Mickey Mouse ears.

Mortified she stood stock still as they all chorused in high-pitched voices,

"Hello, PC Gentle!"

Her instincts told her to turn on her heel and run from the humiliating scene. Instead, she summoned all her energy to force her stunned gaze into a smile – she had no choice but to smile, to laugh even and slap a few blokes on their backs. And, besides, it was funny – hilariously bloody funny, if you weren't on the receiving end of it, and she even accepted a pair of ears that were slipped onto her head.

"Very funny, all of you. Now, which one of you bastards is going to buy me a drink?" she quipped as she started pushing her way towards the bar concentrating on holding back her tears.

Sergeant Morley stepped forward from the gathering, also wearing ears, took her arm and guided her up to the bar. With the show over, the rest of her team turned back to their conversations with the anticipation of the imminent meal.

"What's your tipple, young lady?" asked Sergeant Morley as Sally busied herself by rummaging through her handbag until her drink arrived in front of her. Any Christmas spirit she had managed to summon had now evaporated and she tried not to make it obvious that she didn't want to be there as Sergeant Morley made polite conversation with her. Inspector Creed mingled amongst the crowd selling raffle tickets for which he had given Sally the money earlier in the week to buy the prizes.

She suddenly caught part of a conversation from behind her where they were obviously having a great time.

"Alex, tell the lads about your off-duty arrest last week, you hero cop!"

Sally's head involuntarily turned at the mention of Alex's name. She hoped her reaction hadn't been noticed but, as she turned her attention back to her drink and took a few more gulps, she felt her cheeks colour and noticed the Baroness was looking straight at her.

To Sally's relief, they were soon called to the tables to eat. She picked at her food and drank a bit more whilst Roger's wife recounted tales of their caravan holidays to her as she sat trapped at the end of the table between her and Sergeant Morley. As soon as pudding was served, Sally made an excuse about not liking Christmas pudding and muttered something about getting some fresh air. She pushed her chair back and went to stand up, but the alcohol took its toll and she lost her balance causing her to sit back down rather ungracefully. She was grateful that the Inspector had stood up simultaneously further down the table to announce the raffle draw.

There were only three prizes so Sally stayed put rather than draw any more attention to herself as he called for quiet to reveal the winners. A tin of chocolates was the first prize drawn for and was gratefully won by Roger's wife who was obviously enjoying a rare night out, and also a few drinks judging by the way she skipped to collect her prize. Sally smiled – she was a worthy winner. The Baroness's hippy husband won the second prize and gratefully accepted the bottle of wine across the table. The Inspector held up the final prize: a bottle of malt whisky which raised an "ooh" from the waiting crowd.

"And the winner is..." the Inspector paused for dramatic effect, "...ticket number 155!"

Sally's face visibly dropped as Graham's hand flew in the air to a chorus of "Typical!" and similar remarks. He was the last person she would have wanted to win the prize she had gone out of her way to choose. Graham stood up from his seat a few places down from the Inspector and claimed his prize to a weak ripple of applause. But, before he returned to his seat, he walked down to the end of the table and stood behind Sally with one hand on her shoulder and the other holding the bottle aloft in victory announcing, "I'd just like to thank Sally for arranging this for me."

"Go on, give her a Christmas kiss then!" shouted someone.

Graham was no more likely to do this than Sally would sit there and take it. She brushed his hand off her shoulder and once again got to her feet pushing her chair back forcefully – and unintentionally causing the back of it to catch Graham square in the groin. She turned round to see him physically recoil and almost lose his grip on his treasured prize. A whoop of laughter erupted as Sally strode towards the exit to her own round of applause.

She sat herself on a low wall at the front of the hotel and dropped her head in her hands. The world was spinning. Ten minutes passed as she considered her next move, shivering in the December air with a frost already visible and rising through her bones. A light drizzle added to her discomfort, and she was just planning her escape by trying to nip back into the foyer unnoticed to fetch her coat when a pair of large feet appeared in her downward gaze.

"You OK, Sal?" came a familiar voice.

She looked up sharply to see Alex, his face silhouetted by the moon – a silhouette that included the Mickey Mouse ears. He must have noticed her focusing on the ears and quickly snatched them off before sitting down beside her.

"Yeah, fine," she replied, wiping under her eyes in the realisation she had been crying.

"Oh, come on, Sal, you're not upset about the Mickey Mouse prank are you? It was just a joke. It's Christmas – and, besides, it's one you brought on yourself. Can't you see the funny side?"

Sally smiled a tight smile and nodded in agreement, shrugging as she did so. Someone had gone to a lot of effort not to mention expense to carry off this latest onslaught. She didn't need too many guesses who that person was.

Alex fiddled awkwardly with the ears and nudged her shoulder with his. "I'm sorry, Sal, I didn't realise it would upset you so much – but – but I could hardly refuse to join in either, could I." He spoke softly with genuine regret which caused Sally to respond, "It's OK," though not very convincingly.

"Sorry it's upset you though."

"It hasn't…it's…" she paused but the alcohol had loosened her tongue, "…it's just on top of everything else that's gone on and having to face turning up here on my own…" She looked away stifling a sob.

"Well, you're not the only one without a partner here tonight."

Sally looked at him confused.

"Ann-Marie's father has been taken seriously ill and she and Max have gone over to see him."

Sally hadn't even noticed – or more to the point didn't want to see Alex with his wife.

"Yeah, but at least everyone knows you've got a partner, and you have at least got someone to share Christmas with."

Sally realised she was slurring her words, and a big fat tear sprang from her eye and began to roll down her cheek. She reached up to wipe it away and her handed collided with Alex's as he reached out to do the same. He clasped her hand in his and, in a joint effort, they wiped the tear before she went to release her grip.

Alex however didn't let go. Instead, he drew his other hand up and held hers between his.

"I'm sorry you're having such a hard time of it at the moment. I really wish there was something I could do but—"

"It's OK." Sally despaired inwardly with herself – couldn't she think of anything else to say? Besides, she wasn't OK.

Alex pulled her to her feet. "Come on, it's freezing out here." Sally noticed he was shivering too. "Come back in and try to have some fun?"

Sally ran her fingers through her hair and blew her nose as she allowed Alex to guide her back inside.

"You wait, things will be much different this time next year. You'll see."

Sally wished she could believe him. Right now, she felt that things couldn't really get much worse.

"Things can only get better as they say," said Alex as if reading her mind. "In fact, listen."

They stopped still and, sure enough, the song with the same title by D:Ream was blaring from the function room. Sally giggled at the coincidence.

"Hey, better not be seen going back in together, eh?" Alex suggested.

Sally shook her head. "I need to go and freshen up anyway," and she ushered him forward before making for the ladies' toilets.

He squeezed her hand reassuringly before disappearing through the function room door. Sally waited for it to close behind him before grabbing her coat from where she had left it on a rail and headed back out into the cold. She couldn't face any more crap tonight.

Having changed into her pyjamas, Sally settled on the sofa to watch the film *An Officer and a Gentleman*. She intended to have a good cry along to it. Things worked out OK for the heroine in the end, didn't they? There was hope for her yet. As it happened, after a further glass of wine, Sally fell into a drunken sleep to be awoken by the sound of her doorbell ringing.

She looked at the clock – cripes, half past midnight – *Who's that at this hour?* she thought to herself. They, no she – she corrected her thoughts remembering she was now single – occasionally got the odd drunk playing knock-out ginger and, after all, it was the Christmas season.

Sally positioned herself behind the lounge curtain where she could see who was standing at the door without being seen herself. Her heart was racing even though she was safe inside. *Hang on*, she thought to herself, *I'm a big butch policewoman* – but she would defy anyone not to be unnerved by their doorbell ringing at that hour. As she strained to see who was there, she pleaded for it not to be Julian turning up with some kind of drunken apology that wouldn't last past the morning. In her drunken and vulnerable state, she worried she might do something that she would regret. Just then, the caller moved into sight.

Alex.

Sally raced to the front door and flung it open to see Alex's back as he walked away.

He spun round on hearing the door open and, on seeing her, took a further step back at the sight he was presented with. Sally saw his reaction and looked down at her crumpled pyjamas.

She smiled and shrugged her shoulders. "What did you expect?" she said, resignedly.

He approached the door and Sally stood to one side to let him in. Neither spoke as he entered her flat and she led him into her dimly lit lounge. They were greeted by Honey who after having a sniff at the newcomer, immediately returned to her bed, obviously not thrilled by such late-night disturbances. Sally and Alex both sat down on the sofa.

"Drink?" she offered as she poured herself another glass of wine.

"Err..." Alex looked round for another glass then reached for hers. "I'll just share yours, shall I?" he said, taking a long gulp.

Sally hugged her knees to her chest, suddenly self-conscious. "Good party?"

"Yeah, you were missed though."

"I'm sure. No one else to 'take the mickey' out of?" she said, defeatedly.

"Why'd you go?" Alex asked with genuine care in his voice.

"Oh, I thought I'd have more fun home here on my own on the last Saturday before Christmas than be ridiculed by my so-called colleagues."

Sally suddenly noticed *An Officer and a Gentleman* was paused on the credits on her television screen, and she quickly picked up the remote control and flicked it off before Alex saw how sad and sorry she was feeling for herself.

"I've had enough, Alex. He shouldn't be able to get away with it." Sally didn't have to mention any names.

With that, a large sob involuntarily unleashed itself followed by another and another. Huge miserable sobs fuelled by alcohol and the presence of a sympathetic being next to her. Alex leant towards her and pulled her close which had the reaction of causing her to cry all the more. He whispered words of reassurance and stroked her hair until her sobs finally subsided and embarrassment took over. Embarrassed for wearing her heart on her sleeve, embarrassed for not being strong enough to cope, and embarrassed for the mess she looked. Of all people, Alex was not the one she would have

107

wanted to see her at such a low ebb.

"Hey, come on. You can rise above all this. Don't let the buggers win."

"Look at me – the buggers have already won. Wouldn't Graham just love to see what a snivelling wreck he's reduced me to?"

Alex held her red, puffy face between his hands.

"You're stronger than this. Perhaps you ought to speak to Inspector Creed about how it's affecting you."

"No, no, I...I..."

Sally didn't even know what she was going to say, but it didn't matter as Alex placed his lips on hers and they shared a long, gentle kiss – a kiss that Sally had been longing for since... well, since the day he had introduced himself to her. It was also a kiss they both knew was wrong.

"I shouldn't have done that. I'm sorry," Alex whispered as they sat with their foreheads touching and hands clasped together between them.

Sally didn't reply. She didn't know what to say. She wasn't sorry, that was for sure.

They sat for a long while in silence both enjoying the private and undisturbed closeness that was so elusive in their working environment. Sally leant back against him with the warmth of his breath against her cheek, savouring the moment which she knew wouldn't be repeated. She vaguely remembered feeling the familiar comfort of her duvet being placed over her and the combined effect of the wine and the exhaustion of the previous evening induced a semi-conscious state which rendered her unable to resist the draw of sleep. The last sound she remembered was that of her front door quietly closing.

Chapter Five

Sally returned to work with some trepidation at the thought of facing her team again – and Alex. She needn't have worried. Unfortunately, Alex's father-in-law had died, and he had taken compassionate leave to fly to France to join his wife and her family for the funeral and wouldn't be back until after the New Year. Sally didn't know whether to be disappointed or relieved – but she realised she was a bit of both, really.

She didn't have much time to mull it over as she was called in to the Inspector's office as soon as briefing was over. With her heart racing as to the reason why she had been summoned, she made her way to his office on the first floor. Was he going to give her a bollocking for leaving the Christmas do – telling her it did little to help the strained relationships with some of her colleagues that she knew he was aware of?

Sally was relieved and delighted when Inspector Creed smiled at her and beckoned her in.

"CID have just had a rape reported to them. I know your probationary attachment to them was planned for later in the New Year but, apart from needing a female on the case, it would be a great opportunity for you to gain some experience in this area." He paused to gauge her reaction. "Do you fancy helping out, Sally?"

"If you think I can be any help," said Sally excitedly, but doubting her capability.

"Of course you can. Take every opportunity offered to you young lady. Listen and learn! Now, go and find Detective Constable Stott – he's waiting for you."

The excitement and flattery at being asked was mixed with butterflies and nerves as Sally made her way to the CID office. She knew who DC Mike Stott was. He was a detective with a lot of years' service behind him. His strong Yorkshire accent made him stand out in this part of the world, and a large red drinker's nose also helped him to stand out from the crowd. He had helped her out with a stolen cheque job a couple of weeks ago, and Sally knew she would learn a lot from him. She also felt a pang of guilt at feeling excited about benefitting in some way from someone's pain and anguish.

Sally stopped at the open door to the CID office, unsure whether she should walk in or whether she should knock and wait. Mike was on the phone at his desk and waved at her before reaching over to the next desk to pull a chair up beside his, indicating for her to sit down.

The office was filled with desks which, in turn, were piled with paperwork and box files with the odd family photo peeping through the chaos. She wound her way between the tightly packed desks and perched on the edge of the seat she was being offered. As he spoke on the phone, Mike passed her a pile of papers which she took eagerly and started to read.

The victim was an eighteen year-old girl called Helen who was in her first year at university. She had been to the Christmas Ball and invited a fellow student back to her room where the rape had taken place. There were only brief details at this stage, but the girl knew the name of the suspect. Mike was following up his whereabouts on the phone.

Mike put the phone down and turned to Sally. "Right, Sally, isn't it?"

Sally nodded nervously. She really wasn't convinced that she would be much help.

"Typical fresher rape we've got here – albeit a bit late in the term."

Sally looked confused.

"We get two or three every year. Young kids away from home for the first time. No parents to keep an eye on things. Get themselves tanked up on cheap student union booze then they get a bit carried away and Bob's your uncle – after which the girl cries rape."

Mike went on to explain that another typical feature of a fresher rape was that it was reported a week later so there were little or no forensic opportunities.

"She's had time to dwell on it, talk to her friends or, as in this case, her family, and they've encouraged her to report it. Some of them are genuine attacks but most, I'm afraid, are reported in sober regret – afraid of the reputation they may have earned or feel guilty about the boyfriend at home if they've had unprotected sex."

Mike must have noted Sally's look of disapproval at his take on the whole issue.

"Still, we treat every incident as the real McCoy until we have the evidence to suggest otherwise."

Sally visibly relaxed and shuffled the papers awkwardly. He gave her a list of actions: do some background checks on the suspect's name and call the scenes of crime officers and arrange a time to meet them at the university halls of residence.

Sally set about her tasks. She phoned the Crime Scene Office first and arranged to meet them at the university in an hour. Mike only had an approximate date of birth for the suspect so, although exact checks weren't possible, the Police National Computer would come up with names of men whose dates of birth were close to the one estimated. The check however revealed 'no trace' indicating that it was unlikely that the offender had been in trouble with the police before.

Mike walked across to the fax machine. "The university have confirmed he's a student there but they want a signed authorisation from the inspector before they'll give us his personal details. He'll be home for the Christmas break now and we're about to give him his worst Christmas present ever – a day in our cells…" He raised his eyebrows in a 'that's how it goes' fashion.

Arrangements had already been made for the victim Helen to be interviewed later that afternoon. The procedure for sexual offences was that the victim's statements were taken in a designated recovery suite which was set up in a regular house on the outskirts of the city, providing a more relaxed setting than the interview rooms at the police station.

Sally fetched her coat and followed Mike to the car. He explained that, although there was nothing to be gained by a medical examination of Helen due to the time that had passed, they would still examine the room to attempt to prove that the offender had at least been in there, should he deny that fact.

The campus was deserted as the security guard led them to Helen's room.

"Always the top floor!" Mike puffed as he followed Sally up the three flights of stairs. "Don't think I've ever been to a job in a block of flats and not had to climb t'bloody top!"

Sally looked back at his sweating face which was now the

same colour as his nose. He reached up to loosen his tie.

"Come on, you can do it!" she encouraged as she bounded up the stairs two at a time.

"S'all right for you young uns. Wait till you get to my age," he grunted with some effort as they finally reached the door of Helen's room and where he stood wiping the beads of sweat from his brow with his handkerchief. They stood back as the security guard took out his master key and pushed the door open before standing back himself and allowing them to enter.

Sally stepped inside. It was a typical female student's room: an eclectic mix of study materials and homely trinkets. As Helen had described to the officer who had taken the initial report, her red taffeta ball gown was still hanging on the outside of the wardrobe.

As Sally stood in the doorway, she couldn't help but envisage this poor girl's ordeal that had happened within yards of where she was standing. She wondered whether the student had put up a fight or whether she had resigned herself to her fate, paralysed by alcohol and fear.

"I'll bet she wants to move to a different room when she comes back," Sally observed. "This will just be full of awful memories for her."

"Yeah, if she comes back at all," agreed Mike. "Some just don't cope and want to start afresh somewhere else."

"What a waste. It'll be too late to start at another uni. She'd have to wait until next September." Sally shook her head.

"Aye, heard you were one of those graduate types yourself. Can't beat a degree in life and common sense though, can you?...of course, there are exceptions," he added, aware that he may have just caused offence.

Sally smiled politely. She was getting used to the many similar comments she had received from other colleagues about her graduate status – and she was also beginning to understand why, realising that she had led a pretty sheltered life so far. She had never experienced most of the scenes and scenarios in this job that she was presented with on an almost daily basis. It was certainly an eye-opener and she knew this was exactly why she had joined up.

The radio crackled and they were told that the crime scene investigator had arrived outside. Sally offered to go down and let him in.

Mike gratefully accepted. "Go on then, y'whippersnapper. Your legs are much younger and fitter than mine!"

Sally wondered whether she should object to being spoken to by a colleague as if she was his granddaughter but decided to err on the side of caution and disappeared down the stairs.

Sally was glad to see it was Ben. She had been to a couple of jobs with him before, and he obviously lived for his job and was intense about his examinations.

"It's like searching for treasure," he had explained on their first meeting. He was keen to share his knowledge, and Sally's genuine interest prompted him to give David Attenborough-type commentaries as he went about his examination – much to her amusement and interest. Mike wasn't so interested. He'd seen it all dozens of times before. He retreated to the landing and hung out of the window with a cigarette.

"I gather there may be a condom in situ," Ben stated as he opened his aluminium briefcase and took out his camera to start his inspection of the room.

Sally nodded in acknowledgement. "Possibly in the bin."

She winced at the thought of his task.

"Do you wanna recover that then – save on paperwork for me?"

Sally went to laugh at the suggestion but checked herself as she realised it was a genuine request.

"Are you serious?"

"Yep, here's a pair of gloves. If I seize it, I'll only have to hand it to you and then have to write a statement saying that I did. As you're here, it makes sense for you to do it, and anything else that needs seizing."

Sally pulled a face and looked at the ball gown thinking that it would also be an important exhibit.

"I guess so."

Ben passed her a pair of rubber gloves and pointed at the bin under the desk. "It's all yours."

The way he said it made Sally realise that he wasn't trying to make a fool of her. She had learnt to be wary after her experiences with Graham and his gut-wrenching set-ups. Ben was just letting her know that it was a dirty job but somebody had to do it – and that somebody was her.

Sally pulled the gloves on and made towards the bin. Sure enough the condom was there and she helped herself to an exhibit bag from Ben's briefcase. He made her job easier turning his back and busying himself with giving his full attention to the bed.

With the used condom safely bagged, Ben offered Sally a pair of protective goggles. "Here, put these on and I'll show you the smeg lamp in action."

Sally had heard about the 'smeg lamp', nicknamed as such because the rays from it in a darkened room highlighted, amongst other things, semen, and before further forensic tests could be carried out, it was a good initial indicator of whether any sexual activity had taken place.

Ben pulled the curtains, shut the door and switched on the lamp before shining it over the duvet cover. Immediately, several patches glowed menacingly at them. He pulled the duvet back and similar patches were visible on the undersheet.

"Bingo!" he sang. "I'll let you seize the duvet cover and sheet too, shall I?" he said, taking his goggles off before pulling back the curtains and putting the lamp away.

"I'd love to, thanks!" Sally giggled as she reached for some plastic bags to place them in. She called Mike in to help her bag them up.

"So, we're 'appy the alleged act took place then?" he commented as they told him of their findings so far. "That's the easy part. Now we just 'ave to try to prove whether it 'appened without 'er consent. That's the stumbling block, you see, Sally. It's always t'same: the offender's word against the victim's. We don't often get independent witnesses to such intimate acts." Sally listened intently as Mike continued, "The law currently stands on the offender's side. The decision to send an innocent man to prison for life is a fine balance against the life sentence of a victim who has to carry the burden of a life-changing violation against her as she watches her attacker walk free." He took his handkerchief from his pocket again and wiped his furrowed brow.

They finished bagging up the exhibits as Ben packed up his kit and they all walked back to their cars, having called the security guard to lock up behind them.

"Just time for a bit of lunch before we speak to the young girl, eh, Sal?"

"Sounds good to me," replied Sally, suddenly realising she was ravenous.

In true CID style, they stopped off at a pasty shop. Nothing healthy for the likes of DC Stott – he was renowned for his unhealthy lifestyle and was loath to change his ways, despite the ribbing he got from those brave enough to tease this stalwart officer.

Soon they were on their way to the recovery suite. They arrived at the same time as Helen, her mum and a female DC, Debbie, who was specially trained in dealing with sexual offence victims. Sally didn't really know what to expect but was surprised when she saw Helen was a normal-looking petite and pretty girl. Pale and wide-eyed, she was hugging a big chunky cardigan round herself. Sally felt sorry for her in the knowledge that she was about to have to reveal the finer details of a very personal and intimate experience to a total stranger.

They all introduced themselves and then Debbie gave them a short tour of the house. Sally followed them since she had never been there before herself. From the outside, it looked like any regular semi-detached house in a quiet cul-de-sac. Inside was pretty normal too, with a kitchen and playroom downstairs as well as the lounge where Helen would sit to give her statement. Debbie outlined to Helen what was going to happen as they walked up the stairs and showed her a room furnished as another lounge, a room that had been converted into a doctor's surgery and a bathroom. The last room was an office where Sally and Mike could work from whilst the statement was being taken.

Debbie took Helen back downstairs and settled her with a cup of tea ready to start her statement whilst Sally led Helen's mum to the upstairs lounge. She was shell-shocked by the whole series of events and had obviously been crying.

"How could someone do this to my baby?" she implored. "She's never even had a serious boyfriend before and now this. How will she ever recover and have a normal relationship in the future?"

Sally didn't know the answers and felt pretty ineffective with the limited advice she could offer. After all, how could anyone move forward from this? It was never going to go away and be forgotten, and would undoubtedly have a lifelong effect on this young woman. Her mum looked crushed with the realisation of this and the feeling of helplessness for her child.

Before Debbie started the statement she popped back upstairs and joined Mike and Sally in the office where Mike formally introduced the two female officers. He explained that Sally was a probationary officer and that this was her first experience of a rape investigation.

"In that case, I could ask Helen whether it would be OK for you to sit in whilst I take the statement?" Debbie asked. "It would be good experience because, as a female officer, you're bound to be asked to take a rape statement at some point."

"That would be great," enthused Sally, looking round at Mike for reassurance.

"Go for it, lass! All good experience. I'll take a quick statement from Mum whilst we're waiting" he replied encouragingly before reaching for his cigarettes and heading for the door.

Sally tried to hide her delight when Helen agreed. Not wanting to appear too enthusiastic, in the circumstances. Sally chose to sit in a single armchair just to the side of Helen and out of her direct eyeline hoping she would forget she was there.

The interview started. Helen's memory of the events was sketchy due to the alcohol. She could remember the events leading up to leaving the student union and then heading back to her room with the male student whom she knew as Mark Yardley and was in his final year at the university. They had engaged in some heavy petting and then she thought she had fallen asleep. The next memory she had was waking up with him on top of her, having sex. She didn't protest or fight. She couldn't explain why. She had been stunned and completely dumbfounded, and allowed him to finish before he had fallen asleep beside her. She had then got up and gone to a friend's room where she stayed until the morning when she asked her friend to go to her room and ask Mark to leave. He had left without protest. She hadn't told the fellow student what had happened but, instead, waited until she had returned home and told her older sister, who had in turn told their mum.

Debbie finished writing the statement and then discussed the medical checks that were advised in these circumstances before giving Helen a pile of leaflets offering emotional support, should she need it. Sally fetched Helen's mother and found herself choked as she watched them hug each other. Both clearly relieved the ordeal was over. The girl looked sapped of strength and held on to her mother's arm. Sally looked at the pair whose lives would never be the same again – drawn into a myriad of unanswered questions of whys and what ifs.

Mike joined them and outlined the procedure of what would be happening next. "We'll be looking to arrest Mark in the next few hours." Helen buried her head into her mother's neck at the thought of this and its repercussions. "When we have an account from him, we'll consider sending various items off for forensic examination. We'll need a statement from your other daughter," he indicated to Helen's mum, "and we'll also get one from the girl who asked Mark to leave just in case Helen gave them some information at that early stage that she may have forgotten now." He looked at Helen before clarifying, "we need to make sure we have every bit of information you see?"

Sally wasn't sure how much of this information Helen and her Mum were taking in. Mike handed them his card telling them that he would keep them updated and that they could contact him at any time. With that, Debbie escorted them to their car and left them to try to make sense of what life had thrown their way.

Mike made a call before they headed back to the station. CID officers were waiting for his call as they now had an address for Mark and arrangements were in place for him to be arrested by his local constabulary and brought to Bath as soon as they had the nod from Mike.

"Are you alright to stay on duty? You can interview him with me if you like?"

Sally looked at him in awe. "Me? Are you sure?"

Mike smiled reassuringly. "Course, nothing like the real thing for gaining experience."

Sally had no plans for the evening and was flattered at being asked. They had a long wait while Mark was brought to the police station, during which Sally phoned her mum to ask her to walk Honey for her.

Mike explained to Sally that in rape cases like this, the main stumbling block was often being able to prove whether or not the victim consented to what had happened and that this was difficult when it was one person's word against another. He continued that they relied heavily on forensic and medical evidence to assist them in a charging decision but because this wasn't always immediately available, many solicitors advised their clients to make 'no comment.'

Sally was intrigued. She was going to meet a rapist. What was he going to look like? Was he going to look like the rapists on the intelligence bulletins that were circulated from time to time? One thing was for sure: she hoped Mike would give him a hard time in his interview and, if she was brave enough to speak, she would too.

Later that evening, Mike and Sally stood in the corridor of the custody suite waiting for the detention officer to bring Mark Yardley from his cell to the interview room. They had given a disclosure of the facts to his solicitor who had in turn had the opportunity to consult privately with Mark. When Mark came into view round the corner from the cell corridor, Sally was stunned. He was just a kid, his sallow face pale with fear. He wasn't much taller than Sally and of a slight build. He looked like his world had just fallen apart.

Mike shook hands with Mark and opened the heavy door into the interview room. Sally followed him in and stopped short behind him as Mark looked round the windowless room, its walls lined with dimpled, soundproof tiles. His legal representative was already lounging in one of the plastic chairs, looking dishevelled in a suit that had seen better days and a fat tie hanging loose against his unbuttoned collar. He waved his arm towards the empty chair intended for Mark who stumbled forward and took his place.

Mike immediately sat down and prepared the tapes whilst explaining to Mark what to expect during the interview. Mark nodded in silence and stared alternately at Mike and at his hands clasped on the table in front of him.

The tapes were switched on and the interview started with

Mike going through the standard introduction and caution, reason for the arrest and purpose of the interview. Mike introduced all the people in the room and, when he indicated Sally, Mark jumped at the sight of her having obviously been in such a state of shock that he hadn't noticed her until that point. He took a deep intake of breath and blew out, puffing his cheeks as he did so. This was a young man under stress and deservedly so, thought Sally, though she couldn't help feeling a slight pang of sorrow for him for what he was about to go through. Mike had briefed Sally on his interview plan and encouraged her to ask anything she felt was relevant. Sally had nodded, trying to show enthusiasm but at the same time thinking that she wouldn't dare open her mouth.

Mike asked Mark to tell him everything he could about the night in question.

"No comment," came the barely audible reply.

Sally despised his attitude. *What a coward*, she thought to herself. *What a typical man. They really start early these days.* She wanted to reach out, shake him and shout at him telling him of the devastating effect his actions had had on that poor girl and her family.

Mike continued by relating Helen's account of the rape, intermittently stopping to offer Mark the chance to make a comment if he wished. Mark continued to heed the legal advice he had been given to say 'no comment' gradually going redder and redder in the face and shifting uncomfortably in his seat as more lurid details were described. Mike persisted with his interview plan whilst Mark's increasing distress became obvious, glancing at Sally and hiding his face in his hands. His breathing became more and more erratic and, when Mike announced that they had recovered the condom from Helen's bin and reached into a file beside him on the desk to reveal the offending item for all to see, it was a step too far for this boy.

"Enough, enough!" he shouted, standing up, scraping his chair away and putting his hands out in front of him. The three remaining occupants of the room all started at this unexpected outburst. But no sooner had he spoken than he crumpled back into the chair and leant forward on the table with his head in his hands and started to sob.

"I didn't do it. I didn't rape her...I'm not a-a rapist!" and he dissolved into childish sobs.

The legal representative, looking interested for the first time since the interview had started, leaned forwards towards his client and stated, "Can I remind you of your legal right and my advice to you to remain silent."

"I don't want to remain silent. I want to tell them how it was! I didn't rape her!" Mark opened his hands out, palms upwards, pleading with the officers as he cried tears of obvious frustration.

The solicitor was now on the edge of his seat. "Mark, I have advised you to make 'no comment'," he reiterated.

"I don't want to make 'no comment'," Mark shot back at his only ally. "I want to clear my name – I did not rape her!" He banged his fists on the table and looked straight at Mike. "We both wanted it. She never told me she didn't. She was egging me on! She never said 'No'."

The solicitor made another feeble attempt to intervene, but Mark put his hand up making it clear that he had made his mind up and wanted to talk. Mike suggested the interview should be suspended while Mark spoke to his legal representative again. The tapes were stopped and Mike and Sally left the interview room to allow Mark to talk to his solicitor in private.

123

The detention officer informed Mike and Sally that Mark's parents were in the reception area and were wanting an update as to what was happening and whether or not their son was going to be allowed home with them.

Sally volunteered to speak to them but, by now, was feeling confused by what she had seen and heard. She had been so convinced that he was one hundred per cent guilty when she walked into the interview room. Now she wasn't so sure.

Mark's parents were in obvious pain and anguish. His mother pleaded with Sally, her face drawn in agony at the thought of what her son was going through. "He isn't that kind of boy. There's been a terrible mistake. I know he wouldn't do this."

She grabbed Sally's arm and looked her in the eye. Sally wanted to reassure her that everything would be all right, but she wasn't in a position to offer such assurances. Instead, she told them that Mark was fine and they were taking a break in the interview for him to speak to his solicitor.

"Can I see him – pleeease?" Mark's mother pleaded but Sally could only tell her that, as he wasn't a juvenile, this couldn't be allowed. The woman collapsed into the chair behind her and let out a low primal groan demonstrating the utter helplessness she was experiencing.

Her husband put his arms around her and looked at Sally. "Tell him we're here and that we love him," he managed to say before burying his head in his wife's hair and joining in her grief.

"We shouldn't be too much longer. He'll be released on bail as soon as we've finished," Sally related what Mike had told her, suddenly overcome with sympathy for the ordeal they were also going through.

Her attempt at reassurance only served to prompt another low groan from Mark's mum as Sally made her way back to the custody suite.

As she reached the door, it was flung open in front of her and Mark's solicitor flounced past her without looking at her or saying a word. Sally continued into the custody suite looking quizzically at Mike.

He explained that Mark was back in his cell after sacking his solicitor and was going to continue unrepresented. "In my experience, it's an indication of innocence. He doesn't want to play the solicitor's word games. He wants to protest his innocence."

They had to wait for the inspector to come down and speak to Mark. Sally was aware that this was a requirement of the Police and Criminal Evidence Act when someone has changed their mind about legal rights whilst in custody – just to check they aren't doing it under duress. The inspector was satisfied with Mark's decision and he was brought back to the interview room.

Led by Mike, Mark went through the alleged rape minute by minute in cringeable detail. His face was the colour of beetroot as he described how Helen had put the condom on him. He maintained eye contact with Mike as he gave his account whilst wringing his hands and running his fingers through his hair, as if trying to remove the accusation from his soul.

Sally watched this troubled boy in a new light. This was a young man in torment who didn't know which way to turn to try to prove his innocence. It was obvious to Sally that both the accused and the accuser were trapped in the same downward spiral where both were telling the truth but with conflicting views on the version of events.

When Mike had finished cross-examining him, Mark leant back against the chair, looking like a broken man or, more accurately, boy. His eyes were hollow with fear. Sally had asked a few questions but they were minor points which he willingly clarified for her. The bottom line was that he also had a vague alcohol-confused memory of the night, but he was adamant that the act had been a consensual one and that Helen had even provided the condom.

Mike explained to Mark that he would be released on police bail whilst further enquiries were made which would include speaking to Helen again. He also gave some reassurance that these enquiries shouldn't take too long since, as he wasn't disputing that sex had taken place that night, there would be no need to submit any items for forensic analysis.

Just as with Helen, Sally wasn't sure how much of this Mark was taking in judging by the shell shocked look on his face. She led him out to the front office where his parents still sat in silence, staring into space. They both jumped to their feet when they saw their son appear through the door. Mark's mother immediately wrapped her arms around her son and Mark, too exhausted to protest, bent his head into her neck in an innate response to the stress of his ordeal.

Sally explained to them what was required of Mark: that he must return to the police station on the date specified and that he must make no attempt to contact Helen, directly or indirectly. Mark barely had the energy to stand as he nodded in agreement to the conditions of his bail and was led from the station in his mother's arms.

Sally waved at Stumpy who released the door letting her back through into the staff area where she leaned against the wall, taking a deep breath and closing her eyes. She

126

was exhausted too. She had been through a roller coaster of emotions herself today and was confused by the overload of information she had been presented with.

Mike appeared from the custody suite. "You alright, Sal?"

Sally shook her head at him, showing her bewilderment at the day's events.

"Come on, let's go back to the office and sort our paperwork."

She followed him and was grateful for the cup of tea she was offered. She realised it was nearly midnight and that she hadn't eaten since their pasty at lunchtime. She was ravenous and weary from the intense concentration of the day.

Mike was also tired and completed the bare minimum of paperwork, suggesting that they go home and get some sleep before starting again in the morning at 8am.

"Unless you want to go for a quick drink?" he enquired, looking at his watch. "I know a little place in town where we can still get a pint at this time of night."

Whatever his intentions, Sally didn't have the energy for anything but to make her way home. She crawled into bed wishing, and not for the first time, that she had someone warm and familiar to cuddle up to, though Honey was a willing substitute. Sally was too tired to even notice her hunger and slept fitfully until her alarm told her it was time to get up.

When she arrived back in the office, she sat and talked the case over with Mike. He told her that this was a typical scenario that she would encounter time and again in her career.

"There are two sides to every story, Sally." Mike gave her the wisdom of his long service. "That's the trouble with the demon drink. Helen genuinely believes she's been raped because she has no real memory of the event. Mark truly believes she consented, and we have to prove beyond all reasonable doubt that it happened without her consent to be able to convict him. The Crown Prosecution Service will never take this to court. Still, we have to pursue all the lines of enquiry before we get to that stage." He passed Sally his notebook. "See if you can trace the friend who told Mark to leave. I'll arrange to speak to Helen again and make an appointment to take a statement from her sister."

Sally took the notebook and reached for the phone. She had to be impartial – though she really didn't know which side she would take if she had to. What she did know was that one girl's life had been devastated by the belief that she had been raped. And that a young man's life had been equally devastated as a result of his arrest for a crime he truly believed he hadn't committed – a crime that carries a life sentence. He would also have to live with the knowledge that his arrest would lie on file for the rest of his life and that the news would inevitably spread amongst his peers and cast an unwelcome shadow over his final days at university. There were no winners, only losers in this cruel game.

Chapter Six

Sally turned her efforts towards mustering up some Christmas spirit in time for her sister's Christmas party. Cathy and her partner, Steve lived in a bijou residence and always hosted a lavish get-together on the 23rd December, having offloaded Sally's young nieces Nancy, aged five and Ella, aged three on to their grandmother for the night. There was always a big build-up to the party, even for the children who enjoyed the preparations almost as much as going to stay with their Grandma whilst the party took place. Jean always had a little party for them at her house and made a big effort making sure they didn't feel left out and were happy to leave the adults to their celebrations.

Sally decided to treat herself to a complete new outfit, including shoes, and made a hair appointment for the morning of the party.

She went straight to Cathy's from the hairdresser, to help her prepare. She was glad to have been asked to help as it meant she wouldn't have to turn up on her own. However, she needn't have worried as there were plenty of single people there and she managed to forget all her troubles for a few hours and enjoy herself.

Though admittedly a little hungover, Sally was in better spirits when she met up with Uncle Jack for lunch on Christmas Eve.

As he did every year, he asked her all about her family's plans for Christmas. It was clear he would have loved to have joined them, but they both knew it wasn't possible.

Uncle Jack insisted on paying for lunch and presented her with a beautiful gold bangle inlaid with pale turquoise mother-of-pearl.

"Uncle Jack," exclaimed Sally, "it's beautiful! Thank you!" She leant forward and hugged him. "I couldn't have chosen better myself," she gushed, putting it on and holding her arm out to admire the bangle.

"Ah well, it's not difficult choosing for you. You've the same tastes as your mother – and I know she would love it too."

Sally knew he was correct on all counts, and the thought lingered in the air between them. It was such a waste of lives, but Sally had used all her powers of persuasion to try to reunite them and she had accepted that it wasn't going to happen.

"So, what are your New Year's Resolutions?" Sally tried sounding upbeat to deflect their tandem thoughts.

"Give up the ciggies, of course!" her uncle replied, tapping his packet on the table in front of him and smiling at her mischievously.

"Again?!" Sally leant back in fake surprise. He promised this every year, and every year he failed saying that they and his drink were his comforts and he couldn't do without them.

"What about you? What New Year's Resolutions have you got, poppet?"

Sally raised her eyebrows and shrugged. "I guess I have to knuckle down and master this new career of mine."

"That's the spirit! You'll be a sergeant before you know it; then you can boss all of them around!"

The thought of promotion was appealing, but she had to get her two years' probation out of the way first – and that seemed a long way off.

"And I've got a hot date lined up for next week!"

"Attagirl. Who's the lucky chap?"

Sally had been asked out by one of the blokes she had met at Cathy and Steve's party. She only had a vague recollection of him, and that was only because he was French and had an unusual name: Claude – and also because he was a little arrogant. Still, she thought she would give him a chance in the absence of any other offers and had arranged to meet in the week between Christmas and New Year, for a meal at Franco's, of course. Sally decided to return to Franco's to rid herself of the demons of the last visit and to show Franco that there was life after Julian. And, without wanting to be too pessimistic about the date, at least she could guarantee she would enjoy the meal.

The date didn't start well. During their pre-meal drink at the Crystal Palace pub, Sally had already decided that Claude was a non-starter. She kept saying to herself 'Claude the Fraud' as the accent he had had at the party had disappeared. When Sally questioned this, he blushed and said that he found girls were suckers for accents.

Not this girl, thought Sally to herself as she smiled back politely and tried to feign interest in his work as an air traffic controller. Since Sally had decided this was going to be their first and last date, she told him that she was a teacher and was able to answer the few questions he asked her based on her previous experience. It was a story she had planned to utilise whilst sussing people out, before revealing her potentially controversial occupation.

"Ah, Sally, Sally! How are you this evening?" Franco greeted her as they entered the restaurant.

"Oh fine, thanks," Sally replied non-committally and gestured towards Claude. "This is Claude."

"Ah, Claude! Welcome to Franco's Trattorio. Come, come." Franco summoned them diplomatically to an entirely different part of the restaurant from her last visit and sat them on a curved cushioned bench against the wall with a small circular table in front of them.

Once they were seated, Franco handed them a menu each and Claude the wine list. Claude scanned the list briefly and, without bothering to consult Sally, ordered a bottle of house white. Then he excused himself and headed for the gents'.

Sally made a face at Franco indicating she was having doubts already over her choice of date, causing Franco to clap his hands together with amusement.

"Oh, Sally, I hope this one treats you well. You deserve nothing less than the best," he enthused as he made his way back to the kitchen.

Sally laughed resignedly and sat fiddling with the cutlery, wondering how best to end the evening when something caught her eye on the bench where Claude had been sitting. She leant round to see what it was.

She took a sharp intake of breath when she saw, lying there in all its glory against the red velvet seat, a packet of condoms still sealed in its cellophane wrap.

"Fuck, fuck, fuck!" Sally said to herself under her breath. Her heart was racing and she made a split-second decision. She picked up the condoms, placed them in Claude's empty wine glass and then stood up, reaching for her bag.

"Oh, your turn now, is it?"

132

Sally jumped as Claude's untimely return scuppered her plans to leave the restaurant alone.

"Oh, er, yes," she replied, eyeing her coat and knowing that the toilets were in the opposite direction to the way out. She turned and walked towards the ladies'. Hardly able to breathe, she glanced over her shoulder as she reached the toilet door. Claude was engrossed in the menu, his beady eyes shielded by the menu card. She turned back and, after spotting an escape route, took a sidestep towards the kitchen and disappeared through the door.

Franco looked momentarily surprised. Sally didn't usually frequent his kitchen unless she was on duty.

"Franco," Sally whispered loudly and lurched towards him grabbing his ham-like forearms for reassurance. "My date isn't going well and I need your help."

Franco beamed at her and seemed to understand why she was gabbling at him in his kitchen. He was obviously enjoying the moment and chuckled as he guided her to the back door. Rossana, who was preparing food nearby, shook her head but smiled good-naturedly.

Sally stood on the step outside the back door still clutching Franco's arms and looking anxiously at the door leading to the restaurant, fearful that Claude would appear after her. "Franco, can you keep my coat for me – I'll pick it up in the week?" she said in a conspiratorial tone.

"Of course, of course, *tesoro miei* – it is not a problem."

"And, Franco, can you do me another favour?"

"Anything for you, Sally. What shall I do?"

Rossana appeared beside them holding out one of her coats and placing it around Sally's shoulders. "It's cold, Sally. You'll catch a cold. Here."

As Sally gratefully accepted the offer, slipping the coat on, she continued, "Can you offer my date a glass of wine before he goes?"

"No problem at all!" chuckled Franco, looking mildly bemused. As Sally slipped out into the courtyard, she looked back once more to see Franco walking back inside shaking his head and laughing with Rossana, both revelling at their part in the conspiracy. She wrapped the coat around herself against the chill night air as she ran along Old King Street before hailing a taxi from the corner of Queen Square. Once the taxi had moved off, she lay across the back seat and howled with laughter and relief.

Sally enjoyed a quiet night in on New Year's Eve with her mum. They'd enjoyed watching the celebrations on television with a bottle of bubbly and retiring to bed almost as soon as Big Ben had stopped chiming. A lazy morning followed where Sally's mum spoiled her with a cooked breakfast and they enjoyed a stroll with Honey before Sally left to start her late shift. Although Bank Holidays offered the bonus of double time, it didn't always suit those with families to work at this time of year. Sally had volunteered to work the shift. She had nothing better to do and the money would come in handy.

When she arrived at work, Sergeant Morley told her that Basher had phoned in sick. *Typical*, she thought. *Hungover, more like!* She smiled a knowing smile at Sergeant Morley.

"You choose who you'd like to offer the shift to," he said as he passed her a piece of paper which had the team's contact numbers printed on it.

Sally studied the names in front of her. Several were eliminated due to being away on leave so she plumped for

Dan who was also the one who lived closest to the station and although was married, did not have children providing a valid reason to stay at home. She dialled his number and waited for an answer. Few would turn down the offer of double time when the carrot was actually dangled in front of them. After a few rings, a female voice, presumably Dan's wife, answered with a sharp, "Hello?"

"Oh hi, it's Sally here from the police station. Can I speak to Dan please?" she chirped in a voice she hoped sounded friendly.

The woman didn't reply. Instead, she heard her say as she passed the phone to Dan, "It's for you. It's one of the tarts you work with."

Sally was somewhat taken aback by the woman's obvious lack of effort to conceal her words or opinions and, when Dan croaked a "Hello" down the phone, Sally couldn't resist letting him know she had heard, "That was nice. Did I meet her at the Christmas do?"

Dan was suitably embarrassed and Sally heard a door slam in the background.

"Sorry, Sally. She's err...she's err..." He couldn't think of a suitable explanation so Sally interjected, her tone making it clear that she wasn't impressed.

"Yeah, whatever. I was phoning to say there's a late shift up for grabs today but maybe I'll try the next on the list—"

"No, no, I'll have it." Dan interrupted. "Thanks, Sal, thanks for phoning. I'll be there in half an hour. Err, sorry again, Sal." He added before placing the receiver down.

Sally did the same and sighed. What gratitude from Dan's wife. Sally had just given her an opportunity to pay off a considerable amount of their Christmas credit card bill and all she had got in return was verbal abuse. It was something Sally was learning to take in her stride. Some women just couldn't cope with their partners working so closely with the opposite sex. Besides, Sally mused, since Dan wasn't blessed with good looks by any stretch of the imagination, Mrs Fry shouldn't flatter herself that her husband was attractive to anyone but her.

It was a quiet shift and Sergeant Morley joined Sally on her stroll around the city. There were only a handful of shops open and, as darkness drew in, the Christmas lights glared in the near deserted streets as a reminder that the festive season was not over yet.

After grub, Sally headed out alone. She made for the top of town and enjoyed a tour of the Circus and Royal Crescent before heading back towards the city centre. As she passed the back of Franco's, she noticed the back door was open and made a beeline for it, grinning to herself at the thought of the last time she was here.

"Hello?" she called out and spotted Franco at the same time. He beckoned her in.

"Hey, you don't have to come in the back door as well as leave through it, you know. You are a wicked girl!" Franco greeted her with his customary kiss on each cheek. "Happy New Year, *stellina mia*!"

"Happy New Year to you too." Sally laughed with embarrassment. "How was Claude after I left?" she quizzed Franco, wincing at her own question but at the same time having a sadistic need to know.

Franco could hardly relate the events through laughing and said that Claude had been stunned when Franco hovered the bottle of wine over the glass containing the condoms.

Apparently, Claude had frozen with horror at the sight before declining the wine and making a sharp exit.

"Look there." Franco nodded towards the kitchen window sill where the cellophane sealed packet was displayed.

"It's so funny. Madonna! Even Rossana could not stop laughing!"

He saw that Sally was looking a little uncomfortable, though she was still smiling. It was a hilarious tale, and he embraced her again in a fatherly hug. "Oh, Sally, this year is going to be your year. I feel it in my bones, just you wait and see. Franco can tell these things, you know."

Sally hoped he was right.

"Come on. I teach you how to use Franco's cappuccino machine; then you can make us both one." Sally took off her coat and hat and draped them over a stool whilst Franco showed her how to froth the milk before she made two perfect cups for them.

"Ah, you see, you should come and work for Franco. You are a natural!"

Sally climbed onto another stool and rested her elbows on the counter in front of her before placing her chin in her hands and replied, "Well, you never know, I might just take you up on that!"

With Franco bustling around her, she enjoyed hearing all about his upcoming trip 'back home' in the New Year.

Sally had barely finished her cappuccino when her radio burst into life, bringing her back to reality. A vehicle obstructing the tradesman's entrance to the Assembly Rooms in Alfred Street. Sally picked up her coat and hat and put her cup in the industrial dishwasher – she really was quite at home at Franco's.

"I'll come and collect my coat later in the week when I'm

off duty, if that's OK?" Sally asked Franco referring the coat she left behind on the night of her disastrous date.

"Of course – no problem Sally." Franco replied smiling as she stepped back into the chill air. She headed back up to the top of the city where a party reveller had no doubt made the right decision to leave their car following the New Year's Eve party that the Assembly Rooms always hosted. Unfortunately for them they were about to pay for their late decision.

Sally knocked at the door of the Assembly Room's security office. Security guards were notorious for getting excited about minor occurrences, and this one was no different. He rushed out ahead of Sally, obviously wanting to make sure the car was towed away before the owner could return. Sally followed him, noting his uniform which was couple of sizes too big for him and, combined with the weight of his fully-equipped utility belt, caused the last two inches of his trousers to trail on the floor.

"Here it is," he announced proudly. "We've got another function tonight and the caterers need to get in here."

Sally turned her attention to the red MG parked halfway across the service bay. Red MG? She took a few steps back to look at the number plate – could it be? Could it **really** be?

Yes, it was! It was Julian's car! Sally's heart was pounding. She could just call him and save him the £120 recovery fee. She could, but...Sally radioed the vehicle index through to the Control Room and requested the tow truck. The Control Room replied with the keeper details: Julian Locke and still registered to her flat!

Trying to keep her hand steady, she filled in the Fixed Penalty Notice and scribbled an illegible signature that Julian wouldn't recognise before slapping the yellow ticket in the middle of the windscreen. Sally retreated to a nearby doorway and willed the tow truck to hurry up, praying that Julian wouldn't turn up before it arrived.

Revenge is so sweet, she thought to herself. She was relieved to see the tow truck swing round the corner after not too long a wait. The driver had the car off the ground in no time. This meant that, even if Julian turned up now, he couldn't claim it back without paying the recovery fee. Sally called out to the driver, above the sound of the hydraulic lift, that she had been called to another job. The driver nodded and Sally strode away almost at running pace. Mission accomplished! She allowed herself a churlish giggle at the thought of what she had just done and the thought of Julian's reaction when he discovered his beloved car was gone.

At the end of Alfred Street, she stepped into another doorway to take a final look and watch the truck drive off. She peeped out from her hideout but immediately reeled herself back in as running towards the car from the opposite direction was Julian, waving his arms manically at the truck driver. Sally's joy was immediately quashed when she noticed a woman running behind Julian. She recognised her as 'Fabulous Fiona' as Sally had nicknamed her, a hotshot recruit from his office whom Sally had been introduced to at the last boring corporate dinner she had been to – and had taken an instant dislike to. She liked her even less now.

Sally took her hat off and clasped it to her chest for fear of being spotted. She needn't have worried and, in fact, should have known that Julian would only have eyes for his 'baby' which was now dangling twenty feet off the ground and being manoeuvred over the flatbed of the truck.

Sally could feel her pulse throbbing in her temple as Julian shouted at the driver and gesticulated wildly. She saw him take his wallet out and attempt to show the driver the contents in an effort to dissuade him from driving off. The driver shook his head and shrugged at Julian before tightening the harness which secured Julian's pride and joy to the flatbed and jumping into the cab.

As they helplessly watched the truck drive away, Fabulous Fiona tried to put her arms around Julian in an attempt to console him. This caused Sally to wince but she was somehow comforted as Julian reacted by shrugging the woman off like a petulant child and stepping out into the road to hail a passing taxi.

Sally tried to be pragmatic about seeing Julian with another woman. If she was going to find out that Julian was seeing someone else, it was as good a scenario as she could have imagined. She even managed a smile as she headed back to the station for the end of her shift secure in the knowledge that she had earned for herself on double time what Julian would have to pay to get his car back. That would be one to tell Uncle Jack!

Sally took a week's annual leave early in the New Year. She caught up with some of her old teaching friends and had a couple of nights away at Jackie's during which they saw a few others from training school. Jackie was more than happy for Sally to take Honey who enjoyed being thoroughly spoiled. This single life wasn't altogether bad.

Or so Sally thought until she arrived back at her flat. There on the doormat inside the front door was Julian's key signifying that he had moved the last of his belongings out. Sally put her bags down and picked up the key, staring at it in the palm of her hand for a long while. That was it then. It really was over.

She leant back against the wall of the hallway and slowly slid to the floor. The key slowly lost its focus as tears obscured her vision. She buried her head into Honey's soft fur.

"Oh, Hun, it really is just you and me now, girl."

Honey responded by licking the salty tears from Sally's face, thinking this was a new game Sally had invented.

"Don't know what I'd do without you," wept Sally as Honey started her own game of bounding between the hook where Sally kept her lead and back to where her owner sat holding her face in her hands. Sally didn't hold back and allowed the tears to come in loud, unadulterated sobs.

When she had composed herself she rearranged the furniture in the lounge to try to fill the gaps left by the removal of Julian's things. She was quite pleased with the finished result and placed Honey's bed in front of the radiator, which she knew she would approve of.

Sally returned to work knowing that she would have to at last face Alex after the events on the night of the Christmas do. However, he wasn't at briefing which Sally found odd as she had expected him to have returned from France by now.

"Alex not back yet?" Sally asked Ruth casually after briefing had finished. She could feel her cheeks getting hot as she waited for Ruth's answer and tried to busy herself with checking her pocket notebook.

"Haven't you heard? A place came up on the drug squad and he's gone straight over to Bristol."

"Oh right." Sally tried to sound calm as she felt the blood drain from her body. *Oh my God*, she thought to herself. When

141

was she going to see him again? She couldn't and shouldn't contact him. She felt somehow hollow as she tried to imagine what it was going to be like coming to work and not even seeing him now.

Heading out on the streets with her head swimming from the news of Alex's unexpected departure, Sally made for Franco's. She needed to talk to someone. She told Franco of Alex's sudden transfer, trying not to give too much away about her feelings towards him. Franco listened as he bustled about his kitchen and Sally couldn't help but think he knew exactly how she felt. If he did, he was diplomatic about it and gushed appropriate sympathetic responses, and Sally was grateful for this.

She headed out to move some beggars on and to check out an alarm that was going off at the Model Shop – nothing too taxing but it kept her moving as the weather had turned cold and it was threatening to snow.

"Foxtrot Bravo 1759."

"Go ahead," Sally replied, pausing to see which direction this call would take her in.

"Can you return to the station and speak to the sergeant please?"

Sally's heart skipped a beat. The last time she was called in by a sergeant was when she got into trouble over that passing-out dinner business. She wondered what this could be about.

"Noted. En route," she replied as jauntily as she could knowing that everyone else monitoring the radios would know she had been summoned by a sergeant. Her mind worked overtime wondering what this could be about as she made her way back to the station.

Sally walked straight into the sergeants' office without

taking her hat or coat off. She was keen to know what fate had in store for her this time. What was she going to say if it was something about Alex? There was nothing to tell, she decided.

Sergeant Morley was sitting alone in the office.

"Sergeant Baron called me in?" Sally enquired, assuming it was her who had summoned her.

"Ah, Sally, come in a moment." Sergeant Morley got up and closed the door.

Christ, here we go, thought Sally, her breath quickening as she sat down in the chair offered to her.

"Sally, I've just taken a call from the hospital. The nurse said that a Jack Walker has been admitted; said he was a relative?"

"Oh, my God," exclaimed Sally, jumping to her feet. "Did they say what was wrong with him? Did they say he was alright?" Sally was almost nose to nose with Sergeant Morley as she demanded this information. "He's my Uncle." Immediately tears welled up in her eyes. She had to go to him.

"I...I think he may have had a stroke, Sally. Here, give me your radio and take the rest of the shift off."

Sally didn't need telling twice. "Thanks, Sarge," she said as she threw her radio on the desk and ran to the locker room.

Her mind was racing as she drove to the hospital. Would Aunt Bridie be there? Of course she would. Should she tell her mother? Of course she should.

She arrived at the ward and beckoned the staff nurse to a side room, afraid of bumping into Aunt Bridie. "I've come to see Jack Walker – I'm his niece Sally. He's been admitted with a stroke, I think."

"Ah yes, I'll show you to him." Neither of them moved as the nurse continued, "I must warn you that he's going to look very different from normal – and he won't be able to speak to you."

As Sally's face creased in distress, the nurse reached out and gently touched her arm. "We caught him early so we're hopeful of a good recovery. Come on, be brave for him. He's over here."

The nurse headed out from the side room, expecting Sally to follow her but paused when she noticed the look of horror on Sally's face. Sally leant back against the wall suddenly feeling the effects of shock at what she was hearing.

"Hang on – err, it's-it's his wife, my aunt – she wouldn't approve of me being here," Sally explained.

"Don't worry." The nurse walked back towards her. "We've spoken to his wife and she is travelling back from her holiday in Ireland. She can't get here till the morning." She ushered Sally into a ward bay where Uncle Jack lay.

Sally looked at the pale and motionless figure lying on the bed. He was lying on his back, his head tilted away from her and his left arm dangling lifelessly through the bed rail. She walked up to the bed and gasped as she saw her uncle's contorted face. He was barely recognisable. A large tear rolled down her cheek as she took his nearest hand in hers.

"Talk to him, he might be able to hear you," said the nurse.

"Uncle Jack, it's Sally here," she said softly as she lifted his hand through the bed rail and held it up to her face, giving it a gentle squeeze. "What have you been up to?" She tried to sound light-hearted but wasn't sure she was succeeding.

"Did you say you're Sally?" asked the nurse.

"Yes," replied Sally."

"Sally Gentle?" confirmed the nurse.

Sally nodded, still stunned at the sight of her uncle with a drip attached to his arm and a metal-framed contraption with a fabric sling hanging above the bed.

"There's a note on his medical records for you to be contacted as a next of kin along with a Bridget Walker. I guess that's his wife who's on her way back from Ireland?"

It hadn't even gone through Sally's mind why she had been contacted. She smiled down at Uncle Jack. "You wily old thing, you!" She managed a chuckle before quickly realising that she wouldn't be able to visit easily once Aunt Bridie was back.

She said the same to the nurse.

"I'm the staff nurse, Angie Moreton. Come and see me before you go." She smiled kindly at Sally. "It's probably best not to stay for too long just now though. He needs to rest."

"OK," Sally replied, her gaze fixed on Uncle Jack's face looking for a glimmer of recognition.

The nurse left them alone. Sally drew up a chair and sat with her elbows resting on the bed, Uncle Jack's hand still encased in hers. She held it to her face, wetting it with her tears. Apart from a couple of faint flickers of his eyelids, there was no response from him. She had dreaded this day when they could no longer engineer their clandestine meetings. She worried about what lay ahead and feared that she would not be able see him when he came out of hospital.

Ten minutes later, Sally approached the nursing station, trying to compose herself before speaking.

"Hi, Sally. Are you OK?" asked the staff nurse. Sally raised her eyebrows and nodded unconvincingly.

"Here's the ward's contact details. I'll let the other staff know what the situation is." She handed Sally a compliment slip as she spoke. "I can see that this is going to be an awkward situation but, as he has specifically requested you, if you call beforehand, I'll make sure that you can visit out of hours if that will help?"

"Thank you," said Sally gratefully taking the piece of paper. "What...how...is he going to be OK?" Sally didn't even know what questions to ask.

"It's difficult to say at this early stage but, from the CT scan, it looks as though the stroke was in the right-hand side of his brain which, as he is right-handed, is an advantage. His speech may be less affected than if it had been his left side."

Sally looked back at him, the strain showing in her face as the staff nurse continued, "It's a long road ahead, and he'll need all the support he can get to make a good recovery."

Sally nodded and tried to smile at the reassurances she was being offered.

"Do I take it you're a policewoman?" she continued, nodding at Sally's uniform. She had taken her civvy jacket off in the muggy temperature of the ward revealing her uniform which was minus her tie but in her haste she had forgotten to take off her epaulettes.

Sally nodded again, slipping her jacket back on suddenly feeling self-conscious.

"Well, that's easy then. Pop in when you're out on patrol. The visiting times to avoid are on that slip I've given you. You can always make out that you're here on official business if you bump into your aunt...?"

"That would be great. Thanks," Sally replied, genuinely grateful for the extra lengths this woman was going to for her.

"That's OK, moral support is often the key to recovery from a stroke. He's going to need you."

Sally wandered back to the car park, suddenly overcome with tiredness. She drove back to her flat where she lay on her bed and stared at the ceiling wondering how to handle the situation. How was she going to deal with Aunt Bridie and what was she going to do about telling her mum?

Honey was overjoyed to see her and Sally once again was glad to bury her head into her soft fur before drifting off into the welcome relief of sleep.

Chapter Seven

Over the next two weeks, Sally spent most of her free time at the hospital with Uncle Jack – always checking that the coast was clear first. It was an emotionally draining time trying to convey a positive outlook whilst playing cat and mouse with Aunt Bridie, though it appeared that she didn't spend much time at the hospital. Sally didn't object.

She was saddened to see the empty shell of the lively Uncle Jack she knew and loved. His face seemed expressionless despite her best efforts to make him smile. His speech was also slurred which made him frustrated and tired as Sally struggled to understand him.

She was painfully aware that he found it humiliating when she offered to help feed him, but she tried to be matter-of-fact about it to make it less demeaning and embarrassing for him. It was a strange reversal of roles from the rock he had been for her. She truly felt for him and was acutely aware of the lack of dignity his condition had forced upon him. The staff got to know her and kept her up to date with his progress. His recovery was going to be a long process, and it was hard to accept the Doctor's prognosis that he was unlikely to ever fully recover. She tried to keep his spirits up and spent hours reading the newspaper to him as his eyesight and concentration had been affected. Although she wasn't entirely sure how much he was taking in, he seemed to appreciate her efforts.

Sally had also been battling with her conscience, deliberating over whether to tell her mum and, if so, how. Her mind was made up for her when, one afternoon, Uncle Jack seemed to be agitated and even more frustrated than normal when he tried to speak to Sally. In the end, Sally asked for a piece of paper and a pen and was taken aback when he scrawled 'Jean' in laboured handwriting.

"You want me to tell Mum about you?" she asked in amazement.

Uncle Jack nodded in reply.

"About you being ill?" Sally clarified.

He nodded again looking at her intensely.

"I'll have to explain everything about us – that we've been in touch for such a long time."

Sally searched his face for a reaction but his illness caused him to give nothing away. He just nodded again, maintaining eye contact with her. He extended the index finger of his right hand and stabbed it weakly onto the bed.

"'Ere," he repeated, "'ere."

"You want her to come here?" Sally asked, not knowing whether to laugh or cry as Uncle Jack nodded in response.

As Sally assured him that she would arrange it, making sure that it was a time when they would avoid Aunt Bridie, he dropped his head in to his good hand as tears sprung from his eyes.

"Mum, I've got something to tell you." Sally tentatively broached the subject the following day.

"What is it, dear?" her mother replied, hanging up the tea towel on the rail on the front of the oven and turning towards Sally.

Sally noted the worried expression on her face and decided to come straight to the point. "It's Uncle Jack, he's had a stroke…"

"Oh my…" Jean stumbled towards a kitchen chair and slumped down, the colour draining from her face.

"He's OK. Well, he's not really OK, but he's recovering."

Sally began to explain that she had kept in contact with Uncle Jack but, before she could continue, her mother interrupted.

"You think I don't know that?" she said as her eyes welled with tears. "I've known all along that you've been in contact with him, because I know you so well and from the questions you've asked me. But I didn't want to interfere in case it caused any problems and stopped you seeing him." She blew her nose and looked at the picture she had of him on the kitchen dresser.

Sally put her arms around her. "Oh, Mum. He wants you to visit him."

Jean pulled sharply away from Sally's hold and looked at her, the confusion clear in her face. "H-how can I? Your Aunt Bridie." She dissolved into tears at the impossibility of the situation.

"I've been visiting him out of hours to avoid her. The hospital staff have been really good about it."

Sally made them both a cup of tea and, whilst they sat and drank it, told her mum all about her and Uncle Jack including his wish to have her informed as a next of kin if just this situation arose. Jean was reluctant at first about the idea of visiting, but Sally insisted that it was Uncle Jack's request and she finally agreed for Sally to pick her up the following morning.

They were both nervous as they walked into the ward. Sally walked on ahead and found Angie, the staff nurse and double-checked that the coast was clear.

"Yes, go on. He's had us spruce him up and sit him in his chair. It's really helped perk him up!"

Sally led her mum to the ward bay then stood aside unable to do any more than watch the scene unfold in front of her. Jean slowly walked up to the bed and, for several minutes, no one said a word as she leant over her brother and sobbed into his shoulder whilst he put his stronger arm around her and held her to him. Eventually, Jean moved away but crouched beside him cupping his face in her hands.

"My little brother," she kept repeating and he tried his best to say, "Jeanie, Jeanie" in response. Sally stood with tears rolling down her face. Angie spotted her and made her way over. Sally couldn't talk but smiled at Angie and gave her the thumbs up as she approached her. Angie glanced at Jack and Jean still holding each other and staring into each other's faces, and bit her bottom lip, also moved by the scene. She walked towards them and reached for the curtain which divided the beds and whispered, "Sorry we can't give you any more privacy. Glad it's going well" as she pulled the curtain across to shield them from the neighbouring bed.

The swish of the curtain caught the attention of the reunited siblings, and Jean held her arm open to Sally who moved forward to join them in their silent reunion. Angie appeared through the curtain with another chair and Jean sat herself in front of her brother with their knees touching and hands clasped together. Sally was perched on the end of the bed.

After a round of nose blowing and face wiping, Jean

151

began to shake her head, repeating, "Why? Why? Why have we left it so long?"

Uncle Jack reciprocated by shaking his head too and stroking her hair. There were no answers and they knew the future held more problems for them but, for now, they could be together. Gradually, a stilted conversation began with Sally acting as interpreter for Uncle Jack as she was more used to his speech. With the aid of a notebook, they covered a variety of subjects including the death of Sally's father which prompted another round of tissues.

They kept the visit short as Uncle Jack tired very easily, but he made Jean promise that she would come back which she agreed to with a final flurry of tears. The reunion was well timed as, in a week's time, Sally was due attend her two-week police driving course which meant it would be difficult for her to visit outside normal visiting hours. She was reassured that Uncle Jack would enjoy regular visits from her mum.

The warm feeling that followed the reunion was dashed when she arrived at work. She had to endure an eternal late shift crewed up with Graham where the atmosphere could have been cut with a knife.

Finally, as 10pm and the end of the shift drew near, Graham steered the car back in the direction of the station. As they sat on the Lower Bristol Road at the crossroads with Windsor Bridge waiting for the lights to turn green, Sally stared out ahead of her thinking how ready she was for her driving course which would allow her to take a turn at the wheel and decide where they went, instead of being at Graham's mercy all the time.

The lights turned green and Graham started to pull across the junction. Suddenly, a car appeared from Windsor Bridge

Road on their left and cut across in front of them, turning right and skidding as it did so narrowly missing the front of the police car. It then accelerated away in the opposite direction behind them.

"Christ!" exclaimed Graham. "Get his number!"

Sally was already craning her neck to look out of the back of the car to note the speeding car's registration.

"Blue Rover Charlie 695...I can't see the rest. It's got too far away." She sighed as she swung back in her seat. Graham had already put the blue lights on and was turning the police car round. He tutted loudly to show Sally how incapable he thought she was.

What little traffic there was at that time of night stopped and allowed the police car to complete its manoeuvre after which Graham accelerated away in pursuit of the offending car.

Sally grabbed the radio handset. "Priority! Vehicle failing to stop. Lower Bristol Road outbound. Just past Windsor Bridge. Blue Rover partial registration Charlie 695 containing a white male driver and a white female passenger." She had at least clocked the latter details as the car had flown past her.

They had travelled less than half a mile in pursuit when the Rover indicated and pulled in to the side of the road.

"Vehicle stopped Lower Bristol Road," Sally informed the Control Room as Graham stopped a short distance behind the car. The couple got out and made their way to towards the police car. Sally and Graham unclipped their seatbelts, got out and went to meet them with, as usual, Sally carrying her traffic pad containing the paperwork that would need completing, whilst Graham stood and watched.

She was surprised, however, when Graham positioned himself with his arms folded midway in front of the couple

153

indicating that he was taking the lead.

"Do you know why I've stopped you?" Graham asked the driver. He was rough-looking, with a shiny bald head, wearing jeans and a Man United shirt. He didn't reply.

Instead the woman took a step forward and said, "I don't know why you're talking to him. I was driving. Look, I've got the keys." She showed the officers the car keys in her hand.

"No, you weren't," Graham retorted with a guffaw. "The reason I've stopped you is because you just jumped a red light and nearly took us out in the process." Graham directed his statement at the man. He then turned fleetingly to Sally. "Fetch the breathalyser," he ordered.

Sally paused and stared at Graham, unable to believe his impudence but, knowing that now wasn't the time to retort, she turned on her heels and dutifully walked towards the car. She opened the passenger door, leaned in and opened the glove box where the breathalyser was stored. As she stepped back out of the car, she caught sight of Graham and the driver grappling before sinking to the ground in a bear hug.

Sally immediately threw the breathalyser on to the passenger seat and ran the short distance to where the two men were lying. The driver was lying on his side with Graham struggling ungainly in an attempt to get to his feet, having been thrown off balance. Sally knelt on the man's thigh and tried to catch hold of one of his wrists with one hand whilst reaching for her radio mouthpiece with her other hand and shouting, "Priority" to summon assistance.

The next few minutes were a blur. Everyone was scrabbling on the floor including the man's partner who was repeatedly screaming, "You can't do this. I was driving. I'm a lawyer! I'm a lawyer!"

As Sally and Graham struggled to restrain the man, the woman leaned in towards Graham and took hold of the strap of his truncheon which was hanging from the pocket of his trousers. As both Graham's and Sally's hands were being utilised to restrain the man, they were unable to stop her. Besides, she acted so quickly. The truncheon slid easily from its resting place and, before they knew it, the woman was waving it menacingly in the air.

Both Sally and Graham winced in preparation for what they expected to follow but, instead of attacking them, the woman turned to the police car and repeatedly beat the bonnet shouting, "You can't do this. I'm a lawyer! I'm a fucking lawyer!"

The sound of a two-tone siren heralded the arrival of another police car, and the woman turned back to where her partner was being restrained on the floor and launched the truncheon at the officers. It glanced off Graham's arm and landed nearby.

Sally was still kneeling on the man's legs, trying to get a handcuff around one of his thick wrists and shouting commands to him as she had been taught in her training. "Put your arms behind your back and stop struggling!"

Suddenly another hand appeared on the man's wrist. "Pass your handcuffs!" said a voice Sally recognised as Neil's.

Sally looked up and was relieved to see that 'the cavalry had arrived' – an in-house term for back-up arriving. Within moments, the man had been trussed up in Sally's handcuffs and dragged off to a patrol car, unwilling to cooperate by walking himself. Graham, sweating and even more dishevelled than usual followed behind.

Having been made redundant from restraining the man,

Sally turned her attention to the woman who was still screaming like a banshee and marched her to another car assisted by the Baroness.

As they did so, Sally said to the woman, "I'm arresting you for criminal damage and assault."

She was midway through reciting the caution when the woman lurched towards her and shouted, "Fuck off, bitch!"

Sally calmly finished the caution and then took the woman by surprise by twisting one of her arms up behind her back and pushing her up against the side of the car. The Baroness was already there with her handcuffs and together they put her in the back of the car, much to her indignation. During the short distance to the police station Sally and the Baroness resisted the temptation to retaliate to the array of threats made to them about what their unhappy cargo was going to do to them and their careers.

Sally had already learned that the best response to such tirades was in fact no response. Getting into a slanging match was futile and not responding seemed to be just as effective in managing the person's anger and was less likely to lead to any allegations of unprofessionalism. It was actually very amusing to sit back and listen to people's drunken monologues and made good evidence when it came to writing up your pocket notebook.

It was a late finish that night by the time all the officers involved had written up their evidence. It was a great feeling of camaraderie as they all sat round the briefing room, laughing at the behaviour and comments of Stella and Wayne Woodcock and relating what they had done to bring particularly Wayne under control. Graham's flowered-up version of events before the cavalry arrived caused Sally a wry smile. Apparently, he had taken Wayne to the ground and carried out a 'Home Office Approved' restraint on him whilst waiting for back-up. Sally couldn't recall anything so orderly but just a lot of thrashing round of arms and legs.

"Did you see what Stella was wearing?" Sally joined in the banter referring to the white leggings that were topped off with a tiny, sequinned, turquoise off-the-shoulder number with a cerise bra clearly showing underneath. Fluorescent pink stilettos had completed the outfit.

"Apart from the council facelift, you mean? Nice," replied Dan referring to the woman's hair which had been scraped back into a tight ponytail high on her head.

The icing on the cake was that another couple who had been walking past the scene at the time were able to verify that it was the man who had been driving. And refusing point-blank to be breathalysed meant he would receive the maximum three-year ban. Sally couldn't wait to relate it to Uncle Jack. He would be interested in every little detail and it would be something to capture his interest and focus his attention.

The cherry on top of the icing was that, as Sally approached the sergeants' office to return her radio before she went off-duty, she was stopped short after hearing her name being used by Graham.

"I was grappling on the floor and Sally made no attempt to get out of the car and help me—"

He was interrupted by the Baroness who declared in an impatient tone, "Oh, for goodness' sake, Graham, from what I saw when I arrived, she looked pretty useful to me."

"Yeah, give her a break, Gray," she heard Neil say. "Anyway, were you born the perfect police officer?"

Sally, although delighted to hear people sticking up for her, gritted her teeth, furious at Graham's incorrect and damaging version of her actions. She heard him 'tut' loudly before he flounced out almost colliding with her as he did so.

"OK, Sally?" the Baroness asked as Sally walked in to the office.

"Yes, thanks, it was certainly an eye-opener." She held up her left hand to inspect the graze she had suffered during the scuffle.

"You hurt your hand?" enquired the Baroness. She took hold of Sally's hand and looked at the fresh blood on her knuckles. "Make sure you put that in your pocket notebook and complete an *injury on duty* form – just in case it's worse than it first looks. And well done, you did a good job out there." She dropped eye contact as she said the compliment, but it was good enough for Sally. She trotted down to the locker room, adrenalin still pumping through her veins from the exciting arrests and feeling bolstered by the comments from the Baroness.

Was the worm beginning to turn, she wondered? She felt good about herself for the first time in a long while and she dared to contemplate whether things were starting to look up for her.

It was the first week in February and Uncle Jack's fifth week in hospital when Sally arrived for one of her visits and Angie took her to one side. They had struck up quite a friendship chatting together whilst Uncle Jack slept. Sally really appreciated the contact.

"We're starting to look towards discharging your uncle," Angie told her.

Sally knew she was going to have to deal with this at some

point but now, faced with it, she didn't know how she was going to cope.

"I take it you will have difficulty seeing him once he's at home?" Angie continued.

Sally looked back at her, her eyes wide with panic at the thought of the difficulties that lay ahead.

"We obviously have some concerns regarding his welfare when he leaves here and were wondering whether there was anything you could do to help?"

"Like what? What welfare concerns and how can I help?"

"Your Aunt Bridie isn't the most patient of people and, although Jack will receive home support, there are concerns that she may not cope...or want to cope." Angie looked at Sally for her reaction.

"Are you saying you don't think she'll look after him when he gets out of here?"

"Not exactly – we're not sure what will happen and it's very wearing having someone to look after potentially twenty-four hours a day."

"But he's her husband. How can she...?"

"I know. I was just wondering how you felt about speaking to her before he is discharged."

Sally's stomach flipped at the thought.

"Perhaps you can have a think about it. It'll be a few weeks before he goes home yet," Angie said as reassuringly as she could, knowing that it was a tough call for Sally.

Sally wandered towards the day room where she could observe Uncle Jack unnoticed as he watched the motor racing, a particular favourite of his. Set up in front of him and waiting for Sally's arrival was the game of Connect 4 which was being used to rehabilitate his hand.

'You're a grown woman now,' Sally said to herself. 'You deal with awkward people every day in your job. You can tackle Aunt Bridie.' She knew she would have to. She took a deep breath and couldn't help but smile when Uncle Jack greeted her with his lopsided smile and reached out for her hand.

The driving course was a tiring but enjoyable two weeks where she honed her skills travelling across several counties. It was also a welcome relief from shifts and the pressures at the station. The driving instructor was a retired policeman who loved sharing his vast experience with the three probationary officers he took under his wing every fortnight. Sally completed the course feeling a more confident and competent driver and couldn't wait to put her new found skills to good use. Her attention occasionally wandered to the prospect of the impending tête-à-tête with the cantankerous Aunt Bridie, but she did her best to push it to the back of her mind until she couldn't avoid it any longer.

The day dawned and Sally turned up at the hospital with a million butterflies whirling in her stomach. Angie nodded to say that Aunt Bridie was with Uncle Jack, as they had planned. Sally's mouth was dry and she took a swig of water from the bottle she had bought from the vending machine on the way in together with a bottle of fruit drink that Uncle Jack favoured.

As soon as she entered the ward, Sally could hear Aunt Bridie's unmistakable thick Irish accent. She paused at the entrance to the ward bay where Aunt Bridie was stood over Uncle Jack's bed with her back to Sally.

"Come on, try and hold it yourself." Aunt Bridie was

guiding a mug with a straw in it towards Uncle Jack's mouth. "You can at least drink by yourself." Her voice was sharp and impatient. She let go of the mug and, almost immediately she did so, it slipped from Uncle Jack's grasp.

"You clumsy eejit!" she shouted as the liquid spilled over the bedclothes and onto the floor.

Sally stepped forward. "Here, let me," she said as she grabbed a handful of tissues from the bedside cabinet and began mopping up the liquid. Aunt Bridie was obviously a little taken aback and stood up when she didn't recognise Sally as one of the nursing staff. "Who are you? I haven't seen you in here before."

Sally stopped and stood still. Both women were facing each other with poor Uncle Jack lying between them, a shocked expression on his face. Sally had discussed the meeting with Angie and they thought that the surprise of the confrontation for Uncle Jack was marginally better than having him worry about it – so he was as unsuspecting as Aunt Bridie of Sally's appearance.

"I'm Sally. How are you, Aunt Bridie?" Sally managed to keep her voice steady and controlled as she looked her aunt straight in the eye. She had only been a young girl when Aunt Bridie used to put the fear of God into her when she regularly chastised both her and her sister causing them to cower in terror. Sally was a grown-up herself now and she was going to make sure she had the upper hand.

Aunt Bridie looked as if her legs had given way under her as the chair behind her took her considerable weight. She stammered, trying to start a sentence a couple of times but was so obviously taken aback that she couldn't speak. Sally smiled sweetly at her hoping that it looked like a friendly smile and not, as it was, a cover for her amusement at Aunt Bridie's shock over the realisation of her identity.

"You – you!" she spluttered, regaining her ability to speak. "So it's you who's been providing all these treats whilst he's been in here," she fired at Sally indicating the bottles of squash and packets of biscuits on the bedside cabinet. She was back in control of herself, her shock turning to anger, and gathering pace.

"Yes, he's making a good recovery, isn't he," replied Sally, keeping calm and changing the subject rather than feeding her aunt's demands for information. She bent over Uncle Jack and kissed his cheek, squeezing his hand as she did so.

"Hello, poppet," he mouthed at her as best he could.

Aunt Bridie was again lost for words. She sat there in silence looking from her husband to Sally and back again.

The moment was interrupted by Angie appearing next to Sally. "Everything OK?" she chirruped.

"Yes, fine thanks," Sally reassured her, again making eye contact with her dumbstruck aunt.

"Great. The tea trolley will be along in a minute," Angie added as she moved away. This prompted Sally to delve into her bag.

"Here's your custard creams, Uncle Jack, and a bottle of juice – and I bought you a couple of new season nectarines. I'll cut one up for you if you fancy one now?" Sally continued breezily, though very aware of the rumbling volcano sitting opposite her. Uncle Jack smiled at Sally, the old twinkle returning to his eyes. He knew exactly what Sally was doing: acting as if she was doing nothing wrong and keeping control of the situation.

Then Mount Etna erupted. "I'll cut it up for him!" Aunt

Bridie spat as she leaned forward and snatched the nectarine from Sally's hand. "How dare you come in here without my permission and take over. You always were a little madam, and look what you've grown into: little Miss Goody-Two-Shoes, suddenly concerned about your Uncle Jack after all these years. How did you know he was in here anyway? Who told you he was ill?" Aunt Bridie paused to take a breath.

Sally wasn't going to reveal that they had been in regular contact or that she was listed as a next of kin. Instead, she calmly and politely replied, "I'm not taking over. I'm just making sure that he's as comfortable as he can be and giving him a bit of company whilst he's in here. Surely you can't object to that?"

Sally was right and Aunt Bridie knew it. Sally didn't need her permission to come to the hospital. It wasn't as if she was adversely affecting Uncle Jack's health. In fact, it was clear that she was aiding his recovery.

That said, Aunt Bridie wasn't happy at her lack of control over the situation. She tried a different tack. "You keep 'that woman' away from him or I'll – I'll…"

Sally knew she was referring to her mother. She avoided looking at Uncle Jack in case he gave it away that she was also a regular visitor and bearer of gifts.

"Aunt Bridie, this is a public hospital and, as long as the nursing staff don't think I'm doing any harm, I would like to carry on visiting."

Aunt Bridie realised that the request was more of a statement and one she had no power to undermine. "Well, make the most of it because you won't see him when he gets out of here," she retorted, venom in her voice.

Sally swallowed hard. She knew Aunt Bridie meant it and

that she would be the winner in the long run. Sally tried not to show her disappointment and turned to Uncle Jack. "Sorry if I've upset you. It's such a shame she can harbour such a grudge after all these years."

She turned back to Aunt Bridie. "I was hoping we could move on. I've never done anything wrong towards you. I was a small child the last time we laid eyes on each other. Your problem is with my mother and I'm not responsible for whatever went on between you two. I don't deserve to be on the receiving end of your anger." She paused. Aunt Bridie couldn't maintain eye contact this time.

"Make sure you look after him properly then," Sally warned, "or you'll have me to answer to" – though how she would carry such a threat through she didn't know. Sally kissed Uncle Jack again and brushed his sallow cheek.

"I'm on nights again this week, so visits will be a bit tricky for me, but I'll be in again soon."

"Ah, that's how you found out, is it? You're a nurse yourself. Well, he doesn't need you or your nursing skills, thank you very much."

Sally had heard enough and walked away without responding to the stinging dismissal. The visit hadn't had the outcome she had wanted, but it was some small compensation that she had at least left with her dignity intact.

Angie caught up with her in the corridor outside the main ward door. "I heard it all, Sally. She was everything you described to me. I don't mind telling you that I'm worried about him when he leaves. Look, here are his GP's details if you can use them to help at all." She handed Sally a piece of notepaper.

"Thanks, Angie, you're a star. I don't know what I'd have done without you."

Sally was desperately worried what the future held for Uncle Jack, and she seemed powerless to do anything about it. Angie tried to reassure her, but both women knew that there were worrying times ahead.

She was glad of the fresh air when she reached the main entrance of the hospital. She wouldn't let Uncle Jack suffer. She just hadn't thought of how she was going to make sure of this yet. She also decided not to relate this encounter to her mum.

Chapter Eight

Uncle Jack's illness had a strange effect on Sally in that it helped her put her troubles at work into perspective, and the likes of Graham and his bullying began to take on a different level of importance. Her confidence was building and, now she had her driving course under her belt, she found herself working with other members of the group crewed up together in a car. She loved the variety of the work this job offered her and she enjoyed turning up for work not knowing what she would be doing, what sights she would see or what people she would meet before the end of her shift. The thought still made her stomach flip but, instead of with nerves as had been the case when she first started, it was now with excitement and anticipation.

During briefing on a cold early shift at the beginning of March when there had been a sharp frost, Sally was given a concern for welfare job where an elderly woman hadn't been seen by her neighbours for a couple of days. She walked into the sergeants' office to collect a set of car keys from the board where they were kept and was just writing her collar number next to the registration on the board when Sergeant Morley followed her in.

"Give me a minute, Sally. I'll come with you to that job."

Sally swung round to acknowledge the sergeant's offer. He winked at her and she knew he didn't want her to go to the address alone knowing that this could be her first sudden death. A sudden death is a term for anyone who has died unexpectedly and hasn't seen their GP in the preceding fortnight.

Sally smiled back at Sergeant Morley. "Thanks, I'll wait for you on the forecourt."

After they had spoken to a few of the neighbours in Bloomfield Avenue, Sergeant Morley smashed a glass panel in the front door, closely watched by the middle-aged woman who had called them. She had rushed out of her house as soon as the police car pulled up, and announced that she was the local neighbourhood watch coordinator. She showed a bit too much interest however when she tried to follow them into the house. It was Sally who had politely asked her to stay outside, explaining that there might be important evidence that could be trampled on and the 'less people the better'. This prompted a "Well done, Sal" from Sergeant Morley as they started to look in each of the rooms.

The air was ice-cold and silent as they made their way upstairs calling out as they went. Sally was pleased to have Sergeant Morley with her as, although she felt calm and brave, she knew she would not have fared as well on her own.

They found the woman wedged behind her bedroom door. She was in just her nightdress with her dressing gown tangled around her body and, from the state of rigor mortis, Sally knew from her training that the woman had been dead for at least twelve hours. Whoever would have thought she would have known that? Sally marvelled at the knowledge she had gleaned in a relatively short space of time.

They searched around the house for details of any family, but the best they could do was call the GP whom they identified from her copious amounts of medication. A female doctor arrived and officially pronounced "life extinct" before the undertaker was called.

Sergeant Morley echoed Sally's thoughts, suggesting they wait for the undertaker in the car which was parked on the drive outside. Staying in the house, knowing there was a dead body upstairs, was an uncomfortable feeling for even the most experienced officers. Sally didn't need asking twice and they were glad of the mugs of tea brought to them by the neighbour who had called them. They sat in the car with the engine running to warm themselves up. The Doctor had given Sally the next of kin details, which she passed to the Control Room since they lived outside the force area. The details would be passed to the relevant force to inform the family. Sally was relieved she wasn't going to have to deal with delivering the death message.

"Are you OK?' Sergeant Morley enquired.

"Yes, I'm fine, thanks. How sad to go that way with no one even noticing. I'm glad I wasn't on my own though. It was quite spooky in there!" They cupped their cold hands around their mugs and silently mused such a sad passing.

The Control Room had called out a boarding-up service to make the door secure. They arrived just as the undertaker did and both worked extremely deftly. Before long, Sally was back at the station. She was standing faxing a copy of the sudden death form she had just completed to the coroner's office whilst eating a sandwich when Neil appeared holding a report form in his hand.

"Ready for the next one then?"

Sally looked up at him puzzled.

"Another sudden death! Come on, I'll do the paperwork!"

What a day! Sally thought to herself as she gathered her coat and hat.

She jumped in the passenger seat beside Neil and read the report form he had passed her. It was another elderly female, but this time the call had come from the deceased's husband.

"Always good to have a WPC with you at a sudden death. You're so much better at TLC than we are!" Neil said as he pulled out onto the road.

Sally liked working with Neil. He was experienced, enjoyed a giggle and, above all, was fair. So many of the others on the team used her junior status as an excuse to volunteer her to do all the paperwork, saying that it was "good practice". Sally, albeit reluctantly, always agreed. Neil, however, took his turn. As a community beat officer who had specific responsibility for a particular area, Sally rarely got to work with him. She was fine about accompanying him to this job. It would be far easier to deal with grieving and shocked relatives if there were two of them.

They were met at the door by a paramedic whom Sally had already met at a couple of jobs.

"Hi, Jim, we meet again!'"

"Yes, but it's never a good time to ask for your phone number, is it." The last time they had met, they had been trying to get an injured drunk into the back of the ambulance and the man had suddenly vomited. The vomit had narrowly missed Sally due to some agile dodging on her part but it had pretty much plastered Jim.

"Well, I hope you've washed since the last time we saw each other," Sally ribbed him as he led them inside to where the woman lay on the floor outside an open toilet door on the ground floor.

"This is sixty-nine year-old Norma Gittings. Seems she keeled over on the khazi," offered Jim in a matter-of-fact voice.

"She was slumped on the floor when we arrived. We've laid her here." He was focused on his clipboard trying to release the forms he needed to hand over confirming 'life extinct'.

"Cripes, what a way to go," said Neil under his breath, causing Sally to suppress a giggle despite the recently deceased woman lying in front of them complete with curlers and hairnet.

"Quite common actually," replied Jim. "One strain too many and you're a goner – so make sure you up your fibre content or you'll end up the same." His dry humour was his way of coping with the situation, and Sally had to turn away and compose herself for the task ahead of meeting the recently widowed husband. Neil was also suffering a fit of giggles which then set Jim off and all three were standing stifling their giggles when they heard a voice behind them.

"Hello, I'm Doctor Hamilton – Mrs Gitting's GP."

Instantly, the giggles ceased and they all turned to see a stern-faced man in a suit carrying a briefcase. He had let himself in via the door they had left ajar.

"Right well, that's me done," said Jim. "I'll be off and let you folks get on with what you have to do. Norma's husband Bill is in the lounge with his sister, and I believe his son is on his way." He spoke briefly to the doctor before picking up his kitbag and making for the door, winking at Sally as he did so.

Sally looked at Neil for something to say and was glad when he suggested that they get on with their search of the body.

Sally was fine with this, her second such search of the day, and they both pulled on some rubber gloves and knelt one each side of the body. All bodies are subject to a cursory search by the attending police officers for signs of anything obvious that would instigate a criminal investigation. They rolled her onto her front. Sally pulled up her nightdress which revealed nothing so they returned her onto her back and checked her front. Apart from being completely flat-chested which Sally thought was due to age and degeneration, there was nothing of note. The doctor was busying himself with the contents of his briefcase and did not hear Neil's comment about 'apple catchers' as he knelt back allowing Sally to check inside the deceased's substantial underwear.

Sally lifted the front of the pants and suddenly jolted backwards, allowing the pants to slap against the body. She looked wide-eyed at Neil who responded by mumbling a "What?" through more laughter.

Sally couldn't speak, but was pointing at the woman's groin. "It's…it's…"

Doctor Hamilton stepped in, took hold of the pants at each side and pulled them down. There, for all to clearly see, was a penis lying innocently on a pair of testicles.

"Oh, my God!" exclaimed Neil in hushed tones.

Now even Doctor Hamilton was laughing. In fact, all three were in hysterics, trying desperately to keep the noise down, painfully aware of the inappropriateness of their behaviour. After a minute or so, all parties had managed to compose themselves and the 'woman' was covered over to preserve her dignity.

"It's seems Norma was in fact Norman." Doctor Hamilton grinned. Neil and Sally were glad he had found his sense of humour. "I'll make a call to the surgery and see what I can find out. I'll leave you to speak to the, err, husband, shall I?" he said with a wry smile.

Sally and Neil stood in the hallway like a couple of schoolchildren giggling and shushing each other, trying to decide how to tackle this tricky situation. In the end, just methodically going through the sudden death form revealed a lot of the history: Norma was Bill's second wife though they had been married for thirty years.

"I lost my first wife during the birth of our son," Bill stuttered through his tears, "and Norma and I were never able to have any more. We never looked into it. Well, you didn't in those days. But my son Tom should be here soon."

Sally let him carry on because she couldn't actually speak but allowed herself to smile at Bill, hoping it looked like a sympathetic response.

"Tom's really close to Norma. Never knew his real mum, of course, and considered Norma his real mum. He's a really good lad." Bill sobbed and reached for his handkerchief. "We're all going to miss her so much." He covered his face with his handkerchief and Sally suddenly felt a lump rise in her throat as his shoulders shook and he wept for his wife.

Neil had retreated to the hallway halfway through Bill's explanation. It was quite clear that he genuinely thought Norma was a woman. Sally stared at the paper in front of her unable to believe that in over thirty years of marriage her true identity had not been revealed. Bill's sister was sitting on the arm of his chair, her arm resting on her brother's shoulder. Sally looked to her for a response. Nothing.

With the paperwork complete, there was nothing more to do than wait for the undertaker to arrive. She was trying to think of something safe to say when, to her relief, Tom arrived. It was an emotional scene and Sally, not wanting to intrude, went and joined Neil in the kitchen who was making tea for everyone.

"They've got no idea!" Sally hissed at Neil.

Neil couldn't reply. He just kept shaking his head, an enormous grin on his face. Eventually he managed to say that the doctor had gone but confirmed that Norma had somehow managed to dupe the surgery for all her, or his, married life as well.

"It's just incredible," Sally mused leaning against the worktop and looking directly at the kitchen table which had been laid for two ready for supper. "Whatever the explanation, they were obviously very much in love and lived a normal life as a couple." She was now shaking her head. "I wonder if the son knows."

"Ask him to come out here and we'll speak to him on his own. He might tell us if he knows that his dad isn't listening."

They carried the mugs of tea into the lounge and then asked Tom if he could come into the kitchen on the pretence of needing to fill in some forms. Sally went through the sudden death form again hoping that the questions within it would elicit a relevant response.

Tom gave exactly the same history and answers as his father before rejoining him in the lounge.

"Bloody hell, Sal, this is a new one on me. I'm not sure what we should do in this situation," Neil said.

The humour of the scenario had waned, and Sally and Neil were in a real dilemma over the right thing to do. In the end, Neil went outside and spoke to Sergeant Morley on the radio. He made the decision for them. Bill and Tom had only known of Norma's death for an hour or so. They didn't deserve to have a second bombshell dropped on them so soon afterwards. Whose job it would be to tell them was up in the air at that time but essentially it wasn't a police matter.

The undertaker arrived and after the body had been loaded into the private ambulance, Neil gave them a brief rundown of the situation to pass on to the mortuary staff.

"Come on, nearly done," Neil said to Sally. "Let's go and say our goodbyes."

They had been there for nearly three hours and were feeling the strain of the odd situation. Conveying their sympathies, they handed Tom details of the coroner's office after which they thankfully left the house.

Before they drove off, Neil turned to Sally and just said, "Bizarre!"

"Bizarre!" Sally echoed and, with that, they drove off screaming with laughter, at last able to let off steam.

After a few minutes they had calmed themselves and began to discuss who should be responsible for breaking the news of Norma's true identity to the family.

"Maybe the coroner's office should do it?" Neil offered.

"Maybe it's better they never know," said Sally.

"Yeah, but how do you get round the paperwork, the funeral, the will..."

They both dissolved into giggles again. The news had already reached the others on the shift due to Neil's earlier conversation with Sergeant Morley. Needless to say, it caused much hilarity at the station and Sally was ribbed about her detective ability at determining someone's gender.

"Remind me not to ask you to come to a sudden death with me again," joked Neil as they disappeared into their respective locker rooms. It was certainly a day to remember and, as she drove to the hospital, she knew it was a tale Uncle Jack would enjoy hearing.

*

174

With her usual treats already in her bag, Sally stopped at the vending machine to get Uncle Jack's favourite juice. When she entered the ward bay, the curtains were drawn around his bed. She wasn't worried. This had happened a few times when he was being dressed, having physiotherapy, or being helped to the loo. She waited looking out of the window for a few minutes and turned with a smile on her face to greet her uncle as the curtains were drawn back. Her smile immediately dropped when she saw a face that wasn't Uncle Jack's looking out from the bed.

"Where's Jack Walker?" Sally grabbed the arm of the nurse pulling the curtain back.

"He left this morning. He self discharged," the nurse explained.

"What? He wouldn't do that! Where's Angie?" Sally asked, panicked by this unexpected news, but Angie wasn't on duty. No one could offer her any information other than Uncle Jack had gone home with Aunt Bridie. Sally knew that Aunt Bridie would have been behind him being discharged prematurely. It was her only way of controlling the contact Sally had with her uncle.

Sally returned home and immediately phoned Uncle Jack's GP. She was met with an obstructive receptionist who wasn't helpful by any stretch of the imagination. She did agree to ask the doctor to phone Sally, but warned her that he probably wouldn't be able to tell her much. She was right. Sally had a very frustrating conversation with the doctor. After she had voiced her worries, she was simply told that at this stage there was no evidence to back up her concerns over Uncle Jack's welfare. She could do no more.

Apart from her own investigation, that is. As Uncle Jack's house was on the London Road, a main route in and out of the city, Sally would frequently drive by to see if she could spot either Uncle Jack or Aunt Bridie. There was also a small lane a short way along on the opposite side of the road where Sally could sit up unobserved and watch for coming and goings. There was little to note. Sometimes the car was there, sometimes it wasn't, but she never saw it or anyone coming or going. It was very frustrating.

Sally's Mum was also very uneasy with the situation, and Sally and she spent hours discussing plans of how they could check on him or even kidnap him – but all these plans seemed to involve breaking the law. Not a good idea in Sally's position, but it set her thinking how she could carefully use her position to her advantage. She managed to catch the postman whilst on duty one morning and to ask him about the occupants of Uncle Jack's house. The postman was happy to divulge that post was delivered for Jack and Bridget Walker; he wasn't aware of any recent changes in the household. That, at least, gave Sally some reassurance that he was still alive. Her imagination was starting to get the better of her.

Two weeks passed and Sally spoke to the GP again. He sounded pretty disinterested and told her that her aunt and uncle would be having support from various sources. This time, Sally tried to insist that he made a note of her phone number, pointing out that she was a nominated next of kin should there be any necessity to contact her, but she suspected he didn't even write it down.

Sally seemed no closer to working out a way to see her uncle. A phone call at work two days later changed all that.

"Hi, Sally, its Angie here, staff nurse from the hospital."

"Is Uncle Jack back in?" Sally demanded, ready to rush out of the station. She felt her breath quicken as she waited for Angie to continue.

"No, but I've contacted the support team to check on how he is doing. Apparently their services have been declined over the past week and they're worried because they obviously think he – or rather they still need assistance." She paused. "Have you managed to see him at all?"

Sally explained that she hadn't despite her best efforts.

"Well, I thought I would let you know. I don't know what to suggest."

Sally thanked her and put the phone down. She didn't need any suggestions. She had heard all she needed to make her take some radical action. She dialled the doctor's surgery but was once again given short shrift by the receptionist: the doctor was midway through his surgery.

The receptionist changed her attitude when Sally turned up at the surgery fifteen minutes later in her police uniform.

"Is it possible to speak to Doctor Carey as a matter of urgency, please?" Sally didn't let on that she was the caller who had been refused access to him on the telephone a short time ago – nor did she say who it was concerning. The receptionist didn't ask any details but dutifully picked up the phone and, within seconds, was leading Sally into one of the consulting rooms. Doctor Carey was equally impressed by the uniform and listened to Sally's concerns. This time he took her seriously and looked up Uncle Jack's details.

"Hmmm. He hasn't had a home visit for two weeks," he told Sally.

"I know that, but why hasn't that been followed up before now?" Sally demanded.

The doctor was undoubtedly on the back foot and mumbled excuses about being busy and that it wasn't his direct area of responsibility.

"Whose responsibility is it then?" Sally sat with her arms folded in front of her, becoming more agitated by the minute.

"Err..."

"Right, how soon can you get to his house?" Sally stood up purposefully in front of Doctor Carey.

He looked at his watch. "As soon as I finish surgery – about 12.30. Shall I meet you there?"

Sally could tell he was sucking up to her now. She looked at her watch: 11.15am.

"That would be great. See you there." Sally let herself out of the consulting room without looking back, making it quite clear she was unimpressed with the care that her uncle had been afforded.

As she walked back through the reception, the receptionist called out a chirpy "Goodbye". Sally barely managed a nod back, aware that she had potentially abused the presence of her uniform to get such prompt service. That was the least of her worries, such was her sense of foreboding about her next mission.

She drove straight to Uncle Jack's house. She was beyond caring about getting into trouble. She wasn't overstepping her role as a police officer. They had a duty to protect life and limb, hadn't they? And she was gravely concerned for Uncle Jack's life.

She walked straight up to the front door and rang the bell, scanning the front of the house for any response or signs of life. All the curtains were drawn.

"Uncle Jack?" she called through the letterbox. She could see a pile of post on the floor inside, possibly too much for one day. Surely he wasn't well enough to go away? Maybe Aunt Bridie was also ill – but no, the car wasn't there. She called again and, when there was no reply, made her way around to the back of the house.

The curtains were all drawn there too. Sally looked for any gaps in them without success. She banged on the windows and called out, but there was no response. She was standing back and looking up at the house with her hands on her hips considering her next move when she heard a voice coming from over the garden fence.

"Hello, love. Trouble, is there?"

Sally was relieved to see the neighbour.

"Have you seen the occupants recently?" she asked nodding towards Uncle Jack's house and willing the neighbour to give a quick and positive answer.

"No, haven't seen anyone for a couple of days. Mind you, I don't have much to do with them due to the lady of the house being a difficult type."

Sally nodded in recognition of what he was saying as he continued, "The neighbour on the other side has more to do with them. I think she may even have a key if that'll help?"

Sally could have hugged the elderly lady who was the neighbour on the other side. She was home and she had a key. Sally didn't hesitate. She put the key in the lock and walked straight in. *Oh God*, she thought, *let him be OK.*

"Uncle Jack?" she called out as she entered the lounge and immediately spotted his pyjama-clad legs which were just visible on the floor beside the bed.

"Uncle Jack!" Sally screamed as she ran towards him. His head and shoulders were wedged between the bed and a sideboard next to it. He was ice-cold to the touch but a weak grunt told Sally he was still alive.

"It's Sally, you're going to be alright," she tried to reassure him. She grabbed the pillows off the bed and pushed them into the gap between Uncle Jack's head and the floor before gradually easing the bed away from the sideboard and releasing him. He slumped onto the waiting pillows and lay motionless with his eyes closed.

"Uncle Jack, can you hear me?" Sally cried as she pulled the duvet from the bed and placed it over him. There was no response as she reached for her radio.

"Priority! Ambulance required!" As soon as she had passed the details, Sergeant Morley called up. He had recognised Uncle Jack's name and told Sally he was on his way to join her. She thanked him and then, not knowing what else to do, she lay down next to her uncle and held him whilst she waited for the ambulance to arrive.

Chapter Nine

Sally was granted a week's compassionate leave following the discovery of Uncle Jack. She suffered a terrible feeling of guilt for not taking more positive action sooner despite her concerns and suspicions. Although everyone else tried to reassure her that she was not to blame, Sally couldn't help but feel partly responsible. However, in some strange twist of reverse psychology, it gave her a new found confidence and she felt that, in future, she would be more assertive, and she vowed she would never hesitate again when she knew her gut feelings were right.

Uncle Jack was very poorly. He had been hypothermic when Sally found him and they were awaiting tests which, amongst others, included tests on his kidneys which could have gone into failure as a result of the twenty-four hours the doctors believed he had been trapped. All the good that had been achieved before he was allowed home had been undone and he faced starting again, and that was only if he made a recovery from this ordeal. It was a worrying time for Sally and her mother.

Doctor Carey, who had arrived as Uncle Jack was being stretchered out of the house, had immediately apologised to Sally for not taking her concerns more seriously. He even visited Sally and her mother at home later that evening to apologise again and explain that their procedures would undergo a review to ensure a similar situation didn't happen again. He was obviously worried about his professional standing, and a further grovelling written apology a few days later was confirmation of this for Sally. She wasn't interested in taking it any further. She knew what it was like to be potentially accountable for decisions and actions in her own job and, in any case, the focus of her blame lay squarely at the feet of Aunt Bridie.

Aunt Bridie had been interviewed by CID officers regarding her neglect of Uncle Jack. She had told them that she had gone on an overnight trip to London to meet up with some visiting relatives from Ireland. Apparently it was a long standing arrangement and she claimed Uncle Jack had agreed to her going. Regarding her refusing assistance from the support team, she just claimed that they didn't need any help and that she was perfectly capable of looking after her husband herself.

A decision as to her fate had been put on hold whilst the long-term effects on Uncle Jack were assessed and a medical report prepared. Whilst Sally and her mum felt that at last some kind of justice was prevailing, they were warned that it was likely that no further action would be taken by the Crown Prosecution Service, considering all the circumstances and the account Aunt Bridie had given. Such domestic matters were rarely pursued. Sally and Jean were frustrated by this and spent many hours talking over the guilt they felt about not acting sooner which had resulted in this sorry situation.

They were at least able to visit Uncle Jack without fear of being caught by Aunt Bridie and March ended with some unseasonably warm temperatures. Both factors helped to lift

Sally's spirits and she tried to be positive and looked forward to being able to take her uncle out in a wheelchair in the grounds of the hospital for some fresh air.

Sally approached her return to work on an early turn shift on 1st April with some trepidation and her wits fully about her, ready for any April Fool's pranks. She intended to keep a close eye on her sandwich box and would think twice before doing anything that was asked of her.

As soon as briefing was over, the Baroness turned to Sally and said, "Sally, see me in the sergeants' office before you go out."

Sally felt her ears start to burn as she became aware of everyone looking at each other together with a few nudges.

What now? thought Sally, as angry about being so publicly summoned as she was worried about the reason for it. She wished the Baroness would think about the consequences of her actions and be more discreet, but she knew this wasn't her style. *If I ever get promoted…*she started to muse. She stopped herself. At this rate, she was never even going to make it past her two probationary years.

Sally finished her tea first and made couple of phone calls. She didn't want the Baroness to know how worried she was about being summoned again by rushing in to see her. It was a good twenty minutes before Sally strolled in to the sergeants' office, doing her best to appear calm and unconcerned.

"You wanted to see me, Sarge?" she said casually as she helped herself to a fresh battery for her radio.

It didn't bode well when Sergeant Morley got up from his desk and made for the door with a pile of papers under his arm. He smiled an unreadable smile at Sally as he disappeared through the door closing it quietly behind him.

Here we go, thought Sally, the butterflies in her stomach mounting by the second.

She let out an audible sigh and turned to the Baroness as she shifted her weight onto one foot resting one hand on her hip and the other on the shelf that contained the individual officer's workboxes. Sally really wasn't in the mood for one of the Baroness's chats.

"What's this about then?" she said, struggling to keep her voice level.

"Sit down, Sally," the Baroness said nodding at a chair on the opposite side of the desk to her.

"I'm alright here, thanks," replied Sally, calmly and politely. She wasn't going to be rude, but she wasn't going to be wholly submissive either.

This would normally have annoyed the Baroness but the ace she had up her sleeve made her ignore Sally's refusal to comply. "OK, Sally, as you like." The Baroness referred to a memo in front of her. "I've been asked to speak to you about..." she paused – whether it was for dramatic effect or not Sally didn't know, "...it has been brought to our notice that you are engaged in an inappropriate relationship with a senior officer." She had played her ace and looked up at Sally for her reaction.

She was pleased with what she saw: Sally's grip on the shelf involuntarily tightened as she stood wide-eyed, unable to react or respond. The Baroness knew she'd got her this time.

The smile that drew itself across the Baroness's face jolted Sally back to life. The two women held eye contact for a few seconds as the Baroness waited for an explanation and Sally's mind raced trying to work out how she was going to deal with this.

The anger in Sally was searing up through her body, knowing that this time she was in the clear. OK, she had no explanation but she knew that the Baroness had got her information wrong.

Sally took a deep breath, fighting the urge to scream at her supervisor. "And which senior officer might this be?" she asked calmly, her face giving nothing away.

"Ah well, I was hoping you were going to tell me that, but apparently it's a superintendent or above. An affair with someone of that rank would offer you the quickest route to promotion ever known!" she chortled triumphantly.

Sally's hands were sweating with fear and frustration but she was determined not to let the Baroness see her lose her cool.

"Well, at least give me the source of the information so that I can clarify the situation."

Now it was the Baroness's turn to be taken aback. She had at least expected a denial even if it was true. "I, err…" She hadn't even thought about the possibility of Sally asking this and was unsure for a split second how to deal with the request.

"Well, I'm going to have to speak to them to get to the bottom of this, aren't I?" Sally said, feeling she had the upper hand in this surreal scenario. She held her hand out towards the memo the Baroness still had in her hand, but she quickly removed it from Sally's reach.

"What's the problem? You do have a name, don't you?" Sally was beginning to doubt the authenticity of the claim.

"Um, yes, yes," the Baroness stuttered. "It's the district training sergeant, Sergeant Delaney."

"Has it got his phone number on there?" Sally asked, taking a step towards the desk to look at the memo. The

Baroness obviously didn't want Sally to see the memo and quite frankly didn't like it one bit that Sally seemed to be the one controlling this conversation. In a flustered state, she began rummaging for a scrap of paper to write the number on before handing it to Sally.

"Thanks," Sally said with false gaiety, taking a step towards the door. "Was there anything else?" she added, looking back at the Baroness who was still trying to compose herself.

"No, no – that was it…"

"Make sure you don't leave that memo lying about then, won't you." Sally nodded towards it in a tone that was an instruction, not a question. She didn't wait for a response.

She opened the door, made her way up to the first floor and found an empty office. After closing the door she picked up the telephone and dialled the training sergeant's number.

To her relief, he answered after just one ring and agreed to see her as soon as she could get across to headquarters. As she walked back down the stairs, she met Sergeant Morley coming up. He looked awkward and embarrassed. Not as awkward and embarrassed as Sally felt.

"Is it OK if I pop over and see the district training sergeant, please? I've just spoken to him and he's expecting me."

"Yes, of course." Sergeant Morley nodded.

"Thanks."

As she continued on down the stairs he called after her, "Ask CID if you can borrow an unmarked car. Take as long as you need."

"Thanks, Sarge," Sally sang back in her best attempt to sound as if she was carefree. The strain was really taking it out of her though, and she used the time travelling to headquarters to gather her thoughts and compose herself for the next onslaught. Even though Sally knew there was no truth in this latest accusation, she was still nervous about what she might hear.

She knocked on Sergeant Delaney's door and walked in after hearing him call, "Come in".

"Hi, Sally, how are you?"

"Not great, thanks."

She had met him briefly a couple of times before: once when he had gone to the training school to introduce himself and again shortly after she had started at Bath. He was in his early fifties and carrying a couple of stones too much weight. The word that kept springing to Sally's mind as she sat in front of him was 'smarmy'. From his demeanour, she guessed he had been quite a lady's man in his day but it seemed to her that he had failed to realise that he was well past his sell-by date. His greying hair sailed close to a Bobby Charlton and his trousers were worn up under his ribcage over which his buttons struggled to restrain the blubber held beneath them.

"What can I do for you then, young lady?"

Sally picked her words carefully. "I'm here to ask for an explanation regarding the allegation of my involvement with a senior officer." She didn't say anymore because she didn't know anymore.

Sergeant Delaney checked his paperwork before replying, "All I can tell you is that I was given some information that I felt needed passing on to Sergeant Baron. That information was that you were seen on an occasion recently at Headquarters being overly familiar with a senior officer."

Sally bombarded him with questions, having to check herself when she realised she was shouting.

"Which senior officer? Who gave you the information? Where was this supposed to have happened?" She was sitting on the edge of her seat leaning onto the sergeant's desk. She wasn't leaving until she got some proper answers.

"OK, calm down, Sally, and I'll explain."

"Calm down?" Sally fired back at him. Far from calming down Sally's anger was increasing. It was beginning to dawn on her from Sergeant Delaney's reaction that he had unwittingly started something that was beginning to reveal itself to be quite different to the full blown affair the Baroness had accused her of. "Do you know exactly what I've been accused of this morning?" she barked at this stupid man.

The explanation was simple. Someone had seen and overheard her talking to Superintendent Derrick Jones when she had visited police headquarters during her driving course. They had deemed her behaviour towards him as overly familiar and decided for whatever spiteful reason to let someone know about it. Sergeant Baron's subsequent interpretation of it had led to this sorry situation.

Sally's explanation was simple too, though she found herself sitting back in her seat stunned and unable to reply at first. The source was right. She was familiar with this superintendent. He had been a close friend of her father's. They had joined the police together and consequently he had known her since she was born. She had gone to see him a few times at home to talk about joining the police. He had helped her with her application form and she had subsequently practised the 'police-related talk' she had to do as part of her interview in his lounge in front of him and his wife. They had applauded her with parental-like praise and told her she would pass the interview with flying colours. He had also been the first to phone and congratulate her when she was successful. He had been able to tell her what her collar number was going to be and where she was going to be stationed ahead of the letter that contained the same information.

Sally related this with unequivocal contempt, especially as Sergeant Delaney also refused to reveal the source of the accusation. When she had finished her explanation, she referred to the earlier fiasco of her passing-out dinner which had afforded her a similar miscarriage of justice. Embarrassingly, Sergeant Delaney was also aware of this incident and tried to make light of it, which had the effect of making Sally even more indignant.

She decided that there was more he needed to know. She went on to recount how she was being bullied by a certain member of her team who seemed beyond recourse and was not brought into line by managers, despite them being aware of both the bullying and the misery it was causing her.

Her voice was shaking with anger as she finished speaking. She could hardly focus and felt like ripping off her tie and epaulettes and slinging them on the desk in front of her in defeat.

She was reassured to see that Sergeant Delaney was clearly taken aback by her catalogue of ill-treatment. He offered to phone Sergeant Baron to give a full explanation of the latest debacle but Sally made him promise that he wouldn't. She wanted to confront her about this. He reluctantly agreed, and she felt confident that he would keep his word.

She went to stand up but, finding herself unsteady on her feet, stumbled back into the chair.

"Let me make you a drink," Sergeant Delaney offered before flustering about at his tea-making table in the corner of his office which was cluttered with a number of open packets of biscuits. Sally didn't want to stay but had no energy left to protest. She was relieved about the noticeable change in his attitude towards her since her arrival in his office. As the kettle started to boil, Sergeant Delaney told Sally about a new procedure that was soon to be introduced called the grievance procedure. "From what I have heard about it, it is for just the situation you have found yourself in. You don't have to necessarily prove what you are complaining about but if you perceive you are being, as in your case, bullied then it will have to be addressed."

Sally accepted the tea and helped herself to two large teaspoonfuls of sugar in the hope that it would help to revive her. She hugged the mug as if her life depended on it. Sergeant Delaney gave her some paperwork about the new grievance procedure. She couldn't help but think he was trying to alleviate some of the guilt he was feeling at having instigated a situation that had been blown out of proportion and caused her such embarrassment.

She thanked him for the tea and said she had better be getting back.

"Sally, I'll keep in contact with you to see how things are going and I'll let you know when the grievance procedure is up and running. I'll help you put your case together if that's what you'd like to do."

Sally nodded non-committally. She'd heard enough of his whining voice. And her day wasn't over yet. As he held the door open for her to leave, Sergeant Delaney suffered a pang of conscience. "Sally, I'm not going to give you any names but, suffice to say, you don't have to look very far for the source of the Derrick Jones' business."

Sally didn't reply but returned in a daze to her car. She just couldn't think straight anymore.

On her journey back, she rehearsed what she was going to say to the Baroness over and over again repeatedly banging her hand on the steering wheel in anger and frustration. She didn't want to get tongue-tied whilst she unleashed her words on her persecutor.

This fucking job and all the people in it, she thought to herself. Graham? It had to be Graham. Bastard. Or was it the Baroness herself? Bitch. Or was it someone else who had it in for her? Sally was at a loss.

When she arrived back in Bath, Sally pulled the car on to the station forecourt and sat for a further few minutes, going over again in her head what she was going to say. As she sat there, Graham walked out of the station. He didn't notice her sitting in the unmarked car. She stared at his ugly form as he lowered himself into a patrol car: his shirt hanging out from the back of his baggy uniform trousers and his tie still clipped to the breast pocket of his shirt where the men tended to hang it whilst they released their shirt top buttons during their grub breaks.

Suddenly her head dropped onto the steering wheel. *Of course it was him!* She immediately sat bolt upright as the sound of the horn from her contact on the steering wheel caused the involuntary reaction. Graham looked across at the car and, when he realised it was her, threw his head back laughing at her expense. Why had she ever thought otherwise? He had been on a two-week senior PCs' course at headquarters at the same time she had been on her driving course. She had seen him in the dinner queue ahead of her that day and had given him a wide berth when looking for somewhere to sit and eat. It had to be him. Bastard. Fat, ugly, detestable bastard.

Fuelled by her fresh realisations, Sally marched straight into the sergeants' office but was immediately deflated when she found it empty. Not knowing what to do next, she dawdled down to the briefing room, slumped down in a chair and held her face in her hands trying to make sense of this unwarranted situation.

"You OK, Sal?" Dan's voice asked from behind her. "What have you been up to now?" he asked good-humouredly which confirmed for Sally that the gossip had already got round her team that she was 'in trouble' again.

She lifted her head and looked up at Dan. Her face actually broke into a smile as she saw that Dan had been caught by 'the boot polish on the headphones' trick. He had been listening to one of his tape-recorded interviews and was now walking around with big black rings circling his ears. He rushed off to check himself in a mirror. At least she had managed to avoid any pranks herself so far this shift – though she would have preferred one of Graham's wind-ups than what she had been subjected to thus far.

Dan, having returned from cleaning himself up, sidled awkwardly up to Sally. "Sal?"

"Yep?" Sally shuffled some paperwork, unable to focus on anything.

"Err...I...errr..."

Sally looked up and found Dan looking at her with a worried expression on his face.

"What's up, Dan? Do you need some advice from Aunt Sally?" she joked, half smiling at the absurdity of her suggestion.

"No, err...it's...err..." He shuffled from one foot to the

other and ran his fingers uncomfortably through his hair.

"Come on, Dan, it can't be that bad. What is it?" Sally asked, sensing the worst.

"You would have found out soon enough but I know that Graham has sabotaged your locker. He-he got me to stand guard whilst he did it and I...I..."

Sally scraped her chair back growling, "You bastards" in a low-pitched voice she found difficult to control.

As she headed for the door of the briefing room, he grabbed her arm and swung her round. "I'm sorry, Sal. I didn't want to do it. It was a rotten idea, but you know what he's like...if I hadn't agreed..."

Sally had heard enough and shook her arm free before racing to the locker room.

As she landed at the bottom of the stairs, she was travelling at such a pace that she was unable to stop herself and she careered into Rich Dunbar who had just stepped from the corridor leading to the locker rooms. As she righted herself, she realised Rich's right hand had landed squarely on her left breast. She looked down at it and grabbed his wrist shrugging his hand away before continuing towards her locker room.

"Sal," he called after her, "I'm sorry. That was a genuine accident."

"Forget it, Rich," she replied without looking back, "just forget it."

She could smell it as soon as she entered the basement locker room: a foul, throat-clenching stench of something decaying. She flung open her locker and immediately turned away as a wave of nausea gripped her stomach. There, hanging amongst her uniform, was a foot-long mackerel with its bulging eyes staring out at her, its scales slimy and peeling.

"Oh, my God!" she cried as her stomach involuntarily retched and heaved.

She ran back upstairs and fetched a plastic property bag and some gloves. As she passed the sergeants' office, she could see that the Baroness was inside. Sally saw her opportunity. After removing the fish from her locker, she made her way back to the sergeants' office breathing heavily with fear and anticipation. She burst in and slammed the fish down in front of the Baroness.

"I hope you didn't know about this?" Sally asked accusingly and insubordinately of her sergeant. "It was in my locker."

The Baroness screamed and jumped up at the unexpected and foul-smelling delivery on her desk. It was only then that Sally noticed Sergeant Morley sitting at his desk and Inspector Creed standing in the corner by the window. The fish had split inside the plastic, its guts spewing out and oozing into the space inside the bag. In her haste, she hadn't sealed the end and the stench quickly filled the room.

"What's all this about?" Inspector Creed seemed genuinely unaware of the prank and neither, it seemed, did the Baroness which gave Sally some reassurance.

The Inspector stepped forward and gingerly removed the offending creature from the desk and tied it from one of the window catches so that it dangled outside.

"I'll tell you what this is all about," replied Sally, her hands on her hips and her eyes welling with angry tears. "This is the latest in a long and persistent line of so-called practical jokes by one of your highly regarded officers. And if you don't do something about this, I can assure you that I will be taking it further."

Sally was shaking with rage and she could feel her face and neck glowing with flushed anger.

"I'm aware that you have been subject to some mickey, err, taking." The Inspector immediately realised his unintentional gaffe. "I'm sorry, that was a poor choice of words. I'm aware that you have had to put up with some probationary teasing, but I would agree that things seem to have been taken a little too far this time—"

Sally didn't let him finish and she launched into a tirade about the treatment she had received since arriving at the station. For the second time that day, she poured out all that she had been subjected to. She tried to fight the tears but, as she spoke of the months of frustration where she had tried on numerous occasions to address the problems with her immediate supervisors, the tears fell down onto her uniform as she quoted one example after another.

As Sally paused for breath, Sergeant Morley got up and quietly closed the door. Sally then turned directly towards the Baroness. "As for our conversation this morning, that is the second and last time that you will be accusing me of something without checking your facts first."

As Sally fiercely relayed her family history with Superintendent Jones, she watched Sergeant Baron shuffle uncomfortably in her seat. She told how he had helped with her entry into the police, and how she had bumped into him at headquarters which was the first time he had seen her on duty since she had received his call congratulating her. She described how he had planted a kiss on her cheek and enveloped her in the big bear hug he had always done ever since she could remember – such was his pride and pleasure at seeing her in her uniform. Yes, she had called him by his first name but, as far as she was concerned, it was a social meeting, and she would do the same next time.

It was an unpleasant atmosphere. Sally was on a roll and continued to address the Baroness. "I don't know what your problem is, but you seem hell-bent on making my life a misery. You also allow Graham to get away with being an outright bully. Everyone else is too frightened of him to stand up to him. I've told you numerous times and you've witnessed things happening that have gone beyond harmless mickey taking, but you never do anything about it. In fact, you encourage him. He has far too much clout on this team." She directed the last comment to Sergeant Morley who had the good grace to look directly at Sally and nod in agreement, which was more than she could say for the Baroness who stared uncomfortably at the desk in front of her.

"I hadn't realised it had gone this far or affected you so much, Sally. We'll deal with it," Sergeant Morley said in a sympathetic tone.

"Well, if you've finished your graduate's speech and will let me get a word in edgeways," the Baroness started, "despite the fact that I would have never spoken to my supervisors like that with your length of service..."

That was it. Everything suddenly became clear to Sally. The Baroness felt threatened by Sally. There had been frequent derogatory remarks about her being a graduate together with the old adage that having a 'degree in common sense' was more relevant to this job.

"Hang on, Sergeant Baron." Inspector Creed didn't allow her to continue. He walked over to Sally and put a reassuring hand on her shoulder. "We *will* deal with it, Sally. It's going to take time but we will deal with it. I had no idea it had got this out of hand. You should have come to see me earlier."

Both he and Sally knew that it wasn't the accepted channel of communication to speak to an inspector about such things, and it was only her recent blind rage that had driven her to the extreme measure of ranting in front of him.

"What would you like to be done in respect of all this?" the Inspector asked.

Sally didn't respond immediately. She was at a loss to suggest anything and was concentrating on trying to compose herself.

"I don't know what you can do. Graham seems to have so much power over everyone – even the sergeants. Even those who don't agree with what he does are too scared to stand up to him anyway." The tears started to fall again as she realised she couldn't even suggest a solution to this seemingly impossible situation.

"Let me speak to Graham and see how we can put things right," offered Inspector Creed. "In the meantime, finish work now and go and fetch a dry-cleaning docket from the admin office and get all your uniform cleaned. Buy whatever you need to sort your locker out and get rid of the smell and let me have the receipts. And, above all, don't worry. We *will* sort this out."

Sergeant Baron offered a half smile and nodded her head in agreement that the issues had to be addressed, despite not liking one bit that she had been caught out herself.

The Inspector guided Sally out of the office squeezing her shoulder in an attempt to reassure as he did so before closing the door behind her.

How she would have liked to have been a fly on the wall in there.

Sally did as the Inspector told her and left the station before any of her teammates came in. She only saw Dan as she walked out with a bin-liner full of her uniform. He couldn't help but notice her red blotchy face and called out after her, "Are you OK, Sal? I'm really sor—"

She didn't wait to hear him finish. "Get lost, Dan," she replied without looking at him and disappeared through the staff exit. *Let him squirm*, she thought to herself. She hadn't actually named any of Graham's accomplices. She felt bad enough telling tales as it was. But she felt she had done the right thing. She couldn't fight on alone.

Sally couldn't face going home to an empty house. Instead, she went to the hospital where Uncle Jack lay motionless as he had done since he had been readmitted after Sally had found him at home. She sat and poured out her tales of woe, intermittently helping herself to the tissues from his bedside cabinet. She apologised for offloading her sorrows on him and for not telling him before about the bullying she had been subjected to. She finished by saying that, to cap it all, she had got herself a parking fine when she had risked not buying a ticket whilst she nipped into the dry-cleaner's to drop her uniform off. She laughed at her own misfortune.

Her laughter was halted by the touch of his hand on hers. Uncle Jack had moved his 'bad' hand for the first time since she had found him. It was the smallest of movements, but Sally knew he was attempting to curl his fingers around hers in an effort to give her a reassuring squeeze.

This time she was crying with joy. "Hey, you moved your bad hand!"

She had unwittingly spoken loud enough to catch the attention of Angie who rushed over to the bed.

"Everything OK?" she asked, looking at Sally's red and blotchy face.

"He moved his bad hand! He moved it onto mine and tried to squeeze it!"

More tears. The last few months had taken their toll on Sally more than she realised. She looked at Uncle Jack's hand, with its translucent skin, wrapped around hers. It was time to get a grip of her own life. She was glad things had come to a head today.

She left him sleeping and, having realised she was ravenous, picked up a takeaway on her way home which she devoured with a couple of glasses of wine. She fell exhausted into bed and slept the sleep of the innocent.

Chapter Ten

Inspector Creed kept to his word. Graham was transferred to the enquiry office and, although Sally found some reassurance in this, she also worried about the fact that she had stirred up trouble. It was out of her hands now. She had had her say and took a little comfort from the fact that no one on her team made it obvious that she had been wrong to speak up. In fact, there had been a few odd comments in support of her bravery and the resulting action.

A calm month followed, allowing the dust to settle. One sunny morning in early May, Sally's team arrived an hour early for their shift in preparation for the execution of a drugs warrant. Sally made her way down to the briefing room not knowing what to expect, but excited at the prospect of a drugs raid. What she didn't expect was to see Alex sitting there amongst the other drug squad officers. The sight quite literally took her breath away causing her to greet him with an embarrassingly breathy "Hello".

"Hi, Sally. How are you doing?" he said, standing up to greet her and then sitting down quickly when he saw the others looking at them.

"Fine," she answered not entirely truthfully as they smiled across the table at each other. Sally thought he coloured up a little, as she had also done, and busied herself with her notebook.

There was a buzz in the briefing room, an air of anticipation of the impending raid at a derelict industrial site just outside the city boundary where a chaotic gathering of dilapidated caravans and camper vans had set up home a few months ago. Sally was aware that the site had been gradually increasing in size and was undoubtedly a den of iniquity for drugs and stolen goods.

The drugs squad officers were a motley crew. Many of them wore their hair long and faces unshaven to blend in with a crowd. Their sergeant got up and gave a briefing with a plan of the site, what to expect, and what was expected from them. Sally was paired up with Trevor, a typical suave and self-assured CID officer and they were allocated a caravan in the far corner of the site. She was glad to be with an experienced CID officer as she was nervous about making mistakes and, added to that, had a very limited knowledge of drugs.

Alex followed on from his sergeant with a short intelligence input, highlighting the known criminals who were living at the site and what they were likely to find. Sally took the opportunity to look at Alex's familiar face and wondered whether she would have the opportunity to speak to him about the events of the past few months. She knew he would make her feel better about it all and give her the reassurances she longed to hear.

As soon as Alex had finished, Sally followed Trevor to an unmarked car. She rubbed her hands together in a mixture of anticipation and nerves as they moved off in convoy. It was good to be reminded why she had joined the police.

When they were all in position the command "Strike, strike, strike!" came over the radio. The officers ran en masse onto the site, climbing over discarded pieces of vehicles and shopping trolleys. Sally let Trevor reach the door of their caravan first, happy for him to take the lead. He pulled the door which was a stable door design and the top half flew open. He then attempted to gate vault the lower half and failed to clear it, catching his foot on the top. He landed in a humiliating heap inside the caravan before scrambling to his feet shouting, "Police, stay where you are!" in an authoritative tone in an attempt to recover his dignity. Sally diplomatically pretended she hadn't noticed and leant over the half door unbolting it before calmly stepping in.

"What the fuck?" came from a shocked voice from under a duvet on a bed at the other end of the caravan.

The smell hit her first: a rancid stench that filled the confined space and hit the back of Sally's throat causing her to cup her hand over her nose and mouth. It was difficult to identify it exactly but it was a nauseating concoction of sweat, bad breath and damp mixed with the earthy odour of the dying embers from the wood burner.

The couple who appeared from underneath the duvet were understandably aggrieved by such unexpected and unwelcome visitors.

"It's the filth. Hey everyone, it's the filth!" the man shouted as loud as his lungs would allow him after such a sudden awakening.

"Don't bother, mate. Everyone has been woken by us this morning," Trevor advised him in a matter-of-fact voice.

"I'm not fucking decent, you fucking prick. Get out of here!" the girl screamed at them.

Trevor, calm and polite, replied, "We have a warrant to search your caravan. Stay under your duvet for now."

Destiny, as the girl preferred to be called, continued to be obnoxious throughout the search of the caravan; slagging off the police and objecting to the 'control of a state which could strip her of any dignity and render her powerless to exercise any rights that she believed were hers'. There wasn't much to search, but Trevor and Sally picked their way meticulously through the meagre contents of the caravan and personal possessions of its occupants. When Destiny's partner Mincy – real name Peter Brown – and Trevor stepped outside to allow her to get dressed, she continued to give Sally a hard time.

"What're you doing in a job like this?" she demanded. "You could do something much more positive."

"I think I am doing something positive," Sally responded to this belligerent young woman for the first time. "I try to make sure people live within the law and to help others who have been affected by those who have broken the law."

It was a simple statement but Destiny would not be convinced. She lectured Sally that she was amongst a growing number of a disillusioned section of the population, who believed that society could live without laws. Sally enjoyed engaging her in conversation. As with many of those who chose to live this alternative lifestyle, Destiny was from a privileged background and had been privately educated before rebelling against all the expectations of her parents and the ideals that had been drummed into her from such an early age. She eventually reluctantly revealed her real name, Cordelia Humbert-Smith, which enabled Sally to carry out a check on her. She had no previous convictions and, although her partner had a handful of petty crimes to his name, Sally was disappointed not to find anything to prompt an arrest in the caravan.

Not making an arrest turned out to be a fortunate escape for Sally as the other officers who had made arrests ended up spending a couple of hours in the windowless holding room waiting to book their prisoners into custody. A smell of unwashed bodies emanated from the custody suite as Sally entered via the police entrance. She was grateful that she was not holed up in the twelve-foot square antechamber – especially when one of them vomited...

Opportunities for talking to Alex were frustratingly limited. They managed a short private conversation in the custody suite, which had been Sally's reason for wandering down there. She briefly alluded to things coming to a head, but they were joined by one of Alex's colleagues who was ready to leave and didn't pick up on the vibes that they wanted to be alone. Without having the chance to catch up properly, Sally found herself saying goodbye not knowing when she would see Alex again. She watched him drive away from the station and rebuked herself over futile thoughts that her plight meant anything to him or that she should seek any comfort from him.

As she made her way down to the briefing room to see if anyone needed any help, she noticed that the door of the sergeants' office was closed. Her stomach flipped as she remembered the recent showdown in there. *Stick to your guns*, Sally said to herself. *You did the right thing.* That she was sure of, however hard it was to deal with.

When she reached the briefing room, she found Graham leaning over the lectern holding court. He was deep in a discussion about a trip he was planning over the Whitsun weekend at the end of the month – a camping and fishing trip with his football mates. He was in full flow with an audience who obviously shared his passions but, when he spotted Sally, he realised that he was on a sticky wicket with talk of fish and made his excuses before leaving the room. Although she felt this showed she had made some progress in stopping his bullying behaviour, she was left feeling uncomfortable. She busied herself volunteering to book some stolen credit cards and drugs scales into the detained property register for Ruth. As she did so, an idea sprouted in Sally's mind.

As the Whitsun weekend approached, Sally prepared with a spot of shopping in the joke shop in Abbey Green. It was Sally's birthday mid-week and, in keeping with tradition, she made a batch of chocolate chip fairy cakes to take into work. As she and Ruth got ready for their night shift, Sally asked Ruth if she would be prepared to give her a hand. Ruth looked at her confused as Sally picked up the sleeping bag bearing Graham's name, pulled it out of its sleeve and unravelled it on the floor.

"What are you up to, Sal?" asked Ruth, unable to stop the smile spreading across her face.

"Just a taste of his own medicine – or rather a feel of it," she replied. "Want to help me?" She held up two pairs of rubber gloves and a small, brown paper bag from which she produced a sachet of itching powder, like a magician with a white rabbit from a hat.

"Sally!" exclaimed Ruth. She didn't hesitate and knelt down beside Sally, accepting the bag of itching powder from her. As they giggled like schoolgirls, Sally produced two more sachets from the paper bag. They emptied the contents into the sleeping bag and stifled their laughter as they zipped it back up and then rubbed the two membranes of the bag together to make sure their deed was as effective as possible. They hurriedly rolled the sleeping bag back up and squeezed it back into its sleeve before returning it to the corner where Sally had found it, ready for Graham's forthcoming fishing weekend.

"There, revenge is sweet. Shame we won't be there to witness it!" said Sally mischievously.

They made their way to the briefing room with Sally carrying her tin of fairy cakes. No sign of Graham. He was still on enquiry office duties. After briefing, she took the lid off the tin and revealed her home cooking, each topped with a chocolate button, and handed them round. They prompted an 'ooh' and were gratefully received and washed down with the tea that Neil had already made having got in early for the shift.

After briefing, Sally asked if she could stay in and complete a court file. She took her paperwork into the tape summary room from where she could keep a lookout. Before long, and as expected, Graham slithered past the door and into the briefing room. Sally watched him unnoticed through the crack in the door as he picked up one of the two remaining fairy cakes. He removed the paper case and threw it on the table before putting the whole cake in his mouth. As he did this, he reached out with his other hand and took the remaining cake, leaving the room with it cupped by his side, his mouth still bulging. Sally missed the culmination of her conspiracy as Ruth completed the ruse on her behalf. A short time later, Ruth visited the enquiry office pretending to fetch some forms and left her traffic file on the front counter. It was only a matter of time before Graham would find it – and the Post-it note on top in Sally's handwriting.

Ruth, don't eat the cakes with the chocolate buttons on top – I've laced these with (a lot of) laxative in the hope they will reach the right mouth! What a scream!
Sally x

Ruth was loitering in the corridor and was able to reassuringly report back to Sally that Graham was seen rushing to the gents' at which point she slid into the front office and removed the written evidence before he returned looking pale and uncomfortable. The worm was turning!

The Saturday nightshift was unusually quiet and, as the 'zombie hour' set in at around 4am, when her body felt like it was going into shutdown, Sally and Basher parked up in Milsom Street to take a break from patrolling the streets. No matter how many hours of sleep Sally managed to have, the wretched feeling of total fatigue was difficult to fight, however hard she tried. If there was an exciting job on then her body managed to step up a gear or two, but if it was quiet that dreadful hanging feeling where her body was crying out for her bed was one that was becoming familiar to Sally.

As they sat there struggling to keep their eyelids open, a taxi driver pulled up beside them and told them that there was a drunk lying in the road at the bottom of Queen Square. They drove back up Broad Street and turned left along George Street towards Queen Square. They found the man sprawled across the pavement opposite the Francis Hotel with his head in the gutter. Sally parked the car up so that the lights shone on him. They didn't like these self-inflicted and messy jobs. Sally pulled on a pair of rubber gloves as she approached the drunk.

"Jeez," said Basher bending down to have a look at the man's face, suggesting to Sally that it wasn't a pleasant sight. She took a look herself.

Sally couldn't believe it. It was Julian.

She realised it would have been his Summer Ball tonight. She took a step back and stood with her hands on her hips, trying to decide how she should deal with the situation. She couldn't leave him in this state. She wouldn't have left anyone in this state – although she wouldn't have taken the action she was about to take with the average Saturday night drunk.

"I know him," she revealed to Basher. "Look," she continued tentatively, "I know this is a bit unorthodox, but would you mind if we gave him a lift home?"

"Pah!" Basher replied, having checked Julian's vital signs and standing up to face Sally. He also stood with his hands on his hips, but shook his head in disbelief at Sally's request. "If you're happy to clear up any mess he makes in the car."

She looked down at Julian lying in a semi-comatose state. He was wearing a dinner suit, his wing-collared shirt open to the waist, and a trail of vomit down his chin and chest which continued onto the road.

She lifted his shoulder and attempted to rouse him. "Julian, Julian, it's Sally. Julian, can you hear me?"

She repeated herself several times before Julian gradually came to and lifted his head trying to focus on the face calling his name.

"Sal?" He slowly sat up and reached for the handkerchief that he always carried, attempting to wipe himself down. "What...what are you doing here?" he slurred.

"More to the point, what are you doing here? It's four o'clock in the morning. What a state to get in, for God's sake!" she replied impatiently.

Julian groaned and dropped his head back down.

"Come on, if you can get yourself in the car, I'll give you a lift home," Sally offered.

He looked up at her with a dazed expression and made a move to get up but struggled to coordinate his limbs.

"For crying out loud, Julian. What a state to get in," she repeated.

With a huge effort, he slowly managed to get to his feet, and Sally guided him towards the car. Basher was already sat in the passenger seat, looking unamused.

"If you're gonna be sick, just make sure you do it out of the window, OK?" Sally instructed Julian as she helped him into the back of the car and wound down the window in preparation.

Sally despaired at her own benevolence. This was the man whom, just a few months ago, she had sat opposite expecting a marriage proposal. Now, here she was about to give him a free taxi ride presumably back to the woman who stole him from her. *I must be such a mug*, she thought to herself.

She knew his address, where he was presumably shacked up with Fabulous Fiona, as she had been forwarding his post there. No one spoke another word as Sally drove up to Bear Flat to his latest love nest. As Julian sat hugging the door to keep himself near the open window, Sally caught sight of his pathetic lolling face in the wing mirror. She had to check herself and ward off a pang of sympathy for him. He would be so embarrassed when he woke up and saw vomit adorning his corporate tuxedo. Nice.

Sally pulled up right outside his house in Chaucer Road. She didn't care who saw him being brought home by the police.

"You got your keys or will Fabulous Fiona be here to let you in?" Sally couldn't resist this dig as she opened the back door of the car, which was always immobilised with the child lock, and held it open for him to get out.

He levered himself onto the pavement. "What? How do

you…" he started but it was too much effort. "She's not…we're not—"

"Yeah, whatever," Sally interrupted, realising this wasn't the time or the place. Anyway, she wasn't sure she wanted to hear about her successor.

"Hey, I owe you one," he slurred, leaning heavily on his garden gate.

Actually, Sally thought, *you owe me four years of my life that I wasted with you.*

She didn't reply as she couldn't think of a retort quickly enough. This wasn't like her and she put it down to her extreme tiredness. In any case, it would be wasted on him in his condition. She watched him stagger up to his front door and fumble with his keys. He suddenly leaned over and showered the adjacent flower bed with a helping of his corporate meal.

Sally grimaced and stood watching from a safe distance, her arms folded. He stood up and waved his arm at her in a motion that indicated he wanted her to go. She'd seen enough and made her way back to the car.

"Ugh," moaned Basher as they drove off, unwinding all the windows in an attempt to get rid of the smell of stale alcohol and vomit. "You've got some nice friends."

"Not a friend," Sally replied. "Just a sad bastard that I once knew," as she accelerated away.

She missed the sad bastard though.

Chapter Eleven

Seeing Julian again even in his revolting and pathetic state played on Sally's mind for a few days. She couldn't help but replay his reply to her comment about Fiona. Was he trying to deny the relationship or was he saying that it was over already? She was inquisitive to know, but didn't like to admit to herself why. She missed him. It was only natural after four years together. Or was it just the company she missed? *No*, she thought, *it was him*. Her anger had subsided now and she spent more time remembering the good times than the bad. She wondered what good times he had had with Fabulous Fiona. That hurt.

Sally picked up her packed lunch and fussed Honey before locking the front door behind her. Maybe she should consider moving. Maybe that would help her to stop dwelling on Julian. She had little time to reflect on the idea as it was a busy shift. She was crewed with Ruth and they were immediately sent to an artifice burglary in Horseshoe Walk where an elderly man had been distracted by someone purporting to be from the water board whilst his accomplice stole from the house.

Sally and Ruth made their way to the front door through the overgrown garden of the large, Victorian semi-detached house. It was an ideal location for distraction burglars: no houses on the opposite side of the road and not easily over-looked by the neighbours either side. Sally knocked on the large brass door knocker and, after a few minutes, a man who looked like he was in his late seventies shuffled to the door.

"Hello, Mr Yates?" Sally enquired. "You called us about a burglary?"

He looked from Sally to Ruth, seemingly taken aback by the sight of two female officers.

"You've got the Girls' Brigade today!" Sally said, trying to put him at his ease. "OK if we come in?"

Mr Yates beckoned with his hand without saying anything and turned around before walking back down his hallway. Sally looked back at Ruth and grimaced before following him in. The house was dark, unaided by the overgrown bushes which blocked any opportunity for natural daylight to filter through and assisted by the drab, ancient decor. It was like stepping back in time and smelt strangely of the remnants of roast lamb. The carpet was laid in the old-fashioned way, leaving four inches bare either side of the hallway and stairs, and an old-style green telephone with a dial sat on an ornate table in the hallway.

The two officers were led into the kitchen; Mr Yates indicated the room in general and said, "Sit down."

Sally and Ruth surveyed the room. It was like a scene from the 1940s. Busy wallpaper adorned the walls with the odd precarious-looking cabinet dotted around. A stained Belfast sink was full of and surrounded by heavily soiled dishes, a single tap dripping ineffectually onto the top layer. The surface of the kitchen table was obscured by a mass of newspapers and post and topped with more dirty dishes. The cracked linoleum floor was littered with splayed newspapers, the paisley pattern only visible in small areas.

Mr Yates made his way to a battered armchair in front of a standalone gas fire which, despite the time of year, was lit. Two ragged cats lay in front of it basking in the heat. He grunted as he bent to smooth his hand down both their bodies before lowering himself into his chair.

Sally and Ruth looked at each other, not quite sure how to approach this victim knowing that he must have been in a state of shock with what he had just been subjected to. In addition, from what Sally could make out from the first impressions of the house, he was not used to having company – especially that of two young women who could have been his granddaughters.

Sally crouched down beside him.

"Mr Yates, can you tell us what has happened?" she asked in a hopefully soft and reassuring voice.

He turned his head to look at her for the first time. His eyes welled up with tears. "He came in and said there was a water leak and asked me to run the tap." He nodded towards the sink. "I stood here for ten minutes or more. Then I went to see what he was doing and met them on the stairs. There were two of them. They knocked me out of the way and ran out of the house. They've even been in Mother's room…" He couldn't control the sob that punctuated his account and rummaged in his pocket for his handkerchief.

Sally looked at this sad figure. His hair probably hadn't seen water in months, possibly years, and was stuck together in a solid clump with Brylcreem which she could vaguely smell above the overpowering odour of his unwashed body. His clothes were equally unwashed with a threadbare home-knitted jumper bearing remnants of what looked like custard and something brown and unidentifiable, on top of a pair of polyester trousers which also sported an array of food residue.

"Do you think you could show me where they've been?"

He looked at her confused.

"Can you show me where the men went upstairs?"

"Yes, if you want," he agreed, levering himself out of the chair and pausing when he saw Ruth standing by the kitchen door as if he hadn't noticed her before.

Sally stepped in front of him. "It's OK, she's with me," she reassured him, reaching out to touch his arm before stepping aside to allow him to lead the way.

They followed him up the staircase.

"Can I switch the light on?" asked Ruth when they got to the top which was in unnerving darkness. She slipped her torch out of her utility belt and flashed it round the walls. She spotted a light switch in its old, dark brown round casing and reached out towards it.

"Well, only…only if it's not for long," he wheezed back at them, still short of breath from his climb up the stairs.

"Which rooms did they go in?" Sally asked, also armed now with her torch.

Mr Yates pushed open a bedroom door and Sally stepped over the numerous cardboard boxes stacked around the landing to follow him. She found the light switch which buzzed as she flicked it on to find that this appeared to be his bedroom and was a continuation of the state of the rest of the house. The drawers of a large mahogany chest were hanging out with clothes spilling from them and the doors of the enormous 'Narnia' wardrobe were gaping open.

"Have they taken anything?" asked Sally.

214

"From Mother's room…" He nodded, leading her out and switching the light off.

Ruth had hovered on the landing. "That's the bathroom," she said pulling a face which told Sally that she didn't want to go in there.

"Have they been in this room too?" Sally asked with her hand on the handle of another door.

"That's the spare room. I don't think they've been in there."

Sally put her head around the door. The burglars probably had been in there, but there was little to interest them. She shone her torch around the room: more cardboard boxes and newspapers piled thigh-high. Sally looked a little closer into the open cardboard boxes and was astonished to find each and every one filled with exactly the same contents. They were obviously delivery boxes from one of the old-fashioned grocers that were still dotted around Bath. Each one contained two Andrex toilet rolls, a tube of Colgate toothpaste, a bar of pink Lux soap, a tube of Steradent and a bottle of pine disinfectant. This must have been a year's supply untouched and unused.

What a state to get in, Sally thought to herself.

"Have you got any other relatives nearby?" Sally asked, realising that his mother was obviously beyond being able to look after him.

"No, it's just me and Mother," he replied, pausing outside the remaining closed door. "Do you need to go in here?"

"Yes, we'll need to check everywhere the men went," Sally explained, presuming that this was his mother's room.

He was obviously reluctant to open the door, but Sally tried to smile reassuringly and said that they would be as quiet as possible.

Sally pulled a rubber glove from her pocket and slipped it on before opening the door to reveal another dimly lit room. The only light was from a chink in the curtains. Sally stepped inside and shone her torch down on the floor as her eyes accustomed themselves to the gloomy light. She could make out a single bed behind the door which was empty and the back of a large winged armchair which was facing the window. She could see that the drawers and wardrobe doors were also open.

"Your poor mother, she must have been terrified when they came in here," she whispered as she made her way forward to speak to the woman and to ask if there was any possibility of her being able to describe the intruders. She explained this to Mr Yates as she crept forward feeling decidedly nervy in the dim and silent surroundings.

What she found in the chair made her start just as much as Mr Yates's sudden exclamation informing her, "Mother's on the bed."

The chair was empty. Not scary in itself, but the situation and expectation of seeing the woman there together with Mr Yates's sudden revelation made Sally physically jump and emit a brief, stifled scream.

"Oh, I'm sorry," Sally said when she had caught her breath. She was feeling distinctly uncomfortable and looked towards the bed. She couldn't see an obvious human form on it, but it was difficult to make out anything in this light.

"I...I..." Sally still couldn't see anything or anyone as she moved cautiously towards the bed.

"She's there," offered Mr Yates.

Sally looked at him and followed the line of his hand which was pointing at the bed. Sally, hardly able to control her nerves

216

any more and aware that Ruth had retreated to the doorway, aimed her torch onto the bed. It was empty and perfectly made up with a lilac candlewick bedspread. In the middle of it lay a mahogany box approximately ten inches square. Sally took a step closer and was able to read the engraving on the gold plaque on the top.

Naomi Yates
R.I.P

Sally involuntarily recoiled. She was looking at his mother's ashes.

"Let's go back downstairs and I'll take some details from you," she said feeling an urgent need to get out of there, skipping around Mr Yates with youthful agility and stepping out onto the landing. She grabbed Ruth's hand and yanked her towards the stairs.

Spooked by the experience, Sally half ran down the stairs and waited for Ruth and Mr Yates to join her in the safety of the gloomy hallway. She allowed Mr Yates to lead them back to the kitchen, whispering her findings to Ruth as they followed him, shivering with unexplained fear and bewilderment.

In the kitchen, Sally looked round for a suitable place to lean on to fill in the crime report. She gave up and balanced her clipboard on her arm before crouching back down beside Mr Yates in his armchair to talk to him at eye level.

Due to the recent spate of this type of burglaries, as well as taking the standard crime report details, Sally also needed to take a statement from him. She spent the next hour trying to elicit the order of events in as much detail as possible from this confused and upset old man. Ruth disappeared to carry out some house-to-house enquiries with a smirk at Sally knowing what a difficult task she had ahead of her.

It transpired that £3000 cash was missing from his mother's drawer together with a jewellery box which he had seen one of the burglars carrying on their way out. He wasn't sure what had been in it.

As Sally waited for his replies, she took in more details of his kitchen. The grey net curtain ripped at one end was hanging over the windowsill which was piled high with empty cat food tins. He had obviously been in the middle of making his breakfast when he had been disturbed, as lying on the hob of the large antiquated cooker was a grill pan containing plum tomatoes congealing on top of now cold toast. Sally noticed that the grill hanging from the hood of the cooker was still alight and reached out to switch it off.

Sally knew that, once she had finished, he would be left alone to cope with the unnerving events of the morning. He appeared to have no living relatives and no one to help him. He refused her offer to ask his neighbours to come in and keep him company. She had come across such individuals before, and there was nothing she could do about it immediately.

When she was asking for his details for the crime report, she threw in a couple of extra questions – like who his GP was and who delivered his groceries. She was glad that the scenes of crime officer arrived before she had finished as, not being in uniform, she doubted whether Mr Yates would have allowed him in after what had happened. Any trust he may have had of strangers would cease to exist following this incident. She told him that she would make arrangements for the Crime Prevention Officer to visit to advise on his security measures and fit a chain to his door.

When she left, Sally drove straight to Bunce's the grocer's on Charles Street, explained the situation and suggested that they reviewed his order. They were grateful for her visit and agreed to follow it up saying that they rarely saw him as they merely left his order at his door every week, and he came in once a month to pay his bill. Ruth had spoken to his immediate neighbours, who described him as a recluse and revealed that his mother had died over two years ago. As soon as Sally got back to the station, she phoned his GP's surgery and told them he was in great need of support. It was no surprise to Sally that the receptionist sounded unconvincing that something would be done so she phoned social services who assured her that they would look into it.

Sally sat back and sighed. It would be an amusing story to relate to her friends, but how sad that someone could end up like this.

Sally was right. The lads enjoyed hearing the tale of Mrs Yates's ashes. As they stood in the foyer waiting to be stood down at the end of the shift, she was asked to repeat it for the benefit of those who had only just come in. Even Graham stood at the doorway listening in. She enjoyed recounting the tale which caused a roar of different reactions from shrieks to belly laughs. Sally was starting to feel a part of this team and was even looking forward to the team drink that had been arranged for the following Saturday after work to celebrate Neil's fortieth birthday.

The story also got a good reaction from Uncle Jack as she sat massaging his arm and encouraging him to do his exercises. He was at last beginning to show signs that he was aware and listening. Sally was also conscious, however, that it brought to the surface the question of what was going to happen to him and where he was going to live when he was well enough to leave hospital.

There had been some news on that front. It had not come as a total surprise to Sally that Uncle Jack and Aunt Bridie had been contemplating divorce prior to his stroke. He had occasionally made reference to this, but Sally never dared hope that it would actually happen. As part of her attempts to extricate herself from a prosecution however, Aunt Bridie had started divorce proceedings which would result in the sale of their house and allow Uncle Jack to fund the type of accommodation he would require when he left hospital. Although on the surface it appeared callous, Sally and her mother were pleased with the proposal. It meant that they could be a family again and at least something good would come out of this horrid series of events.

The subject wasn't discussed in much detail as Sally and Jean knew Uncle Jack had enough to think about with his rehabilitation. There was a long way to go before sorting out the finances and sale of the house with Aunt Bridie, but it was all underway. They were happy to let Aunt Bridie deal with the house sale as they knew that she wouldn't dare try to undercut Uncle Jack and, besides that, both had solicitors acting for them. Sally had found Uncle Jack a good solicitor from a contact at work, and she had been able to fill the solicitor in on the background that had led to this situation and was confident that he would do his best for Uncle Jack.

She arrived home tired but happier than she had felt in a long time. She wasn't sure that the hand-delivered note she found amongst her post made her even happier or not. It was from Julian.

Dear Sally,
Really grateful for the other night. Will you let me
take you out for a drink so I can say 'thanks'?
Jules

Sally's heart flipped. Was it a good idea? Was there any harm in it? She would love to know what he had been up to. Curiosity was getting the better of her. During the evening, she pondered over the invite – whether she should reply and, if so, how and when. However, she was saved the anguish when her phone rang.

"Hi, Sal, d'ya get my message?" Julian asked breathily without bothering to introduce himself.

"Err, yes, I did." She paused, unsure what to say next having immediately recognised the familiar voice.

"I'm finishing about six so I'll pick you up about seven – that OK?"

Sally was taken aback: firstly, that the invite was being followed up and a date suggested so soon and, secondly, because he didn't ask if she did actually want to go or not. In his usual confident manner, he had assumed the answer would be yes. Sally's conscience told her to say she was too tired or not available but, before she knew it, she had accepted. Her only attempt to wield some control was that she told him she would meet him at the Crystal Palace pub rather than have him come to her flat.

Sally danced around her flat and whisked Honey out for a walk around the recreation ground. She sat on a bench from where she continually threw Honey's ball with the aid of a plastic ball slinger. Honey would do this all day if Sally had the time and patience. Every time she bounded back to Sally, it was as if she had retrieved the ball for the first time and expected suitable accolades. When Sally had decided what to wear, she got up and started to make her way back. Honey, desperate to play on, jumped up at her to appeal to her to throw the ball again.

"Come on, girl," said Sally finding Honey's high spirits contagious, "I've got to get ready!"

It was a strange evening – like a first date, but with everything and everyone familiar. The atmosphere was a bit awkward at first but, before long, they started to relax and conversation between them flowed. They sat in a quiet corner with Sally on a padded bench and Julian on a chair opposite her. They leaned on the table between them and Julian revealed that his time since they had split had not been good for him. His promotion had only been a temporary contract and, whilst he had done well, the directors had decided that in order to see who was best suited, the post had been shared around amongst other promising juniors. Yes, he and Fabulous Fiona had dated for a brief time, but they had decided that it wasn't going to work between them – especially when Fiona was offered the promotion on a permanent basis. Sally had to bite her lip hard when he told her this; she knew he would have found this really hard to cope with. He even told her that he had had his car towed away on New Year's Day. She felt her cheeks colour at this point and changed the subject quickly. Maybe one day she would confess that she already knew this, but tonight wasn't the right time.

When he had finished, Julian asked how she had been. There seemed to be so much to say to each other, and Sally told him all about Uncle Jack and how she had become a dog owner. She briefly touched on issues at work, but she didn't want to go into too much detail and said that things were improving after a difficult start. After his second trip to the bar, Julian seated himself beside Sally on the bench and subtly draped his arm on the shelf behind her. With the tiredness of an early turn mixed with a couple of glasses of wine, Sally soon succumbed to a long, familiar kiss. She sighed as they looked at each other at close quarters.

"I've missed you so much, Sal," he said, stroking her cheek.

Sally wasn't going to admit this just yet. She was understandably guarded. After all, he had left her high and dry particularly when she had been going through a difficult time at work. She had really needed someone to lean on and that someone had been him.

"You don't appreciate what you've got till it's gone, do you?"

"No please," Sally giggled, holding her hand up to stop him breaking into Joni Mitchell's *Big Yellow Taxi.*

It was one of his old jokes to use lines from songs in his conversations and one of the many witty things that had initially attracted Julian to her. It was also one of the things that really irritated her in the end, but the familiarity of it made her laugh tonight.

She could see that this was a good time to end the evening and made her excuses about being on an early turn the following day. They got up to go and she accepted a lift home from him.

"Can I see you again? We've got a promotion evening at the Hilton next Saturday. Do you fancy that? It's a James Bond-themed evening. I'm not sure I need to hire a costume," he added, mimicking Sean Connery's voice.

"I've got a works do myself," she answered, glad of a reason to say no as she would have been tempted if only to flaunt their reunion in Fabulous Fiona's face. *Reunion, reunion? Was that what this was?* Sally asked herself.

They sat in Julian's car outside her flat for some time, kissing and cuddling, before she went inside. She knew they had to take things one step at a time but it seemed a promising start. Honey greeted her in her usual excited frenzy and jumped up on the bed in expectation of a cosy night's sleep. Sally wondered how Honey would fare if she found herself having to share the bed with Julian as well – or, in fact, how Julian would cope...

During the following week, Sally saw or spoke to Julian every day. She made a conscious effort not to call him and was happy for him to do the running as he showered her with flowers and her favourite edible treats. She enjoyed 'dating' again. They had rarely gone to the cinema prior to their split, and they also enjoyed many walks with Honey, catching up on the last few months.

As they said goodnight after one of these walks, Julian cupped Sally's hands in his. "Will you let me take you to The Priory on Friday night to celebrate our reunion?"

The Priory Hotel in Weston Road was one of the most exclusive and expensive hotels in Bath. They had been there once before for a Valentine's meal and it had lived up to the expectations of its Michelin star reputation.

"My treat. How can you turn that down?" he continued.

Who in their right minds would turn down such an offer? Sally thought to herself. "Of course, I'd love to go. Thanks, but I can't be too late as I have to work in the morning." Sally smiled as she marvelled at the change in her life where she had two consecutive social evenings planned after a pretty barren year of socialising so far. It was a good feeling.

She wore her favourite turquoise silk dress that Julian had bought her from Jolly's the last Christmas they were together. She put on the gold earrings inlaid with diamonds that he had also given her and she hadn't worn since their split. Uncle Jack's bracelet, which matched the colour of her dress perfectly, completed her outfit. Julian picked her up in a taxi and, as they drew up on the gravel driveway of The Priory, a doorman appeared and opened Sally's door.

"Ooh, we didn't get this last time, did we," Sally whispered delightedly at Julian before she elegantly stepped out of the taxi – which she noticed was a Mercedes. *How fitting*, she thought to herself.

They were led to a private terrace dining room, an elegant and stately room furnished with ridiculously large oil paintings of men on horseback and bewigged characters sitting on throne-like chairs. The maître d' held Sally's high-backed upholstered chair out for her and pushed it in as she sat down. He unfolded her napkin with aplomb and placed it delicately across her lap before doing the same for Julian.

"I could get used to this!" she said as soon as they had been left alone to study the menu. They chinked their glasses of champagne which had been poured from a bottle already waiting for them in an ice bucket on a side table.

"To us?" Julian toasted in a questioning tone to confirm their reunion.

"To us," Sally echoed before taking a sip of the ice-cold nectar, her eyes sparkling in the light from the decorated candle in the centre of the plethora of cutlery and crockery that filled the remainder of the table.

A sumptuous meal followed with a starter of pressed terrine of organic chicken followed by pan-fried sea bass for

Sally and a salad of stemmed artichokes followed by roast loin of venison for Julian. Each course was exquisitely presented, and a visit from the chef to ensure everything was to their liking made Sally feel like royalty. Their glasses were regularly topped up by their waiter who, on clearing the main course plates, left a dessert menu by their place settings before leaving them to decide on their final course.

"Whoa, I'm not sure I can fit a dessert in. I'm absolutely full to bursting point!" sighed Sally as she sat back against her plush seat and patted her extended stomach.

"You have to have a dessert!" said Julian in a raised tone that made Sally giggle, realising he wanted her to really make the most of this special venue.

"OK, OK, there must be a sorbet or something light that I can force down." She picked up the menu and opened it, still smiling from his desire for her to maximise this rare opportunity.

It was only when she opened the velvet-edged glossy card that she realised why he had been so anxious for her to choose a dessert. Instead of a list of sweet choices, there was a gold sheet of paper which had the following words printed on it:

My Darling Sally,
Would you do me the honour of marrying me?

Sally tipped the card forward, an open-mouthed dumbfounded expression on her face, to find Julian smiling at her holding a small open box which housed *the* ring from Mallory. She paused, staring at the beautiful diamond-cluster ring cushioned on a bed of burgundy silk. This was what she had wanted and expected that fateful night last November.

Why shouldn't it be what she wanted now?

"Julian, I...I..."

"Sally, I love you. I've missed you so much. Will you be my wife?" he implored earnestly, his eyes fixed on hers anxiously awaiting a response whilst reaching for her left hand.

Sally looked from him to the ring and back to him again before a smile spread across her face. "Yes! Yes, I'll...I'll marry you!"

Julian plucked the ring from its plush resting place, got up from his chair and, much to Sally's enchantment, knelt on one knee beside her and slipped the perfectly sized ring onto her finger. After admiring the effect, she leant forward and kissed her fiancé.

Shortly afterwards, the waiter who had been monitoring the events that he was obviously part of, appeared with a look of expectancy on his face, searching his dinner guests' faces for confirmation that Julian's proposal had gone to plan. The smiles evidenced that it had been a success. They were joined by the maître d', and congratulations were offered and delightedly accepted.

They skipped dessert and ordered coffees whilst they discussed how they would tell their families – and when Julian would move back into Sally's flat. Julian then ordered a taxi to take them home and settled the bill. They chatted excitedly about their plans into the early hours of the morning when Honey eventually got fed up with vying for space on the bed and resigned herself to sleeping on the floor.

Despite a lack of sleep, the unexpected and gratifying upturn in Sally's life ensured that tiredness was warded off and the early turn the following day passed without any real drama. There was, however, an air of anticipation amongst the team as they discussed their impending rare night out. Should they have a meal somewhere?

"Eatin's cheatin'," piped up Basher.

"No showing your butt tattoo to the barmaids this time though, Bash, eh?" came another voice followed by a ripple of laughter.

They all rushed to get changed. The girls took longer than the boys, and got appropriate stick for it, which resulted in the blokes being two pints ahead by the time Ruth and Sally joined them. Sally, unable to help herself, had taken her engagement ring from where she had left it in her locker and slipped it on her right ring finger. She couldn't resist wearing it, but wasn't quite sure how to break the news to her colleagues.

Sergeant Morley joined them for a couple of drinks before leaving them to it and they moved on to the Rummer. Graham apparently couldn't make it due to a committee meeting at the football club. He couldn't miss that and wasn't missed by the remainder of the team either. The evening went with a swing...

Sally was learning that as a result of the situations and experiences this group of people encountered together, the camaraderie displayed in a social gathering of such a band of work colleagues was on a different plane to most occupations. There was definitely no room for outsiders in this clique – all the conversation was 'in-talk' relating and discussing all aspects of a police force that Sally was beginning to feel part of. After a couple more stops at the Pig and Fiddle and all squashing into the tiny Coeur de Lion, Bath's smallest pub, a general consensus was reached that they were hungry after all. Sally was volunteered to run up the road to Franco's to see if he could accommodate them all having made them promise first that they would be on their best behaviour. With a few drinks inside her, she merrily trotted the short distance into Milsom Street and arranged with a delighted Franco to fit them all in. She was feeling decidedly tipsy when she returned to tell them all the good news and didn't notice that they had been joined by an extra member as they piled into the restaurant. It was only after she had sat down that she noticed Alex's face smiling at her from the other end of the table.

"You OK?" he mouthed to her. He looked somehow different though she couldn't quite put her finger on it. Maybe she was too drunk to think or see straight. She was glad she was going to be eating soon to soak up some of the alcohol.

She smiled back, nodding her head at him, unable to take in what her eyes were seeing. She put her drink to her lips thinking about Julian and her feelings for this married man she had also missed so much this year. 'Come on,' she told herself, 'you've just got engaged and you're having a great time. It's great that Alex is here to join in.' She glanced at her beautiful engagement ring. Even so, something inside her felt uncomfortable.

Sally saw what was different about Alex when he got up to go to the counter to speak to Franco. He had lost a considerable amount of weight. Despite her inebriated state, she didn't want to look too obvious and make a beeline for Alex so she hung back and waited for an opportunity to speak to him. Whilst she was waiting, she overheard a conversation between Gavin and Dan.

"Bloody hell, what about Alex then?" said Dan.

"What about Alex?" asked Basher, leaning into the conversation having caught a sniff of gossip.

"He's split up with his missis. She's taken the kid and

229

gone back to France. He hasn't taken it very well, poor bloke," explained Dan.

"Fuck me!" replied Basher. "Who would have thought?"

Sally suddenly felt her smoked salmon carbonara rising from her stomach and she bolted for the toilets.

The toilet pan came in and out of focus as she vomited several times. Ruth, who had noticed her go into the ladies' and not reappear within the expected length of time, knocked on the cubicle door.

"You OK, Sal?" she asked as she pushed it open to see Sally leaning against the side partition breathing deeply. "The drink or the food, do you think?" she asked jauntily, glad she had paced herself sensibly.

"I don't know," replied Sally. "I think I'm OK now." She walked to the sink and splashed her face with water, drinking from the tap before trying to focus on her reflection in the mirror.

"Oh God," she said. "What do I look like?" She started to laugh at her red eyes and streaks of mascara down her cheeks.

"Come on," Ruth reached for some toilet tissue and passed it to Sally, "tidy yourself up. You don't want Alex to see you like this—"

She stopped mid-sentence as Sally swung round to face her.

"What do you mean?" Sally demanded, a little more harshly than she had intended.

"I...I d–don't mean anything. It's just that he hasn't been around for a while and...well, I know you two hit it off. I mean, you seemed to get on really well together." She looked at Sally for a reaction, worried that she had said too much.

Sally's shoulders dropped in defeat.

"Didn't you hear he's split up from his wife? You could—"

"I don't think so, Ruth. Julian and I got back together last night. In fact, we got engaged." Sally held out her hand showing her ring as her words hung in the air.

"Oh, Sal. Right, I didn't know." Ruth took Sally's hand and inspected the diamond-cluster.

"Well, I haven't told anyone yet – all a bit unexpected. Hence the ring on the wrong hand..." Sally leant against the row of basins and stared at the floor trying to gather her thoughts.

"Are you going to be OK?"

"Yes." Sally took a deep breath and did her best to fix her make up. "Come on, let's go back out to the others," she said putting a smile on her face ready to brave the scene outside. She emerged to a cheer as they had sussed that she had been ill in the toilets.

"Atta girl," said Dan putting his arm round her shoulder. "You're fitting in just fine. Now, what about another drink?"

"Just a sparkling water please, Dan," she replied, smiling embarrassedly.

"Another red wine for the lady please," he called across to Alex who was ordering some drinks.

Sally accepted the drink from Alex and graciously sipped it. Her head was spinning and she couldn't think of anything sensible to say, so was grateful when Basher came over and started offering his drunken condolences to him slapping him harder than necessary and causing Alex to spill some of his pint.

Sally felt too uncomfortable to listen so casually moved away and joined another group where Ruth seemed unusually to be holding court. However, as she joined them, the conversation halted and Ruth shot Sally an awkward and apologetic look.

Dan and Gavin looked expectantly at Sally before Dan asked, "You got something to tell us, Sally?" with a wicked grin on his face.

With her courage bolstered by the alcohol, Sally decided that they had to know at some point and, after quickly swapping the ring onto her left hand behind her back, held it up for all to admire.

"Call yourselves detectives?" she teased. "I've been wearing it all evening," – she wasn't going to admit it had been on the other hand – "and no one has noticed!"

They all glanced at it and made the right noises: "Very sparkly..." "Congrats..." before they moved on to more masculine matters. In typical male style, they had neither asked who she had become engaged to nor when the wedding was. Sally, feeling more than a little confused, was glad there was no Spanish inquisition and happily joined in with the discussion about the headquarters decision to change the vehicle fleet from Ford to Peugeot.

Shortly afterwards, Ruth announced that she was leaving and Sally, weary from all she had consumed and experienced in the last twenty-four hours, also bid her farewells and left with Ruth. They walked to the taxi rank at Orange Grove together.

Ruth apologised profusely for letting Sally's news out. "It must be the drink. I never usually drink apart from at Christmas."

Sally could tell she was a bit tipsy and genuinely wasn't annoyed. "Don't worry about it, Ruth. They had to know sometime. I wasn't sure how to tell them so you solved the problem for me." Sally sounded more confident than she felt and they walked on in silence.

Fortunately, there were plenty of taxis waiting so the girls said goodbye to each other and got in their respective cabs.

Sally was glad to sit down.

"Where are we going then, love?" asked the driver.

Sally looked out of the window and then at the driver. "Bear Flat, please."

Chaucer Road was too narrow for two vehicles to pass with cars parked either side and, when they arrived at Julian's house, they pulled up behind another taxi. Sally was leaning forward paying the driver when she noticed out of the corner of her eye Julian's front door opening. Maybe he had spotted her arriving, she thought, and smiled out of the window.

What she saw was not quite the welcome she was anticipating. A tall girl in a tiny gold outfit appeared and stood on the doorstep. Sally then took in the sight of Julian who was wearing just his underpants and an unbuttoned shirt reaching out for the girl and pulling her towards him before kissing her passionately, his hands moving all over her body. Sally froze, staring at the couple.

"I need another pound," said the driver before following her gaze. He realised what he was witnessing and waited for her instructions, obviously enjoying the scene.

Julian and the girl eventually parted lips, and she skipped into the waiting taxi. Sally waited until the taxi had pulled away and then asked her driver to wait for her.

"Sure thing, lady. Go steady though, won't you," he advised.

Sally walked up to the front door and rang the doorbell.

It was answered a short time later by a smug-faced and smiling Julian, still in his state of undress, who was obviously expecting to see the Bond girl and certainly not Sally.

His face dropped in a millisecond.

"Sally! What are you—"

Before he had time to finish his question, Sally took a swing at him and smacked him squarely in the face – a face that was smeared in the gold paint that had adorned the body of his Bond girl.

She took a step back, surprised by her own ferocity, pulled her engagement ring from her finger and threw it at his feet like a small child having a temper tantrum with a teddy bear and stamping her feet as she did so. She was too angry to speak which probably wasn't a bad thing in her drunken state, and she turned on her heel and stomped back to the waiting taxi.

"Where now, love?" asked the taxi driver, revelling in the moment after she had slumped heavily in the back seat.

Sally gave the driver her address as she stared at Julian standing shocked and half naked, his arms raised questioningly towards her.

"Bastard," she muttered under her breath.

"Plenty more fish in the sea, love," offered the driver in consolation.

Sally opened the window and leant her hot face outside, closing her eyes against the cool night air which took her breath away as the taxi made its way to the other side of the city.

The team were on a late shift the following day. If she had just been suffering the after-effects of a heavy night out, she would have dragged herself into work – it was a disciplinary offence to be unfit for duty through alcohol – but, as two o'clock approached, she felt she couldn't face anyone or anything. Not only would she have to face the ribbing from her team of being unable to hold her drink but, more importantly, she would have to reveal that her engagement was over as quickly as it had started.

Sally couldn't put a brave face on today. She needed some time off to come to terms with it all. She cringed at the thought of everyone having to know what had happened. Well, not *exactly* what had happened. Oh God, she felt so foolish all round.

There was no other way round it. She waited until ten minutes to two and then phoned the sergeants' office. Her heart plummeted even further when the Baroness answered.

Great, thought Sally. *Just what I need.*

It was clear that Sally was very upset as she tried to explain things to the Baroness who had obviously been brought up to date with the details of the engagement by some early bird turning up for work. Sally decided to just tell the truth: she admitted that she was a little hungover but, more importantly, her engagement had ended as quickly as it had begun. Her trembling voice broke a couple of times as she requested a couple of days' annual leave and then waited for a response. She was relieved when she heard the Baroness agree to her request. She even thought she could detect some warmth in her voice.

"What do you want me to tell the team?"

Sally paused. "I don't know. It's all a bit embarrassing really. They'll presume I'm hungover after last night..." Sally trailed off.

"Up to you, Sally, but if you want me to tell them about the engagement, it might soften the blow for you when you come back. After all, it'll be old news by then..."

Cripes, thought Sally, this was a different woman to the

one who had given her such a hard time since she had met her. Sally wondered whether the Baroness was just revelling in her misfortune or maybe she was human after all. Whatever. Sally decided to let her update the team and just try not to think about it until she went back to work.

She put the phone down and crawled back into bed. She was woken some hours later by the phone ringing. It was her mum. She started to tell her about Julian then stopped. "Hang on, Mum, get the spare bed ready. Honey and I are coming over."

After an evening of crying and reassurance that only a mum can give, together with a helping of rice pudding and jam, Sally spent the night in her old bed – with Honey snoring beside her. In the morning, she felt more able to face the world again. She knew that there would be some bad days ahead but also knew she was going to have to accept that Julian wasn't, and would never be, the man for her.

Chapter Twelve

As summer drew to a close, Uncle Jack's condition continued to improve. He had progressed from walking with the assistance of a frame to walking with just the aid of a stick, and he was at last looking like independent living was within his reach. As expected, no prosecution was brought regarding Aunt Bridie's treatment of her husband citing that it was 'not in the public interest' to do so. Although Sally and her mum were disappointed, they were reassured by the fact that Aunt Bridie was making the divorce easy and the house was on the market. Uncle Jack seemed philosophical about it too; he knew that, despite his ongoing health issues, he would be happier in the company of family who loved and cared for him. He often said there had been a reason for his stroke, and Sally couldn't help but think that maybe he was right.

The day of Stella and Wayne Woodcock's court trial dawned on Friday 9th September, Sally's first anniversary as an operational police officer. Although she hadn't actually given evidence before, she had accompanied Alex, whilst he was her buddy, to court for a case he had been involved in before she started her tutorship with him. He described the magistrates as sometimes bring out of touch with the real world and that he had known them give harsher sentences to drunks who had damaged the city's award-winning flower displays than the shitty little burglars who ruined people's lives and made them too scared to leave their homes after dark. Sally had sat at the back of the courtroom and found Alex's opinions proven when he was giving evidence regarding a fight in a local kebab shop. The head magistrate stopped Alex mid-flow and asked him to explain what a 'doner kebab' was as he had never heard of one before and then continued to call it a 'donor kebab'.

The magistrates' court was in a modern building a short walk from the police station. There was no separate waiting area for the police so Sally and all the others involved waited down in the cell complex until it was almost time for the case to be called. They were all decked out in their 'Number 1s' which was the name given to their best pressed uniform and included their smart tunics.

"Nervous?" asked Neil, knowing it was Sally's first time giving evidence as they made their way up to the public waiting area.

"You bet!" she replied with a smile on her face, feeling excited as well as apprehensive.

"No matter how many times we go to court, we always get nervous – don't know what it is, but you never get used to it. You'll be fine though," he reassured her. "Just make sure you stick to what you said in your statement and if you don't know the answer then say so. Don't look too unsure or be tempted to guess. The defence love that!"

"Thanks," said Sally, smoothing down her tunic and letting out a slow, deep breath to steady her nerves as they reached the public waiting area. A row of oval, padded benches were positioned down the centre with a small side room half way down housing a snack bar manned by the WRVS volunteers. The Tannoy announced that the case of Woodcock and Woodcock was to be heard to Court 2.

Graham gave his evidence first. Other officers and witnesses weren't allowed to sit in the courtroom until they had given their evidence. Sally sat outside the courtroom reading her statement through not knowing quite what to expect. She knew the order of events: that she would be led through her evidence by the prosecuting solicitor and then cross-examined by the defence solicitor. She also knew that she could ask to refer to her statement or pocket notebook but that this was frowned upon as they were supposed to be one hundred per cent sure of their evidence and therefore convincing about their version of the events.

Each witness would be called in turn after which the defendants Mr and Mrs Woodcock would take the stand.

Sally had struggled to eat breakfast such was her state of nerves that morning, and now she was regretting it as she felt decidedly shaky. She asked if anyone else wanted a coffee which was met with a resounding "Yes" and they all piled into the tiny WRVS room where the ladies behind the counter were delighted to see them all. Sally heaped a spoon of sugar in her coffee to boost her energy for what was ahead. However, no sooner had she scalded her mouth with the first sip from the flimsy plastic cup than she heard her name called over the Tannoy. "PC Gentle to Court 2."

Sally silently swore to herself for fear of offending the genteel WRVS ladies and put her cup down.

"Never mind, we'll let you have a complimentary one when you've finished," offered one of the ladies as Sally reluctantly handed over her cup.

"Thanks," said Sally wishing she was already standing

there drinking that gratis cup. She suddenly wanted to just walk out of the building and not face the ordeal that lay ahead of her.

The court usher led Sally into the courtroom itself. It was an impressive sight. The far wall was adorned with the Queen's coat of arms bearing the motto *Dieu et mon droit*. In front of this was the magistrates' bench which was raised some feet above the rest of the courtroom. Down in front of the bench was the clerk to the court's desk piled high with law manuals. The clerk was a tiny man in his fifties wearing John Lennon-style glasses and with a completely bald head. He looked up briefly as Sally walked in before returning to shuffling his papers and saying in a nasal, camp voice, "Ah, you must be PC Gentle?"

Sally nodded at the top of his head as the prosecution solicitor Patrick walked to meet her and indicated the witness box.

"I haven't given evidence before," Sally whispered, reaching out to touch the arm of the only friendly face in the room.

"I'll call the magistrates in," said the clerk, walking towards a door at the back of the room behind the bench which led to the ante-room where the magistrates retired.

"If you could just hold fire a minute please, Clive," called Patrick before turning back to Sally. "Don't worry, I'll lead you through it. "Here's the bible and oath, or this is the affirmation," he said, handing Sally a bible and a card with writing on both sides.

She turned it over and back again: bible...oath...affirmation? She couldn't remember anything from training school.

Patrick noticed the panic on her face.

"Are you going to swear the oath on the bible or say the affirmation?" he asked slowly.

"Oh, the oath, yes, the oath," Sally gabbled back, repeatedly turning the card over trying to work out which was the oath.

Patrick turned the card to the correct side and put his hand on her shoulder guiding her into the witness box. "You'll be fine," he whispered.

Sally wasn't so sure.

"Thank you, Clive. We're ready now," Patrick informed the clerk.

As they waited for the magistrates to appear, the court usher placed a plastic cup of water in front of Sally. She picked it up gratefully and took a sip aware that her hand was shaking. She looked at her surroundings. Down each side of the courtroom was a narrow area sectioned off with an oak barrier containing a row of seats facing inwards. A slightly raised platform formed the dock at the end of the row nearest the magistrates, where Sally was standing on one side and the Woodcocks on the other. They sat looking nonchalantly at her. She smiled briefly at them because she didn't know what else to do. In the centre of the room, behind the prosecution and defence bench, were three rows of blue upholstered, cinema-style folding seats. These were separated from two more rows of seats at the back by a walkway allowing access from the entrance on Sally's side of the room across the back of the courtroom. The only natural daylight was from the glass panels which formed part of the sloping roof.

Sitting on the end of one of the back rows was Graham looking relaxed, having finished giving his evidence. He didn't look at Sally but busied himself picking at a scab on his arm.

The court usher who was sitting near the public entrance stood up as the magistrates' door opened and the clerk led the magistrates in.

"The court will stand," announced the clerk.

Those who had been sitting stood as the magistrates swept in and took their seats at which point everyone else, apart from Sally and the Woodcocks, sat back down. Sally looked at the magistrates: two men and one woman. They all looked very self-important and of retirement age.

The clerk stood up and instructed the Woodcocks to sit down. He then introduced Sally and indicated to her that she should swear the oath. Sally cleared her throat and managed to get through it without tripping up.

Patrick then turned to her and said, "PC Gentle, I gather you were on duty on the night of the 29th January of this year in company with one of your colleagues, PC Butterworth. Is that right?"

"Yes," said Sally, holding on to the dock in front of her as she directed her reply to the magistrates.

Patrick then took Sally step by step through her statement to which Sally replied confirming that the facts were correct. She was aware that her legs were shaking and felt uncomfortably cold.

She exhaled a sigh of relief when Patrick said to her, "Thank you, PC Gentle, that will be all."

She went to leave the dock forgetting that she still had to be cross-examined by the defence, prompting the clerk to ask her to remain where she was.

"Oh, sorry," she blurted. She cursed herself. She had just made such a novice mistake. She blushed and looked at the female defence solicitor who was staring at her, an annoyed look fixed to her prim little face. This woman had obviously taken lessons in power dressing and wore a sharply tailored, black pinstripe trouser suit with her dark hair in a neat bun worn high on her head.

"PC Gentle, am I right in thinking that, in these cases where several police officers are involved in an incident, you sit and write up your evidence together?"

Sally was immediately put off balance by this opening question and wasn't sure how best to answer it. Was the solicitor going to try to say that they had fabricated evidence together? She didn't know what to say and looked at Patrick for inspiration, but he had his head down busying himself with his papers.

Sally decided to tell it how it was. "Yes, we all sit in the briefing room and do our statements at the same time." She thought the phrase 'at the same time' sounded slightly better than 'doing them together'.

"And it was the same in this case, was it?"

"Yes," replied Sally, trying to think what this might or might not be leading to. She disliked this hoity-toity woman already, and she had only asked her two questions. She desperately wished she could just walk out and not face any more cross-examination. This wasn't an option though. She had to see this through.

Miss Hoity then went on to ask Sally to describe how the Woodcocks had come to the notice of the police. She allowed Sally to continue up until the point where she had seen Graham and Mr Woodcock go down to the ground.

At that point, Miss Hoity interrupted. "Can I stop you there, PC Gentle." She handed some papers to the clerk who in turn handed them to Sally. "Could you read on from that point from your statement of evidence? I've marked the point where I would like you to start."

Sally was more than happy to do this. It was easier than trying to remember the events and what she had written. She finished the passage Miss Hoity wanted and looked up expectantly at her.

"PC Gentle, are you sure they are the correct version of your actions at that time?"

"Yes, they are," said Sally firmly. She couldn't work out what this woman was fishing for. She didn't have to wait long.

"Your colleague PC Butterworth, the officer in the case today, has stated that you, in fact, stayed in the police car during the alleged scuffle."

Sally swallowed involuntarily. She was completely taken aback by this revelation. She wanted to turn to that slimy bastard sitting in the back row and scream at him, "Why the fuck did you say that?!" But she knew why. She cast her mind back to the end of that shift and the comment she had overheard as she had approached the sergeants' office where Graham had tried to criticise her actions. She was boiling mad at him. How spiteful and unprofessional was he? He knew only too well that she had only returned to the car to fetch the breathalyser on his instructions and that she had rushed to his assistance when she saw them go to the ground.

"Do you want to think again about your whereabouts during that time?"

"I...I..." Sally stumbled. "It happened as in my statement that I have already read out to you. I had returned to the car to fetch the breathalyser at PC Butterworth's request but I didn't stay there. I went to assist with Mr Woodcock as soon as I saw him start to fight."

"Ah, now there's my point. My client Mr Woodcock, in fact, denies any scuffle or public order offence and states that it was PC Butterworth who took him to the ground and that he was in fact compliant thereafter and cooperated with all that was asked of him."

Sally stared at Miss Hoity trying to take in what she was saying.

"What I am saying, PC Gentle," Miss Hoity continued, enjoying Sally's obvious discomfort, "is that PC Butterworth's account is correct because, in fact, my client, once he was taken to the floor, did not struggle and, as such, there was no need for you to go to your colleague's assistance."

Sally remained dumbstruck. She could feel the colour rising through her face and felt completely on her own. A strange out-of-body experience allowed her to watch the scene from a bird's eye view above the courtroom where she appeared as a tiny and frightened bird whose wings had been clipped preventing it from escaping.

"Wasn't that the case, PC Gentle?" Miss Hoity brought her back to earth.

Summoning all her energy to find her inner strength, Sally prepared herself to stick to her account – because it was a true and accurate account of what had happened.

"No, no, it wasn't," Sally insisted. "Mr Woodcock was struggling violently and I was helped by other officers to restrain him."

After several futile attempts and abrupt questions from Miss Hoity in her attempt to make Sally change her mind and convince the magistrates that her evidence was inaccurate due to her relatively short length of service, Sally was dismissed from the stand. As she stepped out of the witness box, she picked up the cup of water and gulped it as she walked to the back of the room, quenching her parched throat.

She looked straight at Graham. If looks could have killed, he would have withered there in front of her but, of course, her cowardly colleague was busily engaged in chewing his fingernails. She sat down gratefully – at the opposite end of the row to Graham. She wanted to lie down and close her eyes, such was the feeling of exhaustion that overcame her.

She didn't care if it was obvious to the court that she wasn't happy with Graham. *What a bastard*, she thought. How she hated him. Why? Why? Why would he do this? It really wasn't going to help convict the Woodcocks. She suspected he hadn't thought of that particular consequence of his actions, he had purely set out to belittle her.

Her thoughts were interrupted by the Tannoy: "PC Matthews to Court 2."

Sally didn't know whether to stay and risk being further humiliated by another conflicting account or to stay in the hope that Neil's evidence would back up her account. Her attention was caught by Graham's chair flipping up. He was making for the door. He'd obviously seen what he wanted to see and wasn't going to bother to listen to Neil's evidence.

Patrick had also noticed Graham getting up and summoned the usher. By the time Graham had skulked to the door, the usher had caught up with him and Sally heard him asking Graham to remain in the courtroom at Patrick's request 'in case there were any other queries'. Sally suppressed a smile as he trudged reluctantly back to his seat.

Neil took his place in the witness box, picked up the bible without being asked and gave his oath. He stood tall and smart with an air of confidence, his hands held in front of him as he waited for Patrick to start.

Sally waited eagerly to hear his evidence. Her heart was

beating madly as she wondered which version he would give.

She felt herself slowly relax as she heard that it was virtually the same as hers. She hadn't realised just quite how tense she had been. As he reached the point where he assisted Sally in cuffing Mr Woodcock, Sally purposefully looked across at Graham.

She wanted to shout, "Did you hear that, you lying weasel?!" He was no better than Mr Woodcock himself who was obviously enjoying a day out that was beginning to look good for him and his wife in view of the conflicting evidence.

Patrick sat down which prompted Miss Hoity to stand up. She went straight in for the kill.

"PC Matthews, you say that you arrived at the incident having been summoned over the radio. Can you just remind the court of the scene you were met with?"

Neil again related how he had arrived to find Mr Woodcock on the ground struggling violently, with Graham at his head and Sally leaning on his legs, trying to get control of him. He repeated how he had helped Sally cuff him to the sounds of Mrs Woodcock shouting that she was a lawyer.

Miss Hoity then tried the same tactic she had tried earlier with Sally questioning what he claimed to have seen.

"Are you sure the female police officer was assisting with the alleged struggle?"

"Yes," replied Neil confidently. "I used PC Gentle's handcuffs to restrain Mr Woodcock."

Sally's heart started to beat fast again, this time with excitement, not fear.

"Are you absolutely sure about that, because your colleague PC Butterworth says in his statement that she remained in the police car for the majority of the incident?"

Neil shot Graham a look. Sally couldn't resist doing the same. Graham crossed his legs, one arm folded across his chest and the other holding his hand up to support his chin. He ran his tongue over his teeth and shifted uncomfortably, his focus held on the defence solicitor's back.

"Perhaps he was mistaken due to the confusion that was reigning at the time," Neil offered, "but I am in no doubt that PC Gentle was there in the thick of it because we cuffed Mr Woodcock together."

It was as much as Sally could do to restrain herself from crying out with relief – either that or running over to Neil and hugging him. She decided that neither option would look very professional.

After a few more questions, Neil was released from the witness stand. Miss Hoity had discovered he was not as naive as Sally and that he gave her short shrift when he realised the crux of her argument.

By this time, it was nearing lunchtime and the court adjourned for an hour. As Neil marched out of the courtroom, he tilted his head at Sally to follow him. He led her into the WRVS room and swung round to face her.

"Did that really happen in there?" he asked incredulously.

"I got it worse than you. She was accusing me of making up my evidence!"

"I can't believe that stupid prick," he ranted, referring to Graham. "He might just have lost us the case by casting doubt on the evidence. Stupid sod."

With that, he spotted Graham trying to sneak out unnoticed from the courtroom and sprang out after him. Sally loitered inside the WRVS room and strained her ears to hear what was said.

In hushed tones, she heard Neil say, "You prick. You stupid fucking prick. Just what are you trying to prove, Gray? If you've got any stupid fucking personal grievances then you fucking sort them out outside the job. You made us all look like a bunch of pricks in there. I can see those Woodcocks walking out of here scot-free – and then who'll have the last laugh? Honestly, Graham, I don't know what your problem is, but don't get me involved in it."

Sally dared to peep out at the scene. Neil was standing close to Graham, a finger pointed at his chest. Graham was looking at the floor, his hands firmly in his pockets. He didn't answer but just shook his head.

"You're gonna have some serious questions to answer back at the nick over this," Neil continued. "Christ! Sally has done nothing to deserve all the shit you give her and now this. Well, this is really below the belt."

With that, Neil returned to the WRVS room where he stood remonstrating at Sally about how they had been made to look unnecessarily stupid and that the court process was bad enough without their own colleagues making a mockery of them.

Sally didn't know what to say apart from that she felt partially responsible for causing this case to probably crash and burn. Neil tried to reassure her that she was in no way responsible, and suggested they went to get some lunch. They went down to the cell complex, leaving their tunics there and put their civvy jackets on to walk the short distance to the city centre.

They didn't have long and, in any case, Sally wasn't hungry. Neil fumed about Graham as they sat in a sandwich shop in Northumberland Place. Sally picked at her sandwich before they made their way back. As they had already given their evidence, they weren't actually required to return, but they had been released from their normal duties for the whole day and they both felt the need to see the case through – and to see what damage Graham had done to the Crown's case.

When they returned, Patrick was waiting for them. He was very diplomatic about the morning's events and discussed with them whether the prosecution case would benefit from asking Dan and Sergeant Baron to come to the court to give their evidence. Their statements had originally been accepted by the defence and they weren't required to attend the hearing. A decision was made to hear the evidence from the two civilian witnesses, Mr and Mrs Heath, who had been walking nearby when Mr Woodcock was being restrained, and to then review the decision.

The trial restarted. Mrs Heath was able to say that Mr Woodcock had been driving but, as regards the scuffle, she said that there was a lot going on and she didn't really notice who was where or what any individuals were doing. She was, however, able to confirm that Mrs Woodcock had shouted that she was a lawyer and had seen her being escorted to a police car by two female officers.

Mr Heath then took the stand. Sally smiled as he also stated that Mr Woodcock had been driving and went on to describe how the 'small, blonde female officer' was sitting on his legs trying to put his arms behind his back. As Mr Heath left the witness stand, Patrick looked back at the officers and gave them a nod. The trial was back on course. Neil nudged Sally, giving her a thumbs up.

Then the Woodcocks themselves were called.

Miss Hoity led Mrs Woodcock through her evidence. Mrs Woodcock had obviously got her best gold puffa jacket out for her court appearance to impress the magistrates. With it, she had coordinated a pair of tight white jeans and finished it off with some red platform sandals. She wore her hair in the same 'council facelift' style bedecked with a gold scrunchie hairband. Her neck, ears and fingers were adorned in heavy gold jewellery, the value of which probably exceeded the remainder of her and her husband's assets combined.

Sally studied Mrs Woodcock, who looked a good ten years older than her actual age, whilst she continued to claim it had been her that had been driving and that her husband had not resisted his arrest and had in fact been cooperative throughout. She did, however, admit to damaging the police car and throwing PC Butterworth's truncheon at him because he was 'beating up her husband'.

Miss Hoity nodded to Mrs Woodcock, "Thank you Mrs Woodcock. Please remain standing." With that Miss Hoity sat down and reached for the plastic cup of water in front of her. An amusing scene followed where she misjudged the distance and tipped the cup over, spilling the contents over the surface. She jumped back onto her feet and grabbed her bundle of case papers with one hand and vainly tried to sweep the water away with the other. Patrick valiantly came to her rescue and deftly mopped the spillage up with his handkerchief. She thanked him profusely her crimson cheeks testimony to her embarrassment as the magistrates looked on disapprovingly.

Patrick then turned his attention to Mrs Woodcock. "Mrs Woodcock, every witness so far has described how you repeatedly shouted, 'I'm a lawyer'. Can you tell me how long you've been practising as a lawyer?"

"I'm not," she replied moodily, scowling round the courtroom.

"Do you mean that you're not a lawyer or you are not practising at the moment? Perhaps you could clarify this for the court?" asked Patrick innocently as if he truly believed she might be a lawyer whilst attempting to coax her into a false sense of security.

"I ain't a lawyer," she said almost inaudibly.

"Then why, Mrs Woodcock, did you repeatedly tell the officers you were?"

"Because they were beatin' up my husband, weren't they? They shouldn't be allowed to get away with that."

"And you believed telling them you were a lawyer would help, did you?"

"Well, yeah," she replied, shrugging her shoulders.

"And what do you do for a living, Mrs Woodcock?"

"I don't. I'm unemployed, aren't I," she stated resignedly.

Patrick left this thought hanging in the air and changed tack. "Mrs Woodcock, can you tell me who was driving when the police stopped you?"

"The police didn't stop us. We stopped of our own vul... vol...we stopped because we wanted to."

"And who was it who was driving before you stopped and before you spoke to the police officers?"

"It were me, weren't it?" She frowned at Patrick.

"Mrs Woodcock, do you hold a full driving licence?"

"No," she replied, sighing.

"And do you hold a provisional driving licence?"

"No," she said under her breath.

"I'm sorry, I didn't catch your answer."

"No," she repeated, slightly louder.

"In which case, you will not have any insurance to drive the car, will you?"

"No," she said, rolling her eyes up to the ceiling with impatience.

"Yet you are still maintaining that, on the night in question, you were driving the car without a valid licence or insurance and that it was not your husband?"

"Yep." She nodded.

She stuck to her story throughout. She remained adamant that she was driving and that she had done so despite not having a driving licence or insurance because her husband had had too much to drink and they thought that it was the better option for her to drive uninsured than for him to drive over the limit. It was a plausible account for someone of her ilk, and all because they needed to get back for the babysitter which they had paid for and thus couldn't afford a taxi.

Mrs Woodcock claimed she was sorry that she had damaged the police car and thrown the truncheon at PC Butterworth and that she had learned from her mistakes. Even Patrick couldn't resist a smile at that one.

"I was just really angry at the way they were treating my husband," she explained with a sulky look on her face. It was clear that she hadn't known any other way to react to the situation. Sally felt a pang of sympathy for this woman.

Finally, Mr Woodcock took the stand. He was dressed in his best jeans and a polo shirt that had been ironed in places and displayed the Guinness logo front and back.

He related a tale of police brutality and also tried to convince the magistrates that he and his wife had chosen the sensible option by allowing her to drive since he would have been over the limit.

With all evidence heard, Miss Hoity gave her summing-up speech where she gave an overview of the evidence emphasising the strengths of her case. She focused on the facts that not only had the couple taken the sensible option for Mrs Woodcock to drive, albeit this involved breaking the law, but she also pressed home the point that the police officers' evidence being so different cast doubt upon the whole case and, indeed, of who in fact was driving. They were mistaken in thinking it was Mr Woodcock.

Miss Hoity spoke well and left the court in no doubt that the evidence was inconsistent. The magistrates retired to consider their verdict. Sally and Neil left the courtroom to get a cup of tea whilst Graham stayed in his seat.

Sally felt physically and emotionally drained and talked over the possible outcomes with Neil. Nothing was for certain, that was for sure, and the Woodcocks' future hung in the balance.

The magistrates returned after almost an hour of deliberating. The Woodcocks were asked to stand as the head magistrate turned to them to give them their verdict. Mrs Woodcock looked round at the officers and smirked, obviously feeling confident that the outcome would be in their favour. Sally held her breath, praying for justice to be done. The smirk was quickly wiped from Mrs Woodcock's face and replaced by a look of utter disbelief as the magistrate announced that they had both been found guilty on all counts. Neil grabbed Sally's leg with excitement and she felt her whole body slump with relief.

Mr Woodcock was convicted of failing to provide a sample of breath and given the maximum three-year ban and was also convicted of Section 5 Public Order for which he was given a year's suspended sentence. Mrs Woodcock was convicted of the same public order offence, a common assault on PC Butterworth and criminal damage to the police car. In addition to being required to pay £50 compensation to PC Butterworth and £300 for the damage to the police car, she was also given a suspended one-year sentence having been given the benefit of pleading guilty to these offences. The magistrate then lectured her about the fact she was lucky not to have been convicted of attempting to pervert the course of justice with her claim to have been driving. She looked back indignantly. She had no respect for the law or its advocates.

Immediately the magistrates had left the room, Graham stood up and walked across in front of Neil and Sally towards the door.

"Result!" he said without looking at either of them. "And I'm fifty quid up!" before disappearing through the door.

"Yeah, no thanks to you," Neil retorted but too late for Graham to hear.

Patrick approached them, smiling. "Well, that was an interesting one. What was all that about with PC Butterworth?" he looked from Sally to Neil inquisitively.

"Oh, he's just an arrogant sod who doesn't deserve that fifty quid," replied Neil.

"Well done, Sally." Patrick turned to her. "You coped well there. You stuck to your guns and it came right in the end."

"Thanks," replied Sally gratefully before their attention was caught by the Woodcocks' raised voices.

"You told us we would get off with it!" they heard Mrs Woodcock screech at Miss Hoity.

Neil immediately stepped forward and asked the couple to leave the courtroom.

Mrs Woodcock took another breath before starting again but Neil got in first. "Now, Mrs Woodcock. We don't want any more trouble, do we."

Mr Woodcock took her arm and led her towards the door. She shrugged him off sulkily and gave the officers a filthy look as she left the room.

"I don't think we've seen the last of her, have we," offered Patrick as he watched the couple start to bicker in the tiny entrance foyer to the courtroom. He turned back to the officers and continued, "I'm having dinner with your superintendent tonight. I'm sure he'll be interested to hear about this case." He looked mischievously at Neil and Sally before thanking them and returning to his desk to file his papers.

Sally walked out of the courtroom wearing a beaming grin and chatting animatedly to Neil. Although exhausted, she felt relieved and ecstatic that neither Graham nor the Woodcocks had won.

She was so caught up in the moment that she didn't notice Alex rushing into the waiting area and almost collided with him.

"Hi, Sally!"

"Alex…hi…" replied Sally, the fixed grin still stuck to her face.

"Wow, there's the look of a newly engaged young lady – who's presumably just won her first court case?!"

Neil, sensing the need for diplomacy, brushed Sally on the shoulder, said he would meet her back at the nick and disappeared down the stairs to the cell complex.

"Errr, yes, you're right about winning the court case… but I'm, err, I'm not…well, it turned about to be the shortest engagement ever which is a bit embarrassing, isn't it? And I'm back to being sad and single." She shrugged but was at least able to stay smiling.

"Well, join the club! But hey, Sal, I'm sorry to hear that.

That's sounds tough. Are you OK?"

Before she could answer, the usher called Alex's name.

"Can you hang on?" he asked eagerly. "I've just got to swear out a warrant and I'll be back. Will you wait?"

"Sure," Sally agreed, noticing that he was still looking drawn and hadn't regained his weight since his split with his wife. She walked to the window and sat on the window seat overlooking North Parade. The trees were starting to show signs of autumn's arrival with their leaves edged in shades of brown. She could just make out Neil as he wound his way between the streams of children leaving the school next to the court building. They were skipping and dodging each other full of the joys of life and pleased to have been released from school for the weekend. Sally's heart fluttered at the thought of Alex so obviously keen for her to wait. She was keen to wait for him too.

After quarter of an hour, Alex appeared through the courtroom door and immediately scanned the waiting area for Sally. She got up and walked towards him, unable to stop herself from smiling with obvious pleasure at seeing him.

There was a moment of awkward silence, both scanning each other's faces for signs of what the other was thinking and feeling.

Alex spoke first, holding his one free hand up with his fingers splayed. "I can't hang round. I've got to get back with this warrant," he indicated the paperwork in his other hand, "but-but, Sal, can I call you…or, err…"

"Sure," said Sally, hardly able to hide the excitement bubbling up inside her.

He apologised for keeping her waiting and then having to rush off as she scribbled her number down for him.

"Are you OK though, Sal?" he asked as they made their way to the cell complex together.

"Yes, I'm fine. Things are going better at work so that makes everything easier."

"Well, you certainly looked part of the team at Neil's do. I was disappointed that you left without having the chance to speak to you properly."

"Hmmm," replied Sally, "think I overdid it a bit that night," not wanting to remind herself of the sorry events of the latter part of the night when she had left the gathering.

"Glad to hear things are going better at work. How's Butterworth treating you?"

"I'll need a good hour to bring you up to speed with all that!" Sally giggled. *That's a good sign*, she thought to herself. She could now actually laugh when his name was mentioned and not feel like crying or screaming. "And he caused a stir in the case today, but I'll tell you all about it some other time."

"OK, I've gotta dash, but I will ring you – soon!" Alex squeezed her arm before walking towards the car park. She walked out to the road but couldn't resist looking back. Alex raised his hand having been caught doing the same – she waved back animatedly and returned to the station with an unfamiliar flutter in her stomach.

Chapter Thirteen

Sally didn't have to wait long. She took Honey for a walk as soon as she got home whilst her dinner was cooking and then phoned her mum to tell her about her day. She was delighted to hear that the sale of Uncle Jack's house was going through and he would be able to take up the place in the sheltered housing in Selborne Close that they had found for him near to her mum. After she put the phone down, she dozed off in front of the television. She thought the phone was ringing in her dream before she jolted herself awake and picked up the receiver.

"Hi, Sal, it's me!"

Sally, still half asleep, paused to recognise the voice.

"It's Alex," came a hesitant voice.

"Alex! Hi!" Sally replied, perhaps a bit too eagerly. "Sorry, I'd nodded off. I'm exhausted after today."

"Yeah, I couldn't wait to hear all about it so thought I'd give you a ring."

Sally outlined the case and the traumatic events of the day that culminated in the final victory. Alex listened with interest and punctuated her account with guffaws and obvious enjoyment.

"So that was my first experience of giving evidence. I can't wait till the next time," Sally joked.

"It won't be that bad next time," Alex reassured her.

"If you can get through that ordeal, you'll be able to cope with anything. Wait till you have a Crown Court case – that's even more scary!"

"Thanks for that!" she chided.

An awkward pause followed as they finished the topic of courts; then they both started to talk at once. Sally stopped and waited.

Alex restarted. "So dare I suggest we meet for a drink?"

Sally was glad he couldn't see her: her faced screwed up with delight and punching the air in excitement. She got up and started pacing the room. Honey got up from her basket and thought she was in for an extra walk so Sally got down on her knees and smoothed her whilst she agreed to a drink. They deliberated about where they should meet, both aware without actually saying so that they wanted to keep things under wraps for now.

"Why don't you come here?" offered Sally, worried that this was too forward and aware of her heart thudding as she waited for a response.

She was relieved when Alex replied with, "I was hoping you were going to say that. I didn't want to invite myself and I'm still getting my bachelor pad in some kind of order."

They agreed on the following Wednesday evening before chatting easily on a variety of topics as they had done when they worked together. After hearing her yawn and appreciating the demanding day she had endured, Alex said goodbye and Sally put the receiver down.

She stood in front of the mirror in the hallway and watched herself pull an excited face before calling Honey and heading for her bedroom. Despite her exhaustion, Sally wasn't able to get to sleep quickly. Her mind was buzzing with all the events of the day – and what she should wear on Wednesday night.

Sally decided not to say anything about the court case at work. Graham would have written his statement long before the April Fool's saga, and it wasn't something that could be changed after it had been written. In any case, she doubted it would have crossed the sly and lowly man's mind to try to make amends. It was obvious, however, that Neil had spoken to the sergeants as the Baroness passed comment on the good result and that she heard Sally had had a difficult time.

In her work file, Sally found a message sent via the driving school offering her a late-notice, one-day crew bus course – in two days' time. Sally immediately dismissed the idea and closed the file but, as she reached up to return it to the shelf, she thought again. *Come on, Sally,* she said to herself, *prove to yourself and everyone else that you can do it.*

With that, Sergeant Morley appeared in the office. "Hi, Sally. I've put a message in your work file about a crew bus course. We've got enough on duty that day if you fancy doing it?"

Sally thought to herself, *It's now or never, girl,* and hot on the heels of her court success, and the arrangements for Wednesday evening, she reached back up for her file and took out the paperwork. "Yes, that would be great, Sarge. Thanks."

She signed the sheet and took it to the front office to fax it over to the driving school. It was sealed.

To Sally's surprise, she really enjoyed the day. Driving the twenty-one foot-long bus was easier than she thought and was actually quite fun. She shared many laughs and jokes with the same instructor who had taken her for her initial driving course. She returned to work the following day a fully-fledged crew bus driver and looked forward with nervous anticipation to trying out her new found skills.

Nervous anticipation also prevailed as her evening with Alex arrived. After walking Honey and having finally decided what to wear, she tidied her flat and struggled not to have a courage-inducing glass of wine whilst she waited for him to arrive. The doorbell rang at 7.30 on the dot, and Sally opened it to find Alex standing there holding a bunch of cerise carnations and a bottle of white wine. She gratefully accepted both with a smile that belied the fact that she liked neither of these gifts, but marvelled at how much there was to get to know about each other.

Honey was there to greet him too.

"Hi, Honey, I'd forgotten about you!" He bent to fuss the dog who immediately rolled onto her back asking for her tummy to be tickled.

"Come on, Hon," said Sally, mildly embarrassed by Honey's uninhibited display of her undercarriage.

"Am I allowed to say you look a tad more attractive than last time you opened the door to me?" he asked light-heartedly, feeling as nervous as Sally at the prospect of them being together for the first time as a potential couple.

"Thanks," said Sally, looking down at the outfit she had thought long and hard about, and laughing at the pyjama-clad fright she must have looked last time.

They moved into the lounge where Sally had put out some wine glasses and crisps. She didn't know where to start with the conversation but thought it was probably good to ask about his wellbeing first since they hadn't touched on this in their phone call earlier in the week and it had been on her mind since.

"How's things with you? You know, with Anne-Marie and Max?" she asked as she poured wine for them both.

"Not great, it has to be said. There's no chance of a reconciliation, I know that for sure. But I have tried and failed to persuade her to at least come back and live here so that I can see Max more easily and so he can go to school here. She won't change her mind though; she's determined to stay in France. She says losing her dad has brought it home to her how much she misses her family and wants to be with them – more than she wants to be with me. Things hadn't been great with us for a while. She was always hankering to go back and just couldn't settle over here. We'd worked at it, but it obviously wasn't to be."

"That's really sad," sympathised Sally. She understood just what Ann-Marie meant, having lost her own father. "It must be tough, especially not seeing Max."

"Yes, that's the hardest part. I can't tell you how much it hurts having seen him every day of his life for four years and then not being able to for weeks on end. It's not as if he's just down the road and I can pop in and see him after school or anything."

Sally could see that Alex was struggling with his emotions. She wanted to wrap him in her arms and make him feel better, but it was too soon for anything like that and, besides, she couldn't help with the heartache he was obviously suffering.

"Come on," said Alex, "enough doom and gloom. Tell me what's been happening at work. I want to hear all about it."

For the next few hours, Sally related the whole saga surrounding April Fool's Day and how things had started looking up since. She too got close to tears as she related how low and helpless she had felt. She told him all about Uncle Jack's illness and how she had found him close to death, and of her brief reunion with Julian. Alex sat and listened and commented when appropriate and laughed in all the right places.

"Wow, you've really been through it, haven't you," he said when she finally finished.

"Yeah, what a pair we are!" said Sally, slapping her hands on her thighs in acknowledgement of this statement. This was interpreted by Honey, who was lying at their feet, as an invitation to jump up. She leapt onto Sally's lap and stretched her front paws across the short distance to Alex. Alex shuffled closer to close the gap and, in doing so, their shoulders touched. They looked at one another sitting awkwardly side by side before Alex lifted his arm and placed it around Sally.

"Is that OK?" he asked gently.

"Yeah, it's fine," she replied, leaning against him. He leaned over and kissed the top of her head. Sally briefly closed her eyes. She couldn't believe what was happening to her.

Alex made her laugh with some of the antics of the drugs squad. She was amazed at some of the situations they got themselves into – which weren't always intentional. She didn't fancy that kind of work and, in any case, any move was a long way off for her just yet. The hours passed in a flash and, as Honey became restless to be let out, Alex said that it was time he should be going.

They both put their coats on and Alex offered to accompany her in walking Honey. Sally willingly agreed and they set off for Primrose Hill. Once Honey was off her lead, Alex reached for Sally's hand and drew her to him.

"May I?" he asked, smiling down at her in the moonlight.

"You may, PC Moon." She smiled.

They stood and kissed for a long while. It was something Sally had dreamt of since their illicit kiss last Christmas, but she had never liked to admit to herself how much she was longing for it to be repeated. They walked back to her flat hand in hand with Honey happily panting beside them. The dog sat and waited patiently at the front door whilst Alex and Sally kissed again.

"Thanks, Sally, I've had a lovely evening."

"Me too." She smiled back at him as they stood close holding hands between them.

"Can we do it again?"

"Sure." Sally shrugged, conscious not to look too keen. "Give me a call."

Honey signalled it was time to go inside so, after one last lingering kiss, Sally closed the door and leant against it, her eyes closed and her head tilted to the heavens. "Thank you, thank you," she whispered.

Alex phoned her the very next day and every day after that when their shifts allowed.

They enjoyed many 'clandestine meetings' as they called them. They walked miles with Honey, getting to know each other in this new role together and gradually discussing how best to go about going public with their relationship. Sally worried about what the station's reaction would be so soon after their earlier relationship failures. Alex was more relaxed and told her that it was none of their business when she voiced her concerns.

Taking things one step at a time, towards the end of November, they decided to brave the outside world and Sally popped into Franco's whilst on duty to ask a favour.

She knocked on the back door and walked on in calling out, "Only me!'

"Oh, Sally, please come in and tell us how our favourite police officer is today!" Franco beckoned her in and moved towards her to offer his welcome.

"What have you got to tell us?" he asked as he kissed her on each cheek.

"Well, actually, Franco, I've got a favour to ask you..." Sally started.

"Anything for you. What is it, my *tesoro*?"

"I was wondering whether I could book a table for tomorrow night?"

Franco put down the mortar and pestle he was preparing a pesto sauce in and wiped his hands on his apron. "Sally, Sally, this is good news, yes? Who is the lucky man this time?"

"Franco, you make it sound as if I've had a long queue of them coming in here!"

"Is it another Cloud the Froud?" He was referring to Claude the Fraud. "Rossana – she still laughs about that and tells the story every time she phones home to Italy!"

"Well, I'm glad to see some good came out of my awful evening." Sally laughed. "No, it's not another Claude. It's a surprise. I'm not going to tell you!"

"Ah, OK." Franco looked intrigued.

"Can we have the table at the back in the corner, please?"

"For you, Sally, anything! Consider it booked!"

"Great!" replied Sally and hopped up on a stool to chew over the best way to prepare the perfect pasta *al forno*.

Sally was surprised by how much the atmosphere at work had improved, and she was loving it. Graham had been moved to the custody suite to act as a detention officer looking after the prisoners. This would not be seen as a positive move but more of an unspoken punishment as it was rumoured the job did not need the skills of a police officer and that it was soon to be civilianised. Sally chose to steer clear of him and, when she couldn't avoid being in the same breathing space as him when she was dealing with a prisoner, she could tell he was uncomfortable. After the court case saga, she now felt she had the upper hand. She knew he wouldn't dare try anything else. His copybook was well and truly blotted. Sally was definitely carrying out her duties with more of an air of confidence these days and loving every minute.

Of course, her relationship with Alex was helping her sunny disposition. She was enjoying carrying the secret and smiling to herself at the thought of their times together.

Sally was looking forward to their meal at Franco's and she was ready and waiting when Alex pulled up in his car to pick her up.

"Oh, my God," she said as she got in, "I can't believe we're doing this. What if we're spotted?!" she gabbled excitedly despite the fact that any normal couple would have 'come out' by now.

"Well, at least it would solve the problem of how to come out, wouldn't it."

"Hmm, true," said Sally, but she preferred to be in control of her own destiny.

Franco spotted them walking into his restaurant hand in hand. His reaction made them laugh. He was just beside himself with joy.

"I knew you two were made for each other! I knew it from the moment I saw you together. Rossana! Rossana!" He pushed open the kitchen door and beckoned his wife. She came quickly at the sound of his excited voice and beamed as he held his arms open towards a laughing Alex and Sally.

"Look, Rossana, they are a couple! *Che coppia adorabile!*"

"Oh, Franco," Sally said, embarrassed but pleased at his reaction as she led Alex to her chosen table. Franco rushed over and pulled the chair out for her and, after pushing it in, picked up her napkin and opened it with an exaggerated motion, smoothing it on Sally's lap before repeating the process for Alex.

He fetched a bottle of wine for them and filled their glasses before moving away backwards saying, "I'll leave *piccioncini miei* to decide what you like to eat. You call me over when you are ready to order." He rolled his tongue on the 'ready' and bowed to them before disappearing through the kitchen door.

Sally and Alex were left giggling at his obvious approval of their relationship. Sally just hoped their workmates would have the same reaction.

Alex seemed to be reading her mind as he said, "I bumped into Dan today. He asked if I'd be interested in going to the team Christmas do..." He allowed the words to hang in the air for a few moments. "Might be a good ice-breaker. What do you think? It's on the 16th, isn't it?"

"What, you mean go together?" Sally asked as her mind wandered back to last year and the humiliation she suffered in providing such unintentional entertainment for her colleagues.

"They're going to find out at some point, aren't they?" he asked reassuringly and taking one of her hands in one of his.

He was right. And, besides, they might as well go and front it out with them all than be found out skulking about in secret.

"You're not embarrassed to be seen with me, are you?" he asked.

"No, not at all," Sally defended herself before realising he was joking.

Far from it, she thought to herself looking across at him and realising that actually she did want to be seen with him.

"OK, let's do it!" she said, smiling at this man who was managing to take her to a level of happiness she hadn't experienced in a long time.

"Let's drink to that," said Alex, raising his glass. "Tell you what, you go ahead and book for two and leave them wondering..."

It was starting to sound like fun – although she didn't want to make a grand entrance – just walk in and be casual about it. Yes, she was looking forward to it already.

It seemed a long couple of weeks before their 'coming out' and, during that time, Sally, although remaining nervous at the thought, realised it was high time they did so. It was becoming awkward trying to be together and not being spotted. They went further afield to Cheltenham to do a spot of Christmas shopping together where Sally chose a stunning and sophisticated, sequinned, black Jaeger dress for the Christmas do.

The night itself dawned and Alex called for her in a taxi. She climbed in the back with him and exclaimed, "Oh, my God, I can't believe we're really doing this!"

"It'll be fine," he reassured her though she noticed his hand was a little clammy as she held it on the journey to the Menzies Hotel. "And, by the way, you look stunning," he added as he leant over and kissed her.

As they got out of the taxi, they met Neil and his wife

and walked into the foyer together.

"Hey, nice one, you two," said Neil approvingly, stepping back to allow them to enter the function room ahead of him and his wife.

"Ready?" Alex asked Sally.

"Ready," Sally confirmed.

He squeezed her hand as they walked in. It only took a few seconds for heads to start turning and a slight hush descended on the room. Fortunately, the lull was short-lived as Sally and Alex strode with purpose towards the bar where they were met by the team who, apart from being pleased to see Alex, seemed genuinely pleased to see them together. There was a bit of back slapping and a few 'you sly dog' comments and then the moment was over. They were official. Sally and Alex were a couple.

In any case, there was some much more interesting gossip circulating. Dan revealed that Graham had been suspended from duty following an allegation of misconduct at the football club.

"What kind of misconduct?" was the question on everyone's lips. Their natural requirement for information was evident as they speculated whether the misconduct was of a physical nature or whether it was a dishonesty issue. The Baroness was able to furnish them with the required information: it was some allegation regarding Graham receiving 'bungs', and the evidence that he was involved was apparently fairly overwhelming against him.

There was shock and disbelief that Graham could have been quite so stupid.

"At Vauxhall Conference level?" guffawed Basher.

"Was it ever worth it?" echoed Neil.

Sally mused that it was typical that, even when Graham wasn't there, he was able to steal her thunder – but since the information she was hearing brought a satisfying smile to her face, she was happy for the conversation to offer a distraction from the shock of her and Alex turning up together. Besides, she was delighted to hear Graham was getting his just comeuppance.

It was a great evening, during which there was much discussion about Graham. A few more details came out and it looked like he would be lucky to keep his job. It would all depend on the results of the disciplinary hearing which would take place well into next year. He would remain suspended for the time being and possibly be given a desk job somewhere in the meantime if it dragged on for too long.

"Stupid sod." Dan voiced his opinion and most people echoed similar sentiments. Sally stayed quiet, taking a sip of her red wine. She was aware that several pairs of eyes had looked at her for a reaction. She was going to rise above it. He had managed to ruin his career all by himself; he didn't need any more running down by her.

The time flew. Before they knew it, the DJ was playing the last few songs, and Alex led Sally on to the dance floor to join the other couples for the slow dances. There were still a few interested glances in their direction, but this didn't prevent Alex from holding her close and showing them all that this was for real.

Goodbyes were said, and Alex and Sally caught a taxi back to her flat. Without any discussion, Alex paid for the taxi whilst Sally opened the front door and he followed her in.

"Don't take your coat off!" Sally giggled at Alex as she rattled Honey's lead at him. Although both were under the influence of a bottle or two of wine, they were clearly happy with how the evening had gone and were quietly reflective as they walked to Primrose Hill and back.

Honey was relegated to sleeping on the floor that night.

Sally's return to work was met with a few smirks and winks, but she was fine about it – in fact, she quite enjoyed it. Everyone seemed genuinely pleased for them, including the Baroness who spoke to Sally when she went to fetch her work file.

"You make a great couple. I hope it works out for you both."

Sally stared at her at first not knowing how sincere the Baroness was being, but the look on her face showed that she was being genuine.

Sally broke into a smile. "Thanks," she replied affably. She was tempted to add "Glad you approve" but she didn't need her approval – she didn't need anyone's approval. Still, it was good to hear the Baroness say something positive about the relationship, and she appreciated her making an effort to be friendly.

It was Sally's last shift before the annual leave she had booked for Christmas this year, and she was looking forward to taking some time out to relax with her family – and Alex, of course. It was an evening shift and, after a busy first half, the team headed out to the crew bus that was parked on the station forecourt.

"Hey, Sal," called Dan, "your turn tonight!"

She turned round just in time to see the crew bus keys flying towards her. She snatched them with fluke casualness out of the air and retorted, "Fine with me" and turned to open the door.

Her stomach did a flip and she cursed herself for being so outwardly confident when she was in fact shaking in her boots, hoping her bravado didn't backfire on her. She didn't make a good start as she stalled as she went to pull off the forecourt which prompted a good-natured cheer from behind her.

"Come on, Basher, you do that nearly every time you drive us!" mocked the Baroness which was met with some concurring echoes as Sally finally accelerated up Manvers Street. She was in her element – and she was really proud of herself. As she had discovered on the course, the crew bus was much easier to drive than she thought. It was its incredible size that was so off-putting but she relaxed into the task. She knew it would look an impressive sight: a massive beast complete with mesh visor which it wore like a pair of sunglasses propped on the roof waiting to be pulled down to offer protection to those inside – and all this with a diminutive policewoman at the wheel!

Sally drove them around the usual hotspots in the centre of the city and all was quiet. She even managed to squeeze through a narrow gap caused by parked cars and an abandoned taxi in Cheap Street, which was orchestrated with an "oooooh" which rose and fell in acknowledgment of her skill.

"Just the Bennett's Lane challenge to go and you're up with the big boys," called out Dan from the back and beyond of the bus.

She didn't reply but metaphorically picked up the gauntlet and headed the crew bus towards Snow Hill. It was some minutes before everyone clocked that she had taken on the challenge and a ripple of surprise resounded around the bus.

Why am I doing this to myself? Sally asked herself, a feeling of excitement masking the true fear of what she was

273

about to attempt. She reached the bottom of Bennett's Lane and strained forward in her seat to get a view of the summit she aimed to conquer. After taking a deep breath and selecting first gear, her crew started a low 'ohhhhhhh' like a football crowd watching a penalty kick. She blocked out the noise and began the climb whilst the 'ohhhh' intensified.

'Oooohhhh': the sound hit a crescendo as if the penalty taker had hit the posts as a car turned into Bennett's Lane from the top and drove towards them. The lane wasn't wide enough to pass without slowing right down and Sally found herself having no choice but to pull in tight against the narrow pavement and allow the car to pass. She was sweating by now and wished she hadn't been so hasty in accepting the challenge. She bit her lip nervously as she looked across at the Baroness. An encouraging nod towards the road indicated to her that she should and could persevere and spurred her on to continue.

Another deep breath and a controlled, if noisy, hill start as she resumed her quest. At the junction at the summit, she yanked the handbrake on and prepared for her final quest. To the obvious delight of her crew, Sally carried out a perfect hill start and pulled out onto Camden Road with control and poise to a rapturous round of applause. She felt a few congratulatory shoves on her back which caused her to grip the steering wheel firmly to stop them unseating her.

I did it! she said to herself. *I damn well did it!*

Who would have thought, she mused as, behind her, Basher started clapping rhythmically and struck up a rendition of the Beatles' *Drive My Car*. Everyone joined in and Sally looked in the rear-view mirror at the sight of everyone clapping in time as they repeated the chorus swaying from side to side behind her. Even the Baroness was joining in. Sally felt like her heart could burst. Why had she ever doubted her decision to join this merry band? The radio crackled into life, interrupting this auspicious occasion which Sally would remember for the rest of her days.

On Christmas Eve, Sally and Honey stayed over at her mum's. It was just like old times in her old room and she woke up to find a small stocking at the end of her bed and a doggy version for Honey. She woke later than she had anticipated to the sound of laughter coming from downstairs and, still clad in her pyjamas, she went down to find her mum and Uncle Jack sitting in the lounge.

"Merry Christmas, Sally," they chorused.

"Merry Christmas to you too," she said, bending to kiss them both before going to open the back door to let Honey out.

They had a breakfast of smoked salmon and scrambled egg, and Sally had just got herself dressed when Cathy and Steve arrived with Nancy and Ella. The presents seemed to multiply tenfold under the tree and, once Sally and her Mum had served everyone with an appropriate drink and put a Christmas CD on, they sat down to open their gifts to the smell of the turkey cooking.

There were suitable 'whoops' and 'aahhs' as everyone unwrapped their gifts and the children disappeared into the dining room to play with their long awaited toys. Uncle Jack nodded at Sally who took the parcel she had prepared on his behalf from under the tree and handed it to him.

"Jean," he said in a voice that was once again clear and recognisable, "this is for you."

Sally's mum sat down beside him and carefully unwrapped

the gift to find a photograph frame. As she turned it over to reveal the picture, tears sprung from her eyes. With Sally's help, he had managed to frame an enlarged and restored copy of the photo he carried in his wallet.

"Oh, Jack, where did you find that?!" Jean sobbed. "That was our holiday at Slapton Sands. Just look at our faces!" She reached for her handkerchief and dabbed at her eyes. Then, noticing the tears rolling down her brother's face, she handed the handkerchief to him before they held each other in an emotional embrace. Even Nancy and Ella who had briefly reappeared in the lounge stopped to take in the scene – and a moment hung in the air as the adults reflected on the past year and its turn of events that had brought them all together.

The hush was interrupted by the doorbell ringing. Jean went to check on the turkey, and Cathy and Steve smirked at the imminent appearance of the expected guest. Sally disappeared into the hallway and checked her reflection in the mirror before opening the door.

"Happy Christmas, Minnie!" Alex squeaked in a high-pitched voice.

Sally burst into laughter as she took in the sight of Alex standing on the doorstep wearing a pair of blue-sequinned Mickey Mouse ears.

"Happy Christmas to you too, Mickey!" Sally laughed, genuinely amused.

He had just arrived back from a trip to Euro Disney as a Christmas treat for Max. Sally had been anxious about him spending time with Ann-Marie and her family, but his obvious pleasure in seeing Sally again gave her the reassurance she was seeking. Safe in the knowledge that she had taken his Mickey Mouse ears in good spirit, as he stepped inside the door he produced a set of matching red Minnie Mouse ears. He placed them on Sally's head before reaching forward to kiss her. He put the bag of gifts he was carrying down onto the floor and wrapped his arms around her.

"God, Sal, I've missed you!"

They were almost immediately interrupted by her young nieces who had been watching from the lounge doorway.

"Ooohhhh! Sally's kissing her boyfriend!" they shrieked before they ran back inside the lounge to join those who had obviously been entertained by the commentary.

Sally led Alex by the hand to meet her family.

Maybe it hadn't been such a bad year after all.

And who knows what the New Year would bring?

Find out more about the author and her work at
www.sandyosborne.com